Acclaim for
Alex in Wonderland

"*Alex in Wonderland* is a hilarious and utterly compelling story of one man's search for self-identity, independence, and love at the risk of forsaking a family inheritance and rejection. LaCroix has created a story that features a sizzling mix of fast-paced storytelling and lyrical sexuality. A must-read."

—Durrell Owens,
Author of *The Song of a Manchild*

"Tennessee Williams meets Jackie Collins with a dash of Truman Capote in Monsieur LaCroix's hilarious debut novel, *Alex in Wonderland.* Tracking the life of one young, sexy (and perpetually horny) Alex Sumner as he explores the many delights of his burgeoning homosexuality, this delicious novel evokes sultry images of Anne Rice's New Orleans and the bayou country. Alex, scion of a mega-rich, oil baron tycoon, is on the run from a marriage of convenience, arranged by his overbearing, despot of a father, Randolph. Add to that, a thwarted, *Some Like It Hot,* in-drag bus trip to the gay mecca of Key West and a cast of unique characters straight out of *Cat on a Hot Tin Roof,* and you have an undisputed winner! Will Alex escape the oppression of his billionaire father and live happily-every-after and find true love with the brutish Cord? What will become of his bride-to-be Camilla? And just how many sexual escapades can one handsome, Southern boy experience in the span of a few weeks? Michel LaCroix's *Alex in Wonderland* is the perfect novel to read while sipping a mint julep and fanning yourself on the veranda!"

—Michael D. Craig,
Author of *The Ice Sculptures:
A Novel of Hollywood*

Alex in Wonderland

HARRINGTON PARK PRESS®
Southern Tier Editions™
Gay Men's Fiction

Elf Child by David M. Pierce

Huddle by Dan Boyle

The Man Pilot by James W. Ridout IV

Shadows of the Night: Queer Tales of the Uncanny and Unusual edited by Greg Herren

Van Allen's Ecstasy by Jim Tushinski

Beyond the Wind by Rob N. Hood

The Handsomest Man in the World by David Leddick

The Song of a Manchild by Durrell Owens

The Ice Sculptures: A Novel of Hollywood by Michael D. Craig

Between the Palms: A Collection of Gay Travel Erotica edited by Michael T. Luongo

Aura by Gary Glickman

Love Under Foot: An Erotic Celebration of Feet edited by Greg Wharton and M. Christian

The Tenth Man by E. William Podojil

Upon a Midnight Clear: Queer Christmas Tales edited by Greg Herren

Dryland's End by Felice Picano

Whose Eye Is on Which Sparrow? by Robert Taylor

Deep Water: A Sailor's Passage by E. M. Kahn

The Boys in the Brownstone by Kevin Scott

The Best of Both Worlds: Bisexual Erotica edited by Sage Vivant and M. Christian

Some Dance to Remember: A Memoir-Novel of San Francisco, 1970-1982 by Jack Fritscher

Confessions of a Male Nurse by Richard S. Ferri

The Millionaire of Love by David Leddick

Alex in Wonderland by Michel LaCroix

Transgender Erotica: Trans Figures edited by M. Christian

Skip Macalester by J. E. Robinson

Chemistry by Lewis DeSimone

Friends, Lovers, and Roses by Vernon Clay

Beyond Machu by William Maltese

Virginia Bedfellows by Gavin Morris

Now Batting for Boston: More Stories by J. G. Hayes by J. G. Hayes

Alex in Wonderland

Michel LaCroix

Southern Tier Editions™
Harrington Park Press®
An Imprint of The Haworth Press, Inc.
New York • London • Oxford

For more information on this book or to order, visit
http://www.haworthpress.com/store/product.asp?sku=5257

or call 1-800-HAWORTH (800-429-6784) in the United States and Canada
or (607) 722-5857 outside the United States and Canada .

or contact orders@HaworthPress.com

Published by

Southern Tier Editions™, Harrington Park Press®, an imprint of The Haworth Press, Inc.,
10 Alice Street, Binghamton, NY 13904-1580.

PUBLISHER'S NOTE
This is a work of fiction. Names, characters, places, and incidents either are the products of the
author's imagination or are used fictitiously, and any resemblance to actual persons, living or
dead, business establishments, events, or locales is entirely coincidental.

Cover design by Lora Wiggins.
Cover illustration by Robert Bush.

Library of Congress Cataloging-in-Publication Data

LaCroix, Michel.
  Alex in Wonderland/Michel LaCroix.
    p. cm.
  ISBN-13: 978-1-56023-532-3 (soft : alk. paper)
  ISBN-10: 1-56023-532-2 (soft : alk. paper)
   1. Gay men—Fiction. 2. Closeted gays—Fiction. 3. Fathers and sons—Fiction. 4. Conflict of
generations—Fiction. 5. New Orleans (La.)—Fiction. I. Title.
PS3612.A353A79 2006
813'.6—dc22

                                                                        2005010853

For my fellow
Vieux Carré denizens,
Most especially
Samara Poché

CONTENTS

PART THREE

PART FOUR

PART FIVE

Acknowledgments

Most of the people responsible for this book appear in these pages in one guise or another. You all know who you are, and merci beaucoup for facilitating Alex's journey down the rabbit hole.

Special thanks to Robert Bush for his superb cover illustration, Clay Helgren for some eagle-eyed editing, Greg Herren for taking a chance on my story, and the staff of the Haworth Press who could not have been more professional and accommodating

And, of course, to Tom.

PART ONE

"Everybody says 'Come on!' here," thought Alice, as she went slowly after it. "I never was so ordered about in all my life, never!"

Lewis Carroll,
Alice's Adventures in Wonderland

1

Family Ties

Who is *that guy,* Alex wondered, *and why is he alone?*

He only half listened to Camilla's latest wedding rant, far more interested in the dark-haired stranger over his fiancée's shoulder. It was unusual to see someone dining alone at New Orleans's venerable Commander's Palace restaurant, where Alex was a longtime regular, and odder still for someone to cruise so openly. Every time he glanced in the man's direction, he got as good as he gave.

Eventually, Alex couldn't resist venturing a polite nod and a bit of a smile, thrilled when those baby blues flickered to Camilla and back. Raised eyebrows told Alex the stranger was speculating about the brunette babe swarming with DKNY and talking a mile a minute. *Forget her,* Alex thought, wishing he could telepathically send his erotic wishes. *Forget her and focus on me, man. I know you're trying to determine if this woman's my wife, girlfriend, relative, or pal. Been there. Done that.*

"Alex Sumner! Shame on you!"

"Yeow!" Alex jerked his gaze back to Camilla, rudely yanked from his erotic reverie when the toe of her Manolo Blahniks whacked his shin. "What was that for?"

"For not listening to me!" Camilla hissed. "You were a million miles away."

More like two tables, Alex thought. "Sorry, honey."

"Well, you should be," she sniffed.

There was no question that Camilla Spivey was a beauty, but when she was not the center of attention, which was rare if she had anything to do with it, she had the disconcerting habit of wrinkling her nose like a llama. Just now she looked like she was ready to trek the Andes, and if she hadn't been seething Alex would've burst out laughing. He risked giving the handsome stranger a parting glance before refocusing on Camilla. He also rubbed his shin.

"I guess I'm just tired. I didn't sleep very well last night."

"*You* didn't sleep well? What about me? Why, I haven't had a good night's sleep since you proposed. The wedding is just a month away and there are a million details to attend to, and I'm worried that Puddin' Dupree was the wrong choice for maid of honor. It seems like I'm doing all the work because she's never available, and, well, I'm just worn out. You silly grooms don't have to do anything, and you better thank your lucky stars I'm here to do all the worrying for you."

When she stopped babbling, Alex took his cue to say something gallant and smooth her ruffled feathers. "Of course I'm worried," he managed, taking her left hand and grimacing at the three-carat sparkler his father's fortune had planted there. "Plenty worried."

There was far more truth in this than the high-maintenance llama realized. Again the center of attention, Camilla dimpled and metamorphosed into sweetness itself. She could change moods so swiftly Alex sometimes wondered if she was borderline schizophrenic.

"What on earth have you got to worry about, Alex? Surrendering your silly old bachelorhood?"

"Of course not, honey," he replied, feigning happiness in the face of impending disaster. "In fact, I'm counting the days until it's gone."

"Oh, you're just too sweet!" Camilla smiled, dimples dancing until they made Alex dizzy. "It's going to be the most gorgeous wedding ever, darling. You'll see. And afterward, we'll be so happy together!"

Instead of happiness, Alex faced a potent mixture of dread and fear. The marriage was the latest effort of his father, Randolph, to control and direct his life. Since Alex had first toddled, his destiny had been to be another asset for a man who exploited his son as fiercely as he ran Sumner Petroleum, a multimillion-dollar empire based in New Orleans, with rigs and refineries stretching from Texas to Venezuela. Sumner also had vast holdings in shipping, real estate, Louisiana sugar plantations, and Mississippi catfish farms. As long as Alex could remember, he blindly obeyed while Daddy selected everything from

clothes and schools to clubs and his first car. Randolph even chose his
son's college major, and after graduation bestowed a meaningless job
with the family business, all title and no responsibility. Alex occasionally bristled, but always bowed, even when his father took him into
the library, control center for receiving orders, and told him he was to
woo and win Camilla Spivey, daughter of a powerful business associ-
ate and one of the city's most popular debs. Not only was Alex indifferent to Camilla, whom he barely knew when they began dating
a year ago, but there were other reasons he was not interested in a
marriage, arranged or otherwise.

They were summed up by the handsome hunk barely ten feet
away.

Alex had only recently acknowledged his attraction toward other
men. Or as his only gay friend, Jacques "Jolie" Menard, put it, "Tenn
would have said you have a 'certain flexible quality in your sexual nature.'" Since "Tenn" was none other than Tennessee Williams, Jolie
assured Alex that he knew what he was talking about.

Of course, telling his father he was gay would be the equivalent of
murdering a child or a confessing to a $500-a-day cocaine habit. It
was something that the homophobic, racist, archconservative, über
Republican Randolph B. Sumner would not tolerate, much less ac-
cept, so playing the truth card was not an option. That harsh, un-
changeable reality was what gave Alex sleepless nights and made him
wonder how he could take Camilla on a Kaua'i honeymoon when he'd
much rather be banging her gorgeous brother Beau.

"Oh, look," she cried. "There's Bitsy Covington." Her frantic wave
nearly dislodged a passing tray of bread puddings. "Bitsy! Over here,
honey!"

Bitsy was one of Camilla's sister debs and bridesmaids and thoroughly deserved her nickname "ditsy Bitsy." She was the silliest girl
Alex had ever met. She looked around the room trying to figure out
where the voice was coming from before finally spotting Camilla and
hurrying over to swap air kisses. Alex wasn't paying particular attention until Bitsy revealed she was lunching with the nearby mystery
man.

"My cousin Chandler Wilde is visiting from Key West," she announced. She was oblivious to any incestuous implications when she added, "He's so scrumptious I could just eat him with a spoon."

Alex was thinking the same thing as Bitsy motioned Chandler over.

"This is Camilla Spivey and Alexander Sumner, two of my dearest friends!" she announced with a great fluttering of hands. Alex recalled that he had seen her exactly once in the past year. "And they're engaged to be married. Isn't that delicious?"

Chandler smiled. Alex paled.

"Congratulations," Chandler said. He nodded politely to Camilla before making eye contact with Alex when they shook hands. Those blue eyes were even more disarming at close range, and his intense gaze triggered a familiar tingle inside Alex's Jockeys. "When's the wedding?"

"Ju—Ju—" Alex stammered, embarrassed when the word stuck in his throat. He coughed and tried again, knowing the twinkle in Chandler's eye was purely conspiratorial. "June."

"So soon? You must be very excited."

"You have no idea!" Camilla said.

"You're right. I don't."

Chandler's frankness was both unexpected and disarming. Bitsy's flutters and twitters filled the awkward silence that followed.

"Well, I'd just love to catch up, but we'd better order. I'm late as usual and I know Chandler's starving. We were supposed to—"

"She's right," Chandler interrupted. "Breakfast was inedible. I don't know which was worse, room service or the food."

"You're not staying with the Covingtons?" Alex asked. He was fishing for the name of Chandler's hotel when Bitsy unknowingly gushed to the rescue.

"Isn't that the silliest thing? Here we have just tons of room at home and Chandler insists on staying at Chez Royale in that awful old French Quarter. Well, we'd better scoot." More off-target kisses and Bitsy was off, Chandler firmly in tow.

With the lingering warmth of Chandler's hand, it was more difficult than ever for Alex to concentrate on Camilla's endless wedding prattle. She was obsessed with the subject, babbling incessantly about guest lists, caterers, florists, bridal showers, etcetera, ad nauseam. It was all mind-numbingly familiar territory. In fact, Alex couldn't remember talking about anything else since they announced their engagement at the Comus ball three months ago. That particular time and place had been his father's dictate, because all New Orleanians who mattered were present at this most prestigious of carnival events.

Alex did his best to nod and grunt on cue while trying to enjoy the restaurant's signature turtle soup and steal an occasional glance at Chandler. "Mmm-hmm."

The more he looked, the more he liked, and although the insistent throb against his thigh wasn't his cell phone, it gave him an idea. He looked into his lap and pretended to study the caller ID. "It's Daddy," he lied. "You know I have to take it."

Camilla resented the interruption, but whenever Alex's father was involved she was savvy enough to take a backseat. She said nothing as he slipped from the table and found a quiet corner where he could call Chez Royale. His message to Chandler's voice mail was right to the point.

"This is Alex and I know you're not there because we're still at Commander's. This is presumptuous as hell, but I'd love to get together. If that's possible, call me on my cell. Sooner is better than later."

Alex rattled off his phone number and hung up, hoping he hadn't sounded too needy. *God,* he thought. *What's the rush? Couldn't you at least have waited until after you took Camilla home?* He was embarrassed and a little flushed as he returned to the dining room. Camilla remained oblivious, resuming her wedding monologue as though he had never left. By the time he dropped Camilla at her parent's home, his head ached from her nonstop talking, and he was so edgy that he jumped when his cell vibrated.

"Hello."

"Alex?"

His heart leapt. "Chandler?"

"Yes."

"Oh, hi!"

"Got your message, buddy. I'd love to see you too, and yeah, sooner is definitely better than later."

"How about right now?"

"Terrific. I'm in the little cottage at the rear of the courtyard." Chandler's husky voice was even sexier than Alex remembered. "Shall I order something to drink?"

"Just something soft."

"Did you say soft?" Chandler chuckled. "You've got the wrong man, babe."

2

A Walk on the Wilde Side

Because Alex was in such a hurry, the traffic along St. Charles Avenue seemed to crawl, and then there was the familiar nightmare of parking in the congested French Quarter. He finally found a spot three blocks away from Chez Royale, and by the time he got to the rear cottage, the combination of haste, heat, and anxiety soaked him with sweat. He took off his jacket and slung it over his shoulder, embarrassed that his shirt was sticking to him. Chandler didn't seem to mind as he pulled Alex inside and slammed the door.

"Mmmmm . . ." Chandler moaned as they kissed and tangled tongues. He unbuttoned Alex's shirt and rubbed his damp chest. "I love a man who sweats!"

"Me too," Alex confessed, relieved and more excited than ever. "How about we work one up together?"

"You're reading my mind." Chandler smiled and mussed Alex's blond curls as they tumbled into bed. "C'mere."

With tongues and fingers as compasses, the two devoured each other, exploring every inch of their bodies, thrilled with each new discovery. Alex was eager to play submissive first mate to Chandler's aggressive captain, and surrendered to an invasion that left him breathless. Afterward, they leisurely showered and washed away the residue of their frantic romp in the sheets.

Alex knew he should be getting home but indulged himself a little longer when Chandler pulled him back into bed and held him close enough to share heartbeats. These days, the opportunity for privacy and being himself were almost nonexistent, and his comfort was reflected in a sigh of deep contentment.

"Yeah, me too." Chandler smiled. He stroked Alex's cherubic cheeks, still flushed with sex excitement. "You're really something."

"What do you mean?"

"I mean that you just about wore me out. Has it been a long time for you or are you always so insatiable?" Alex didn't respond. "Hey, man! Just ignore me if I'm getting too personal."

"No, no. It's all right." Alex took a deep breath and sighed as Chandler's hand wandered strategically and squeezed. "It has been a long time, and . . . well I haven't had all that much experience."

"Wow! You sure could've fooled me." Chandler's comment wasn't meant unkindly, and Alex knew it.

"And I'm sure you're wondering about Camilla."

"She crossed my mind," Chandler said, fingers deftly working Alex again. Both were somewhat surprised at the intensity and speed of his arousal. "Damn!" Chandler took Alex again, short and rough this time, before lying back and waiting for his breathing to return to normal. "Now where were we?"

Alex sighed. "The wedding. I know it sounds pathetic and ridiculous, but I've never been able to stand up to my father."

"Mmmm. Then I take it that: A, he wants you to marry this girl, and B, he doesn't know you like boys."

"Right on both counts. He's also the kind of man who can't take no for an answer."

"Even when so many human lives are at stake?"

Alex nodded, wondering why he made such a private admission to a perfect stranger. Obviously, those blue eyes that so energized his libido could also search his soul. "What does your mother think?"

"She was kowtowing to Daddy before I was born," Alex admitted gravely. "She never questions him either. No one does. Truth is she's so involved in all her club activities and antique rose gardens that I don't think she's given it much thought."

"Maybe you should tell her the truth," Chandler suggested. "See what she thinks. She might surprise you."

Alex shook his head and then laid it on Chandler's furry chest, toying with a nipple and longing to stay all night. "I wish I could, but I just don't know how she'd react. I'm afraid to risk alienating her."

"Mothers are pretty resilient creatures. Mine was very accepting. So was my father."

"Does Bitsy know about you?"

"I've not come out to any of my New Orleans family, but, God, they must have all been lobotomized if they haven't figured it out by now. Hell, I'm a thirty-eight-year-old bachelor decorator living in Key West. Duh!" Chandler chuckled. "I was going to tell Bitsy, but she's so dizzy she'd probably forget. Then again, I'm not sure she even knows what *gay* means." He studied the fatigue on Alex's face. "I've been there, man, and I really wish there was some way I could help." He brightened. "Want to run away to Key West? I'm leaving to-night."

"I wish I could," Alex confessed. "I wish I could just chuck every-thing, get the hell out of Dodge, and start over again."

"Why don't you?"

At the ripe old age of twenty-six, Alex was too embarrassed to ad-mit that he was totally dependent on his father, that all his credit cards were courtesy of Sumner Petroleum, and, worst of all, that he still lived at home. Nor was he keen to confess that his current predic-ament had him frightened, frustrated, and angry.

"It's way too complicated, Chandler. I know it sounds like a damned soap opera, but it's one of those family spiderwebs no one can escape."

"I understand."

"Thanks." Alex figured Chandler was just being polite, but he ap-preciated the gesture. He brushed the man's lips with a kiss and reached for his clothes. His damp shirt was clammy from the overly air-conditioned room and he shivered as he slipped it on. "I apologize for rushing off, but my family dines promptly at seven and I don't dare be late." He looked longingly toward the bed. "If I had my way, I'd climb back in there and go for thirds."

"I'm flattered." Chandler fished in his wallet for a business card. "I know you're going through a really rough patch, and if you ever want to talk or need a place to hide out, give me a call. No strings attached."

Alex was touched as he pocketed the card. "I appreciate that, Chandler. I really do."

Chandler nodded. "Good luck, buddy."

"Thanks. I'll need it."

They kissed once more, without passion this time, and Alex said good-bye. As he walked back to his car, he couldn't stop thinking about what Chandler said about running away. It was an alternative he had honestly never considered, much less voiced, but as he analyzed the possibilities he felt like Scarlett O'Hara at the end of *Gone with the Wind,* eyes streaming tears as she pleaded with a departing Rhett Butler: "Where shall I go? What shall I do?"

Rhett announced that he didn't give a damn, but Alex knew his father would never be that indifferent. If he ever tried leaving New Orleans, his father would track him down like a dog. Or would he? If he knew his son was gay, would the elder Sumner say good-bye and good riddance? If so, how hard would it be for Alex to start a new life without friends or funds?

The more Alex weighed the possibility he'd never dared consider, the more excited he became. He also became terrified because it involved standing up to his father, something else he'd never done. The wedding loomed like a time bomb. *If not now,* he thought, *then when? This is my life hanging in the balance, and if I don't put up at least token resistance I'm not sure I can live with the consequences.* As Chandler said, mothers are full of surprises, and maybe, just maybe, Daddy would be too.

Only one way to find out.

⟵ 3 ⟶

Pardon My French

Alex's heart thumped as he pulled up before the Garden District mansion he had always called home. People seeing the nineteenth-century Italianate mansion for the first time invariably marveled, but for Alex it was like the gilded cage in that old song, and as he walked across the veranda he was overwhelmed with foreboding, and his excitement faltered. The uneasiness deepened when he went inside and donned a fresh shirt before heading to the library. He knew he'd find his father there, sitting in the same leather club chair, having his usual double bourbon while watching stock reports on television.

Everything was totally predictable, but that was about to change.

Alex paused a moment to muster courage before sliding open the pocket doors and entering his father's inner sanctum.

"Hi, Daddy."

"About time," his father said, pounding his fist against the arm of the chair when he saw that one of his pet stocks had taken a dive. "I was wondering why you took the afternoon off without permission. I was just about to call the police and have them drag the river."

Randolph B. Sumner (plenty of people speculated about what the "B" stood for) was attempting a joke, but Alex never saw him as anything but dead serious. As long as he could remember, his father had been totally humorless, and flaunted a physical demeanor that spoke volumes, even to the casual observer. At six feet three inches he towered over his son, and was impressively fit for a man of fifty-eight, the result of religious workouts at the New Orleans Athletic Club. He also played golf, hunted in the bayous, and deep-sea fished in the Gulf, usually with Alex in tow despite the fact that his son hated all three pastimes. His thick shock of white hair, once as blond as Alex's

13

curls, showed no signs of thinning, but what might have been a handsome face was undermined by perpetual sternness. No one knew if the
look was natural or if it was cultivated to intimidate family and industry rivals, but it succeeded at both. Sumner was a formidable force in
the boardroom, notorious for never cutting a deal unless he took the
lion's share of the profits and for the kind of detailed homework that
kept him a step ahead of the competition. He heard what he wanted
to hear and ignored the rest, and his ruthlessness had built an empire
from the half dozen oil wells bequeathed by Alex's grandfather.

Now, at his peak of power, Sumner B. Randolph was, depending
on who you asked, one of the most hated and admired men in America.

"Well?" he demanded.

Alex braced himself for the lie. "I had lunch with Camilla at Commander's and since I didn't have any appointments this afternoon I
went for a drive. I know I should've called the office but . . . well, I had
some serious thinking to do."

Thick white eyebrows rose. "Oh?"

"We need to talk, Daddy."

Recognizing something new in his son's voice, the elder Sumner
was instantly on the alert. "Want a drink?"

"No, sir."

"Go on then."

Alex took a deep breath, feeling like he could hardly breathe. He
was about to put a lifetime of obedience behind him and march un-
armed into the lion's den. *Do it,* he told himself. *It's now or never!*

"I don't want to marry Camilla."

The silence that followed roared in Alex's ears, and for a moment
he wondered if his father heard him. There was no change of expression, no sign of recognition or acknowledgment, nothing. The first
sound was the clink of ice as his father drained his drink and poured
another one. Alex had seen this brand of silent intimidation in the
boardroom and thought he would scream if his father didn't say
something.

"Did you hear me, Daddy?"

"I heard you, Alexander. I'm just trying to determine why you've suddenly decided a beautiful woman from one of the best families in the city isn't good enough for you. I cannot possibly imagine what reason you might have." He sipped the bourbon and studied Alex over the rim of the glass. "I'm waiting."

Alex opened his mouth to say "I'm gay!" but instead he blurted, "I don't love her."

His father's reaction was arctic but unsurprising. "For God's sake, boy. Is that all?"

Alex hated it when his father called him "boy."

"I thought that was a pretty important factor," Alex replied, struggling to press his case. "I mean, you love Mom, don't you?"

"We *learned* to love each other," his father said. "Oh, I suppose some young fools are nuts about each other, but our marriage was like yours. A merger, of sorts."

Alex was pained by the indifference of the statement. "We're not talking about two oil companies, Dad. We're talking about people's lives, people who—"

"Damned right we're talking about oil companies, boy! Cleve Spivey owns fifty-one percent of Gulf South Oil, and we're looking to put our businesses together as a legacy for you and his daughter."

The truth floored Alex. He knew it of course, but to hear it spoken was both ugly and painful. It also pissed him off. "So this is really all about you and Mr. Spivey, isn't it? You're just looking to expand your empires with Camilla and me as collateral."

His father's eyes narrowed. "What's gotten into you, boy? After all, you'll stand to inherit one of the largest—"

"What do I care about an inheritance if my life is miserable?" Alex was surprised by his daring declaration. No one, absolutely no one, ever questioned the red-faced man glowering across his desk. "Daddy, I—"

"Why, you ungrateful little snot-nosed—"

"You're not listening to me, Daddy!" Alex cried, hastily plumbing his newfound courage to interrupt a man whose temper was mounting like a Gulf hurricane. "What about my personal happiness?"

"This is not just about your happiness!" his father thundered, impervious as usual to other opinions. "We're talking about families here. God *damn,* boy! You're a Sumner of New Orleans. That's a privilege, a noble obligation to be appreciated and honored. It's not something to be thrown away like trash. Camilla's father was King of Rex and your mothers were both Queens of Comus. Your pedigrees are impeccable, and a merger of the two families will—"

"Stop talking about mergers, Daddy!" Alex yelled. "All this phony baloney royalty makes me sick. Who really gives a shit about Mardi Gras kings and queens?!"

Sumner blanched at this unthinkable sacrilege. *"What?!"*

"You heard me!" Alex railed. "I'm tired of being a pawn in some kind of stupid carnival chess game!"

With his father momentarily stunned into silence, Alex continued to state his case. His mother, Karen, was also silent. Drawn by the loud shouts, she stole down the hall and listened just outside the library doors. She was as shocked as Sumner by their son's atypical behavior, but unlike her husband, a smile crept across her face as she listened to Alex dissect New Orleans society and lambaste values he found empty and stifling. As he talked on, warmth stole into a heart she believed was dead.

Alex's voice grew louder, more enraged, as years of resentment and emotional abuse boiled over and spilled at his father's feet. "I'm sick of seeing the same damned faces I've seen all my life and belonging to the same old clubs and going to the same parties and galas. I'm tired of the same fund-raisers and charity balls. I'm sick and tired of all of it!"

His father was a rumbling volcano, his infamous temper on the verge of eruption, but he mentally counted to ten. He was a cold, indifferent man, but he was not blind as he plumbed for the truth behind his son's wildly uncharacteristic behavior. "It's not just about Camilla then. It's more than that, isn't it?"

"Yes!" Alex shot back.

Now was the moment when he should have told the truth, when he should have shouted to the rooftops that he was a proud gay man, not a time to be some pathetic spineless soul to be railroaded into blind obedience and coerced into living a lie. He took his umpteenth deep breath and struggled for control as the words formed deep in his gut and bubbled toward the surface. They were on the verge of explosion when his mother slid open the doors and joined him in the lion's den.

"My goodness!" Karen exclaimed, always the peacemaker. "The whole household can hear you all!"

"What the hell do you want?" Sumner growled.

Karen Sumner was a diminutive, soft-spoken woman who looked like she'd jump if anyone said, "Boo!" Just then, however, something in her demeanor made her loom large, and there was a flash in the gray eyes neither man had seen as she walked right up to her husband.

"I'm proud of Alexander for speaking his mind, Randolph. What's more, I agree with him."

Sumner reeled from his second big shock of the day. "You . . . you what?!"

"I've never especially liked Camilla," Karen confessed. Her words were genteel but their impact was razor sharp. "I think she'll be nothing but trouble for our only child. She's vain and self-centered and manipulative, and despite her impeccable social credentials, I don't want her to be the mother of our grandchildren."

Summer was deadly accusatory. "Why didn't you say something before now?"

"Would it have made any difference?"

His response was nothing if not honest. "No. Because I know more about this than both of you put together." Karen moved beside her son, pleased when he slipped an arm around her waist. The gesture did not go unnoticed. "And don't think ganging up will do any good. Cleve Spivey and I have a gentleman's agreement and, like it or not, the wedding will take place as scheduled."

"Not without a groom," Alex said.

His father drained his bourbon and slammed it down so hard Karen was surprised the Waterford didn't shatter. "Boy, you'd better listen and listen good," he snarled. His voice was low and controlled, carrying far greater impact than a shout because it was such a pure, raw threat. "Unless you want to be cut out of every cent of your inheritance, you'll march down the aisle of St. Patrick's Church on June twelfth and take your wedding vows like a dutiful son. End of discussion!" He stomped down the hall, bellowing at his longtime butler, Jedediah, to serve dinner.

The moment his father issued the outrageous ultimatum and stormed out, Alex decided to leave home.

"Mom," he said, looking around a room that had been the scene of so many painful edicts, "I think I've just had an epiphany."

"Want to share it?"

"I'd rather you be as surprised as me."

"Something tells me your father will be more surprised than you and me put together."

"Bingo!" Alex gave her a quick kiss and offered his arm. "Shall we?"

To dupe his father, Alex dutifully followed him into the dining room and ate his steaming shrimp gumbo as though nothing had changed. It was the only time he remembered a meal being taken in total silence until his father finished and rose to leave. As always, he would have the last word.

"Did I make myself clear in the library, Alex?"

Alex almost gagged on his phony humility. "Yes, sir."

"So you understand me better now?"

More than you know, Alex thought.

"Yes, sir."

"Good boy."

Alex glared at his father's back until it disappeared down the hall, ignoring the hated nickname and focusing on plans to leave. He decided to go that very night, while the fever to escape burned inside his belly, and knew he had only one friend who would understand his dilemma and offer safe haven. As Alex had hoped, a frantic call to his friend Jolie brought an invitation to come over right away and stay as long as he liked. Alex thanked him and grabbed a handful of what Jolie had nicknamed the three basic Ps—Prada, Polo, and Perlis, the latter being pricey local shirts with crawfish logos instead of polo players. He'd just begun stuffing them in his suitcase when his mother tapped at the door.

"It's me, darling!"

Time to share the epiphany, he thought. "Come in, Mom. I was just—"

"No need to explain." Karen registered no surprise when she saw the luggage, and to Alex's relief helped him pack. Her reason was heartfelt and stated with quiet dignity. "You've done what I've wanted to do for years, Alexander. Standing up to your father was a remarkable and courageous act and I am very proud of you. I always knew your moment would come."

Chandler was right, Alex thought. *Mother* did *surprise me.*

"But how did you know something *I* didn't even know?"

She smiled and smoothed an already perfect pewter coiffure. "Mothers always know, my angel."

He hugged her and then stepped back to look into eyes as warm and gray as his own. "You're really amazing, Mom. Especially about Camilla. She's always been on her best behavior around you. How did you know she was such a—"

"Selfish bitch?" Karen finished. When Alex looked shocked, she added, "Pardon my French, dear, but this is an old French town after all." She smiled. "As far as Camilla is concerned, it was pure female instinct on my part, plus another irrefutable reality."

"Which is?"

"What I told you earlier, darling. Mothers always know, and sometimes they even know best." She pecked his cheek affectionately and said, "Now run along before your father figures out we're up to something."

4

Seeing Red

Alex gave his mother Jolie's phone number (grateful that she didn't ask about this "good friend" he'd never mentioned) after she promised to keep it a secret, tossed a couple of Gucci bags in the car, and headed downtown. He experienced a powerful rush of exhilaration as he raced past the clanging streetcars along St. Charles Avenue and crossed Canal Street into the French Quarter. Leaving behind his father's stifling dictates and the Garden District's leaden social obligations was like breaking out of prison. Alex knew there would be consequences for this daring deed, hell to pay in fact, but again he deferred to Scarlett O'Hara: *I'll think about it tomorrow.*

As he turned onto Royal Street, he phoned Jolie to ask him to open the gate to the carriageway alongside the house. He enjoyed another rush as the heavy iron gate swung shut behind him, physically and symbolically sealing him off from the outside world. Alex felt better still when he heard his pet name from somewhere deep in the courtyard.

"Back here, baby doll!"

"Hot stuff coming through!" Alex called back as he wound his way through the carefully orchestrated landscape of palms and bamboo, fountains and lotus pool, all designed to give the impression of a well-manicured jungle. Jolie was fond of telling everyone it inspired the fabulous garden Tennessee Williams described in *Suddenly, Last Summer.* Naturally he couldn't be bothered with the fact that the play was set in the Garden District, not the French Quarter, or that it was written before he met the playwright. Because of Jolie's passion for illusion—the grander the better—Alex thought he would have been wiser claiming to be inspiration for Blanche DuBois, the heroine of

A Streetcar Named Desire, who famously professed, "I don't want realism. I want magic!"

Jolie just never lets facts clutter up a good story, Alex thought with a smile. Lord knows I learned that the first time I saw the guy.

As he plunged deeper into the garden, Alex recalled their meeting at a Twelfth Night party two carnivals ago. He was wearied to the bone of dragging old ladies around the dance floor to the drone of a hopelessly dated band and was plotting escape when he was cornered by the one person he'd been avoiding all evening. Overdressed, half-soused, and old enough to be his mother, Margarita Bishop approached him like a galleon under full sail, ruthlessly intent on plastering her tired, half-bared knockers against his chest and groping his butt for the next dozen dances. Once Margarita caught his eye, there was no escaping, but just as she moved in for the lecherous kill, Alex was enveloped in a cloud of Jean Patou's Joy as a tall fiftyish woman materialized from nowhere and gracefully spirited him away. An infuriated Margarita was left in the lurch with only her hot hands and perpetually damp panties for company.

As he swept his mysterious dance partner across the dance floor, Alex took inventory and remembered seeing the lady earlier. Her slender body was elegantly swathed in vintage black silk Chanel, and she was the only woman wearing black, opera-length gloves and a hat with a fashion veil tucked under her chin. An enormous ruby sparkled on her finger, and it occurred to Alex that he had never seen a ring worn over gloves. He was also aware that everyone in the room was watching them.

"I don't know who you are, ma'am, but thanks for rescuing me from a fate worse than death."

"You are most welcome." Her voice was heavily accented. "I am Tatiana Yussupov, late of St. Petersburg." She cleared her throat. "And I do not mean Florida."

"Russia?"

"Russia."

"Your last name sounds familiar."

"Perhaps you have heard of my great-great-half-uncle Prince Felix Yussupov. He killed the monster Rasputin."

Alex wasn't too keen on history but he was a serious movie buff, and when he watched *Nicholas and Alexandra* for the costumes he inadvertently learned about the wanton monk who helped bring down the House of Romanov. He ran through his cinematic repertoire and mentally screened the scene when Prince Yussupov (Martin Potter) tried to seduce Rasputin (Tom Baker) with a gypsy transvestite (uncredited) before poisoning, stabbing, and shooting the monk to death. Alex had always wondered if the prince was gay.

"Really?"

Tatiana waved a gloved hand in dismissal. "Is nothing."

They danced in silence while Alex racked his brain to find a conversation topic. In desperation he mentioned Margarita who glowered at him every time he and Tatiana danced by. "I take it you know Margarita Bishop."

"I only know that the peasant insulted me once in her tacky gallery. I never forgave her, so when I saw her about to swoop down on another helpless young man, I intervened." She glared daggers through her veil. "Lecherous old drunk."

Alex chuckled. "Well put."

They ended the dance and began another. Tatiana eventually picked up the conversational gauntlet and told Alex about her former hometown, lapsing into Russian and French when she wanted to make a point. He didn't follow everything but was fascinated nonetheless, mostly because he'd never met anyone with such an exotic provenance. She was so captivating, in fact, that Alex forgot about the cute red-haired waiter who had been suspiciously attentive. It was just as well, he thought. He had an unbreakable rule: never cruise in uptown society, even if it was only the help.

As Jolie put it: "Don't shit where you eat."

"Dance me toward the door, dear boy," Tatiana whispered, "and we'll both escape this dreadful wake."

Ever mindful of manners, Alex asked, "Shouldn't we say good-bye to our hosts?"

"Why? They're as boring as their party."

"Good answer," Alex chuckled. "Why did you come?"

Tatiana shrugged. "Friends insisted."

"So you're not alone?"

"I came with my son, but he left with some young people about an hour ago. I don't mind taking a taxi."

"Where do you live?"

"These days I'm staying with my brother Jacques Menard. Perhaps you know him. He lives on Royal Street in the French Quarter."

"I don't know anyone in the Quarter," Alex confessed, "but I'd be happy to drop you off. It's still early and I was thinking about heading downtown for a drink anyway. I wouldn't be here, but it was important to my parents."

Tatiana beamed. "What a dutiful son."

Alex glanced around the room and spotted his mother. "I'll tell them I'm leaving and be right back."

"Perhaps you'll stop in for a nightcap," Tatiana suggested. "I have some divine Russian pepper vodka, and I promise I'm no Margarita Bishop."

Alex smiled as she squeezed his arm. "I'm sure you're not, and that sounds like fun."

Tatiana smiled. *"Bon."*

As he walked Tatiana to his car, Alex remembered he hadn't introduced himself. "Forgive my bad manners. I'm Alexander Sumner, but everyone calls me Alex."

"Oh, I know all about you, young man. I don't sweep just any stranger onto the dance floor. You needn't look surprised. I chatted with your parents earlier and they pointed you out. Your father is a rather . . . um, imposing gentleman. I would say he has a great deal of power and influence, perhaps too much for his own good."

Alex was surprised. "That's a lot to decide from a quick chat."

"Some people are name droppers," she explained. "Your father is what I call a power dropper. I've never heard so many politicians and CEOs jammed into a handful of sentences. I'm amazed he hasn't run for governor."

"He'd consider it a step down," Alex explained. "Especially in the power department."

Tatiana's eyebrows rose as she considered the remark. "Well, I must say he makes quite an impression."

"That's my daddy," Alex said. Coming from most sons, it would have been high praise, but the comment was laden with defeat and disappointment. Tatiana made no comment, just clapped her gloves together when Alex opened the car door.

"What a splendid automobile! A Jaguar, is it?"

"Porsche."

"I didn't know they came in red."

"They do if you have a rich daddy," Alex said, embarrassed by his sarcasm. "I'm sorry. That was really tacky."

"You're entitled, young man." Tatiana slid onto the supple leather with a smooth whisper of silk. "My family was rich too before those dreadful communists ruined things for everyone of quality. I've hated red for as long as I can remember." Remembering the color of Alex's car, she hastily added, "Unless it comes in Porsche of course."

5

Trés Jolie

As they drove downtown, Tatiana entertained Alex with vibrant tales about a Russian childhood and the drastic changes since the collapse of communism. She made the short drive seem even shorter, and before he knew it, Alex pulled up in front of a grand 1840s Creole townhouse wrapped in lacy iron galleries. Gaslights flickered alongside a front door flanked with slender Ionic columns. More splendor loomed behind an ornate gate that gave charming but necessary protection in a neighborhood that could turn ugly in the wee hours.

"We've both done good deeds tonight," Tatiana said, taking his arm as they climbed the three steps to the front porch. "I rescued you from Margarita and you've been kind to your elders."

Alex was about to insist she was hardly an old lady when Tatiana handed him keys for the gate and door. Her old-world manners and behavior reminded him of something out of a black-and-white film, and thoughts of old Hollywood lingered when she flipped a switch. A towering chandelier bathed the foyer with golden light, stunning Alex with the kind of dramatic opulence usually confined to movie sets. The vestibule was a sumptuous dream with gleaming marble floors reflecting the chandelier, gold walls and twin, life-sized blackamoors guarding a staircase that swept up to darkness.

"Welcome to *Le Garçonnière*." Tatiana said.

Alex gave her a strange look. "Isn't that an old French term meaning 'house for unmarried men'?"

"Ah! So you Garden District denizens do know something about the Quarter after all." Tatiana sounded pleased. "You're absolutely right. It's what you Americans used to call a 'bachelor pad.' The Creoles built them on their plantations, for stashing lusty adolescents and unmarried gentlemen and thus protecting any unmarried ladies in the Big House. Theoretically, anyway. They were never built in the Quarter. I just like the name." Tatiana flipped another switch and a smaller chandelier blazed in the front half of a double parlor. She indicated a marble-topped mahogany table groaning beneath a forest of decanters. "The pepper vodka is on the far left. It's red like your car. Please help yourself while I freshen up." She paused on the stairs, adding, "If my brother Jacques is home I'll send him down to entertain you while you're waiting. He can be *trés amusant!*"

"Uh, thanks."

Alex had never tasted pepper vodka, and he wasn't sure he liked the burn until after the third sip. He wandered around the room for five minutes or so, examining a costly art and antique collection, until a deep voice floated from the vestibule.

"Alex?"

"Yes?"

Alex faced a tall, slender man in slacks, crisp white shirt, and loafers without socks. Watch, belt, shoes and glasses were unmistakably Prada, and a spectacular emerald gleamed on his left hand. He looked bald until he moved under the chandelier and revealed a mostly shaved head. His exact age was elusive, but Alex found a clue in the patch of silver chest hair.

"I'm Jacques Menard, Tatiana's brother. She'll be back down in a moment." He shook Alex's hand and nodded at the vodka. "I see you've made yourself at home. Good. I think I'll join you."

Oddly enough, Jacques was shorter than his sister, but they shared the same high cheekbones and fine features. He also displayed Tatiana's elegant, continental grace as he poured a shot of vodka, lifted it in Alex's direction, muttered *"A votre santé!"* and downed it. He poured another and sat, a signal for Alex to do the same.

"Tatiana says you met at the Palamaras' Twelfth Night party." Alex nodded. "Terrible bores. And where in God's name do they find those antiquated orchestras? I swear those musicians are too old for Preservation Hall!"

"So were most of the guests," Alex offered.

"Which makes me wonder why a young man like yourself was there."

"My family," Alex said. He shook his head. "Sometimes I could choke on all the requisite noblesse oblige."

Jacques's eyebrows rose. "Do I detect a note of resentment?"

"I just get tired of the same routine, and don't worry, because I'm not going to bore you or myself with it." He glanced toward the stairs. "I certainly see a resemblance between you and your sister, but why are your accents so different? You sound American."

"I'm half. Our father was an American soldier in World War II and Mother was a Russian war bride. They met after the Siege of Leningrad and he brought her to the States. They divorced when I was eleven and Tatiana nine. I stayed here with him, but Mother took Tatiana to Leningrad where she still had family. It's St. Petersburg now of course. Anyway, Tatiana hated the communists but became somewhat obsessed with the Russia of the tsars. Mother was too young to even remember the Romanovs, but my sister took it as a personal cause to keep their memory alive. She was ecstatic when they found the Romanov bones, and for some reason felt personally obliged to attend services when the family was buried in the Peter and Paul Cathedral."

Alex was confused. "Maybe her obsession is because you're related to the man who killed Rasputin."

"Did she tell you that?" Alex nodded. "Well, I adore my sister but I'm afraid she has a vivid imagination. Our ties to the Prince are questionable at best. Mother has a distant Yussupov cousin by marriage, but apparently that was enough for my sister to ignore her given surname and present herself as a Yussupov. I suppose it does no real harm, but I find it a bit embarrassing. I feel far more American than Russian and have never regretted growing up here."

"I guess not," Alex offered. "And what brought you to New Orleans?"

"Amtrak," Jacques said with a twinkle in his eyes.

"Sorry. I didn't mean to pry."

"I was just teasing." When Alex took another sip of vodka and made a face, Jacques said, "That's meant to be tossed down in one gulp. It'll go down much easier."

"So will I," Alex laughed. "I'm feeling it already,"

The two made small talk for another ten minutes, during which time Alex forgot about Tatiana. Jacques was every bit as entertaining as his sister promised and captivated Alex with naughty stories about his world travels. Alex hung on his every word, relishing tales about this outrageous Bangkok bathhouse or that decadent Parisian club. He was especially intrigued when Jacques spoke of being gay as though it was a given. Alex both envied and admired the man's casualness in describing "a dashing Hungarian soldier who quite literally took my breath away and spirited me off to a desperately shoddy hotel on the Left Bank where we broke every commandment imaginable."

Alex's yearning for Jacques's worldliness and contentment with his identity made him want to confess the truth about his own sexual preferences, but paranoia threw up the familiar roadblocks. He tried hard to shrug it off. *After all,* he thought, *this is the French Quarter, not the Garden District, and I'll never see this man or his sister again.* He also told himself to relax, but another shot of vodka only triggered more frustration and confusion. Anticipating a foul mood, he glanced at his Rolex.

"I'd . . . I'd better be going."

Jacques frowned and made a face toward the staircase. "I'm afraid my sister has no concept of time, but I'm sure she'll be terribly disappointed if she doesn't get to say good-bye. Please help yourself to another shot of vodka while I go hurry her up."

Alex spun what he hoped was an acceptable lie. "Actually, I'm supposed to meet some people for a drink, and I'm already late."

"May I ask where you're going?"

Alex wasn't drunk, but the vodka snagged his tongue and he blurted, "Lafitte's."

Jacques smiled at the telltale revelation and cautiously probed. "Lafitte's Blacksmith Shop or Lafitte's in Exile?"

"I . . . I don't remember."

Jacques pushed the envelope. "You know of course that one bar is straight and the other is gay."

"Yeah?" Alex asked, suddenly on the defensive.

Of course he knew. He had been to the gay bar exactly twice, and spent both nights cowering in a dark corner, constantly looking over his shoulder, terrified he would be recognized. Alex swore he'd never return, but he was drawn again tonight by a force he couldn't resist.

Jacques nodded. "It's certainly none of my business, but it's my guess you don't really know which one you want these days."

"You're absolutely right, Mr. Menard," Alex said with exaggerated formality. "It's none of your business. Let me correct that. None of your *fucking* business!"

"Whoa! Sounds like I really hit a nerve."

Alex got to his feet. "I'm outta here."

"As you wish."

Jacques opened the front door and swung the gate wide, but Alex remained frozen in the parlor with a desperately lost look. "On second thought—"

"Yes, Alex?"

"Maybe . . . could I have a cup of coffee?"

"Of course."

Afterward, Alex could never explain why he asked for coffee or why he spent the next two hours confessing things to a stranger he'd never been able to admit to himself, a lengthy, painful litany of fears and anxieties about being homosexual. All he knew for sure was that the more he talked, the less frightened he was and the more relieved he felt. At fifty-two, the worldly-wise Jacques had enough experience to be a solid father confessor with all the right answers. He was also tenacious and wouldn't budge when he believed Alex was being evasive or dishonest. Although utterly sympathetic, he kept hammering away at Alex's tightly sealed Pandora's box until the air swarmed with all sorts of nasty gay bugaboos. Alex's emotional dilemmas were not resolved in one night, but he certainly acquired a much clearer idea of who he was and what he wanted from life.

For that he would be forever grateful to Jacques Menard.

Alex had been so totally immersed in his unexpected confessions that he forgot how he had gotten there until Jacques walked him to the door. "Whatever happened to Tatiana?"

Jacques chuckled. "I always told her she'd be late for her own funeral. Wait right here."

Alex watched Jacques race up the grand staircase and disappear behind the glittering chandelier. When Tatiana returned, Alex squinted in an effort to focus and wondered if the coffee had sobered him after all.

"What the—"

"Hello, darling!" Jacques called in his best Russian accent. He was poised midway on the stairs with black hat and veil back in place. Chanel pumps restored a height Alex noticed when they met. "Tatiana Yussupov. Late of St. Petersburg, and I don't mean Florida, honey."

A smile crept across Alex's face as he realized he'd been had. "Well, I'll be double damned!"

Jacques curtsied grandly and blew him a kiss. "No more secrets, eh, *mon ami?*"

Alex shook his head, fuzzier than ever from the pepper vodka. "So Tatiana doesn't exist and no one lived in St. Petersburg?"

"Or Paris, although I've spent *beaucoup* time in both places. That helped with the research." Jacques tossed the hat and veil aside. "Most of my friends call me Jolie."

Alex's head was exploding with questions. "So you went to the Palamara party . . . dressed as a woman?"

Jolie grinned. "You can call it drag if you like. It's something I do occasionally to amuse my uptown friends. Not all of those Garden District folks are stuffy, you know, and this is our little way of making a harmless tweak and having a royal good time. They love taking me to snotty parties and introducing me as an obscure Romanian Grand Duchess or Lady Edwina Pomegranate-Jones-Hyde-White or some such silliness. There's always some bourbon-soaked dowager or her pompous prick of a husband who wet their pants at the thought of meeting nobility, and I absolutely adore playing the role." When

Alex still looked baffled, Jolie said, "There's also another reason why I do it, my friend."

"What's that?"

"The same reason a dog licks himself, dear boy. Because he can!" He roared at his own joke before adding, "The truth is I'm just a plain old Cajun lad, and to paraphrase Auntie Mame's bosom buddy Vera Charles, 'When you come from Bellefleur, Louisiana, you have to do *something!*'"

6

Homecoming

Memories of that milestone night and the strong friendship it spawned danced happily in Alex's mind as he found Jolie in the gazebo and leaned down to give him a kiss. "I was just thinking about the night we met."

"Ah, yes," Jolie chuckled. "When the rich uptown kid met Mother Russia."

"I was so naive," Alex said, collapsing tiredly into a wicker chair. The weight of the night's events were catching up with him.

"Are you saying Tatiana wasn't convincing?" Jolie demanded, pretending mock anger. "I thought she was *trés magnifique!*"

"Of course she was. Only that accent sounded more like Bela Lugosi in *Dracula*. Or should I say *Dragula?*"

"Fuck you, dollink!" Jolie growled, giving him a playful swat. He nodded toward a silver tray with a chrome art deco shaker, two Rosenthal stemmed glasses, and a small china bowl of olives. Jolie never did anything halfway. "Thank God you're finally here. I've been absolutely perishing for a cocktail, but you know I never drink alone." He filled their glasses, took a generous sip, and sighed. "Mmmm. Sheer nectar!"

Jolie was dying to know why the urgent phone call, but he had promised Alex "no questions asked" and was a man of his word. Besides, he understood Alex better than anyone and knew it was only a matter of time before he learned everything. Sure enough, when Alex started talking it was like the night they met. Two hours and as many martini pitchers later, Jolie had received a play-by-play description of all that had gone down in the Sumner household, tonight and in years past. A good listener, Jolie's response was to loft his martini high.

"Hallelujah! It's about fucking time!" He clinked Alex's glass. "Congratulations, baby doll. I'm very proud of you and, from what you just told me, so is your mother."

"Thanks," Alex said. "I'm pretty proud of me too, but I'm not sure where this is going. In fact, I haven't a clue."

"Well, for one thing you've decided not to be railroaded into a heterosexual marriage built on lies that will surely make everyone wretched, destroy lives, and produce children doomed to divorced parents." He took a deep breath and exhaled slowly. "God knows I've been there, done that." Because Jolie rarely mentioned his son William, the product of a very young, very ill-advised marriage, Alex never fished for more. "Supposedly we're living in more enlightened times where a man doesn't have to marry to hide his true sexuality, but there are still plenty who get caught in the tragic backwash of family obligation and all that crap. You have no idea how much heartbreak you're saving everyone, even your father, although he's too stupid to realize it."

"He sees only what he wants to see," Alex said, sadness creeping into his voice. "Always has. Always will."

"Enough about him!" Jolie said, quick to stem what threatened to dampen an evening of exciting revelations. "It's *your* night and you don't have to make any more major decisions. Just hang around *Le Garçonnière* a while and unwind. Let's see. Tonight's Friday, so you don't have to go to work for a couple of days."

"Are you kidding?" Alex growled. "I'll never work for that bastard again!"

Jolie beamed at the determination in this new-and-improved Alex's voice. "All right then. I'll get on the horn tomorrow morning, not too early mind you, and rustle up a party for tomorrow night. We need to do something to celebrate your personal gay independence day."

"Why wait until then?" Alex beamed, giddy with a surge of good spirits, his and those of the vodka. "Let's go to Lafitte's for a nightcap." He winked and added, "Correction. Make that Lafitte's in Exile."

"That's my boy!" Jolie said. "I'll grab a quick whiz and we'll be off."

Named after Jean Lafitte, the dashing pirate who fought alongside General Andrew Jackson in the Battle of New Orleans, the two bars occupied opposite ends of a block of Bourbon Street in the heart of the gay area. The original, a 1772 French colonial structure at the corner of St. Philip Street, was the oldest gay bar in America until the 1970s when new owners booted out the clientele and turned it into a straight piano bar. In playful protest, the orphaned owners reopened at the other end of the block, installed a campy memorial flame just inside the door, and called themselves Lafitte's in Exile. It was easily the most popular gay bar in the city, and at eleven on a Friday night it was jammed.

Alex and Jolie made a strange couple, the short, curly-haired blond and the tall, bald gentleman twice his age. Both knew there was plenty of son-daddy speculation, but each had his own agenda as they waded into a crowd of all ages, shapes, sizes, and colors, with only their sexuality as a common denominator. Because Chandler's beautiful body and the afternoon's two intense orgasms lingered in his memory, Alex had honestly not been in a cruising mood when he suggested the nightcap. It took about two minutes in this room reeking of sweat, sex, and a soaring testosterone level to change his mind. More specifically, a slender guy with close-cropped brown hair and the requisite Vandyke changed it for him, especially when he flashed Alex a big smile.

"Check it out, Jolie!"

Jolie didn't respond, totally lost in a monitor showing rapid-fire clips from *Mommie Dearest* with Joan hammering Christina while Abba sang "Mamma Mia." Alex nudged him and cupped a hand to his ear, shouting over the din.

"Over in the corner. In the red tee. Check it out."

"Cute as a button," Jolie agreed, "but I have someone else in mind for you."

Alex was surprised. "Who?"

Jolie nodded in the other direction. "Over there by the eternal flame. The gent in the navy Polo shirt and jeans. He's an old friend I've always considered devilishly handsome, and I wish I could personally confirm the rumor that he's more than generously endowed. Not that such things are important of course."

"Only to those who don't have them," Alex laughed.

Jolie rolled his eyes indulgently. "You have a great deal to learn about the gay world, my boy. Those who are not blessed in the penile department have been known to develop other highly desirable talents." When Alex gave him a blank look, Jolie shrugged. "Who am I kidding? I don't believe myself either!"

Alex craned his neck to get a better look through the shifting crowd. After several glimpses, he hit the bull's eye, a deeply tanned guy in his mid-thirties, on the chunky side with a thick shock of prematurely gray hair. His jaw dropped as recognition swept over him.

"Oh my God. It's Duncan Stone. He and Daddy are in the same krewe!"

"Hardly surprising since he's from your neck of the woods. Or should I say your ex—neck of the woods."

"Shit!"

Alex was tormented by the familiar fear that he would be recognized in a gay bar, but Jolie read his mind and responded immediately. "Be logical, baby doll. Duncan's in no position to point fingers and incriminate himself. Believe me, he's been a familiar fixture on the Quarter gay scene for years."

Alex shook his head, stunned by a glimpse of what he might have become a decade from now. Duncan was everything Alex's father wanted him to be: Married to the perfect Junior Leaguer. Father of two children, a son at Tulane, a daughter in Sacred Heart. Membership in all the right clubs and carnival krewes. Season tickets to the opera and a box at the Superdome. The magnificent Garden District mansion on First Street.

"Here's another surprise for you, my pet. Duncan's one of my uptown chums who first suggested I don some royal drag and pay a call on the local gentry."

"I'll be damned!"

"Don't you want to say hello?"

Alex laughed as he saw Duncan in a different, nonthreatening light. "I do now!"

Because of the fifteen-year age difference, Alex and Duncan had only a passing acquaintance, but whenever their paths crossed Alex had drooled. His favorite recollection was when Duncan joined him and his father for a round of golf at English Turn that past summer. The weather had been so murderously hot that they hit the showers after only five holes, and when Alex glimpsed Duncan in nothing but a wet towel, he duly noted a tantalizing tent. The guy had a bit of a belly, but that didn't bother Alex, and the overall erotic image danced vividly in his mind as Jolie led him through the noisy, jostling throng.

"Duncan!" Jolie yelled. "Over here!"

Jolie blocked Duncan's line of vision as he leaned down and kissed him on both cheeks. Then he shouted something in his ear and stepped aside. As Duncan recognized Alex, the shock on his face was unforgettable.

"Alex Sumner! I don't believe it!"

"Believe it!" Alex shouted, grinning as they shook hands and then heartily embraced.

"I'm floored," Duncan said, turning to Jolie. "I've lusted after this lad for more years than I care to think about. He just about drove me crazy when we played golf last summer."

"Really?" Alex was thrilled that Duncan remembered.

"Damned right. I played a terrible game that day because I kept sneaking peeks at you when your old man wasn't looking. When I saw you without your shirt in the locker room I almost threw a boner!"

"I know," Alex said.

Duncan roared with laughter. "Was it that obvious?"

"It was to me," Alex confessed. "And you weren't the only one who got excited!"

Duncan beamed. "So *that's* why you hurried off to the shower?"

"Exactly!"

"Talk about two horny ships passing in the night." He gave Alex a hungry look. "How come I've never seen you here before?"

"I've only been here a couple of times, and I was so scared I hid in a corner."

"Poor baby." Duncan pulled Alex close. "You don't look scared now."

"I probably should be. After all, I've just run away from home."

Duncan was stunned all over again. "What?!"

"It's kind of a long story."

"Not necessarily. Remember, I've known your father a lot of years, Alex, and I can pretty much fill in the blanks."

Alex nodded, relieved. "I guess you could at that."

He returned Duncan's smile, amazed at how relaxed he felt, the ease with which he was talking to an uptown acquaintance in a gay bar. He had always feared this sort of encounter, but now that it was here he welcomed it. No doubt because the man involved was Duncan Stone, someone he'd always admired and now found hotter than ever. He felt like he could melt in those dark brown eyes and hungrily speculated about what raw joy it would be to explore that big, furry body. He could almost feel his fingers tangling in Duncan's silver hair as he pulled their faces together and shared a first kiss.

"What?" Alex leaned closer, unable to hear over the throbbing music. "I can't hear you, Duncan."

"I said let's go to the upstairs balcony and get away from the smoke and the noise."

"Okay."

"No, wait! On second thought, let's go back to my house."

Alex's eyes widened. "Are you crazy?!"

Duncan grinned. "Not uptown, babe. I have a little *pied-à-terre* a couple of blocks over on Dauphine Street."

"Really?"

"Yes, really," Jolie said. To Alex's surprise, he had managed to hear every word. "And there's no place like it on earth. Guaranteed."

"No whips and chains I hope."

"Nothing of the sort," Jolie assured him. "It's just something very clever on Duncan's part and you really must see it for yourself." He looked from one to the other and grinned at the match. "What fun! I feel just like Dolly Levi."

Alex was dying to go home with Duncan, but he was also a man of strong loyalties. He smiled at Jolie. "But I'm with you, kid."

Jolie was genuinely moved and brushed Alex's cheek with a kiss. "That's very sweet, baby doll, but you needn't keep me company. I'll see you in the morning at breakfast."

Alex was both thrilled and embarrassed by the implication. "Are you sure—?"

"Absolutely. As a matter of fact why don't you bring Duncan for breakfast too? We'll make it a foursome."

Alex frowned. "Who's the fourth?"

"That divine little number in the red tee you ogled earlier. I don't know if it's his pecs or my last vodka but suddenly he looks real yummy. What's more, he's giving *Maman* a steady cruise, so now, *exeunt!*"

Jolie blew kisses in their general direction and was swallowed by the crowd.

Duncan was still chuckling when he turned back to Alex. "Ready?" he shouted.

"I've been ready for years!" Alex shouted back.

7

Double Your Pleasure

Alex followed Duncan into the relative quiet of Dumaine Street, pleased when Britney, Christina, Mariah, and Madonna stopped screaming in his ears. It was two blocks to Duncan's house, a tidy duplex dripping with Victorian trim in the 1100 block of Dauphine. In New Orleans it was called a double shotgun, double because there were two sets of front and back doors with mirrored floor plans, and shotgun because of the series of connecting rooms with no central hall. Locals said you could put a shotgun at one end and blow out the last wall with a single blast.

"Nice little house," Alex said.

"Nothing like uptown, of course, but I prefer it for a lot of reasons. You'll see why." He looked from one front door to the other. "Hmmm. I'm trying to decide which half to show you first."

"What's the difference?"

"You'll see."

Duncan unlocked the right front door and motioned for Alex to follow. The inside was dark and remained that way, even after Duncan flipped a switch by the door. A single, naked lightbulb, thirty watts max, flickered and glowed overhead, a weak sun in a shadowy solar system. The tightly shuttered room was completely bare of furniture, as was the next and the next. The fourth room was recognizable as a bedroom only from a mattress on the floor. A folding chair and a rickety chest of drawers completed the funky interior design scheme.

"Well, well," Alex said, trying to make the best of things. "Looks like you're really into minimalism."

"It's more about practicality than aesthetics," Duncan agreed. "Especially if I bring home somebody with a tendency to 'borrow' things."

"What do you mean?"

"First a kiss, and then I'll tell!"

Alex got his earlier wish when Duncan brushed his lips with a kiss. He indulged himself further by tangling his fingers in the wavy silver hair and sharing a taste of his tongue. His arousal was instantaneous and intense, and he sighed with erotic anticipation.

"Mmmm."

"Me too," Duncan said, backing off. "I'd better show you the other half of the house before I'm too busy to find the key."

More intrigued than ever, and seriously excited as well, Alex followed Duncan back outside and waited for him to lock the right half of his house and unlock the left. When Duncan turned on the lights, Alex saw that the two sides could not have been more different.

"Like this a little better, eh?" Duncan teased.

"Wow!"

The front parlor could have been a showroom for Restoration Hardware meets Pottery Barn, a thoroughly masculine retreat with highly lacquered forest green walls, clubby brown leather furniture, and handsome retro lamps. Elegantly framed prints of prizewinning English livestock mixed with nineteenth-century paintings of Louisiana thoroughbreds, and the coffee table held stacks of expensive art books and a trio of antique *santos*. A silk Persian oriental rug tied all the colors together. There was more understated elegance in the dining room, bedrooms, bath, and kitchen.

"I don't get it," Alex said.

It's really very simple," Duncan said, taking Alex in his arms again and studying the troubled gray eyes. "I'm the first to admit I have an enormous sexual appetite, for men that is, and I bring them home on a pretty regular basis. Who they are depends on whether they're taken to the Ritz or the Pits."

Alex smiled at his deluxe surroundings. "This half being the Ritz of course."

"Right. If they're rough trade or hungry little hustler types, which I really don't care for that much but confess to occasionally indulging, I take them next door where there's nothing to steal." He brushed Alex's lips with another kiss. "On the other hand, if they're gentlemen of quality and breeding, such as yourself, I bring them here. It's really just a matter of economics. I only needed to get ripped off once to realize how to solve the problem once and for all."

"Jolie was right. This is amazing."

"So's this," Duncan said, helping himself to a handful of Alex's swollen flesh. "And I can't wait to see it up close and personal."

"Same here." Alex returned the gesture and felt what he'd dreamed about since last summer. As Jolie had speculated, Duncan was enormous. "Damn!"

Duncan nuzzled Alex's neck with a stubbly chin. Alex trembled with the rough sensation. "Let's go to bed, huh?"

"Oh, yeah!"

They left a trail of clothing from one end of the shotgun to the other before climbing into Duncan's towering four-poster bed. When Alex was with a man for the first time, he liked to massage the guy through his shorts before getting to the Main Event, but this one was in such a hurry there was no chance.

"Come here, baby."

With an eye on the prize, Duncan practically tore off Alex's boxers and licked his chest and belly before trailing his tongue further south.

"Mmmm!"

Alex lay back, closing his eyes and floating with the moment. He couldn't believe the man giving him such incredible erotic joy was Duncan Stone, that he was actually living out a fantasy for the first time in his life. It was an exhilarating experience that threatened to spiral out of control and end as quickly as it had begun, until Alex pulled away.

"Easy," he gasped. "You're getting me too hot too fast."

"Is there really such a thing?" Duncan asked. When he noticed Alex's sex-flushed face, he knew the guy wasn't kidding. "Okay then. Your turn." He rolled onto his back and yanked down his shorts, tossing them into a corner and exposing his equipment for the first time.

"Man, what a beautiful package!"

"It's all yours," Duncan said, putting a hand on the back of Alex's head and guiding him to the target. Alex was no expert and promptly choked on the oversized prize.

"Shit, Duncan! It's too damned big."

Duncan was patient. "Just do what you can, baby. It's all right."

Alex was frustrated. "But I want it all!"

"Then go slow and take deep breaths. You'll surprise yourself."

Alex followed Duncan's advice and, after some more failed attempts, slowly conquered the target. He moaned, thrilled with his success, but didn't stop until he'd claimed complete victory.

"That's it!" Duncan sighed as more sexual warmth flooded his body. "That's the way."

Once he mastered the technique, Alex got sassy and gave Duncan a mischievous look. "I was just thinking about Mae West."

Duncan frowned. "Well, that may be the most unromantic thing anyone ever told me."

"Relax, man. She said, 'Too much of a good thing is wonderful,' and now I know just what she meant."

"So do I, baby!" Duncan tangled his fingers in the blond curls as Alex deftly finished the job. "So do I!"

🐇 8 🐇

Monty's Python

The next eight hours were utter bliss. Alex had enjoyed the tryst with Chandler, but the nonstop romp in Duncan's bed was downright phenomenal. Alex had never had sex so many times with the same man, but was secretly relieved when Duncan fell asleep. They both snoozed until the phone rang at 11:00 a.m. Duncan's groggy hello told the caller everything.

"You naughty boys have missed breakfast," Jolie mock scolded. "And you're about to miss brunch. Shall we aim for lunch now?"

Duncan turned away so his morning breath missed Alex. "Want to have lunch with Jolie?"

"What happened to breakfast?" Alex muttered sleepily.

"This happened!" Duncan said, taking Alex's hand and putting it between his warm thighs. He chuckled. "Well?"

"Lunch," Alex grunted, sliding low in the bed and dragging the covers with him so he exposed Duncan's huge morning erection. "Mmmm!"

"What time?" Duncan asked Jolie.

"Noonish. We'll have mimosas in the courtyard and then ramble the Quarter until we find something festive."

"Great. See you then."

Duncan hung up and watched Alex prove that what he'd learned the night before was no fluke. Duncan sighed, thinking he hadn't enjoyed head this good since wrangling with that hunky Cajun from Galliano. He still couldn't believe the history of the hot young man giving him so much pleasure.

"Damn!" he muttered. "If your father only knew!"

"Yeah!" Alex said, going at it with a vengeance. "Let's send him a video and give him a heart attack!"

The fun, albeit of a different sort, continued at lunch. Jolie had a sudden urge for Vietnamese food and drove them to New Orleans East, to the area called Little Saigon where locals in coolie hats worked the rice fields like it was the Mekong instead of the Mississippi delta. They gorged on shrimp spring rolls and a hearty bowl of *pho* before continuing their lazy, serendipitous afternoon. Next stop was the Country Club, a gay venue in a funky neighborhood called The Bywater. It was Alex's virgin visit, and when he learned swimsuits were optional, he embraced his newfound freedom with a vengeance. He announced he was going *au naturel* and insisted Duncan follow suit or, as Jolie put it, *sans* suit. When Duncan protested he was ashamed of his soft belly, Alex assured him that no one would notice it.

"Not when you unleash the python," Alex laughed. Duncan said maybe and went inside the clubhouse to get everyone drinks.

Jolie's eyebrows darted up. "So the rumors are true."

"Absolutely. That's why I nicknamed him Monty."

"Like *The Full Monty?*"

"No, but that's good too." Alex cackled. "Actually I was referring to Monty Python. I swear the damned thing's like a giant snake!"

Jolie grinned. "Do tell!"

"Maybe you'll see for yourself."

When Duncan surrendered to queer peer pressure and stripped bare-ass, Jolie gasped, along with the rest of the Country Club, at what had kept Alex entertained all night. Alex had been right in predicting no one would notice anything above Duncan's crotch. One guy walking the edge of the pool was so riveted that he lost his balance and fell in the water, to the hoots and whoops of his equally mesmerized buddies.

"I've been coming here for years, and I've never seen anyone turn so many heads," Jolie said. "I guess it's just a matter of knowing your audience."

"Not to mention giving them what they want!" Alex said with a laugh. "C'mon, Jolie. You're next."

"No, no, my pet," Jolie replied, stripping only to his Prada shorts and slathering heavy-duty sunscreen on every exposed pore, including his shaved pate. "I subscribe to the Gypsy Rose Lee school of cruising. Promise 'em more, and then don't give it to 'em." He turned to Alex as Duncan waded into the water. "For the love of God! That's the kind of package UPS would have trouble handling."

"Tell me about it," Alex said. "Which reminds me. What happened with Mr. Red Tee? I thought breakfast was supposed to be a foursome."

"We had breakfast in bed," Jolie smirked. "And then he had to be on his merry way, home to Boutte, of all the Godforsaken places. I must say I took full advantage of his youthful charms. He left with a bit of a 'hitch in his git-along,' as they say in Mississippi. And with a new nickname, too."

"The booty from Boutte?"

"Very impressive!" Jolie was amused at being second-guessed. "Learning at the master's knee, are we?"

"So to speak," Alex said, leaning over to give him a buss.

Jolie shook his head. "You truly amaze me, Alex. I mean, you are coming out of the closet with awesome gusto. I am so proud of your newfound self-confidence and, frankly, very happy to be a part of it."

Alex was touched. "I'm not as brave as I pretend, Jolie. Underneath it all I'm still scared to death." His scanned the pool. "On the other hand, I'm also like a kid in a meat market. Just look at all that Grade-A beef!"

He and Jolie watched handsome, red-haired lovers walk by arm-in-arm, shoulder length hair tied in neat ponytails, intimate equipment swinging free in the breeze. A gorgeous black man with a killer bubble butt trailed, and behind him were three gym bunnies with carefully sculpted pecs, abs, glutes, and lats. All were walking ads for Speedos. Of course there were plenty of other not-so-perfect men with bald heads, pot bellies, and hairy shoulders, but Alex admired them all simply because they were announced to the world they were gay and didn't care who knew.

He shook his head. "I just keep thinking of those old T-shirts that said 'So Many Men, So Little Time.' It's true!"

"Down, boy. You're only twenty-six."

"Uh-oh," Alex said as Duncan splashed out of the water. "Hand me that towel, will you?"

"What's wrong, baby doll?" Alex draped a towel over his growing excitement as Duncan headed their way. "Oh," Jolie tittered. *"That."*

"Can't help it," Alex said. "The man makes me crazy." He beamed as Duncan stretched out beside him, deep tan gleaming beneath the sun. "How's the water?"

"Okay I guess." Duncan looked at his watch and sighed.

"Something wrong?"

Duncan shaded his face so he could look into Alex's eyes when he told the truth. "Just the inevitable."

Ouch, thought Jolie.

"What do you mean?" Alex asked.

"I have to go, babe. Felicity took the kids to her folks in Baton Rouge for the weekend and they'll be back at five. I should be there when they get home."

"Oh." The disappointment in Alex's voice was almost palpable. Duncan started to add something, but Alex said, "It's all right. I went into this thing with my eyes wide open. It's not like I didn't know you were married."

"That's my guy," Duncan smiled, relieved. He gripped Alex's thigh and squeezed affectionately. "How about a rematch next weekend? We can even do bad boy fantasies in the Pits if you like."

"I don't care what we do as long as we're together," Alex said. Jolie looked away and rolled his eyes. "Call me?"

"Absolutely. How long are you going to be at Jolie's?"

"As long as he likes," Jolie announced. "Do you want me to drive you back to the Quarter?"

"No thanks. I'll get the bartender to call a cab." Duncan leaned down and gave Alex a lingering smooch while half the Country Club turned emerald with envy. He blew Jolie a kiss, thanked him for lunch, and was gone.

"Go easy, baby doll," Jolie said.

"What do you mean?"

"I mean that you're acting like a smitten kitten."

"So what if I am?" He handed Jolie some sunscreen. "Put some on my back, will you please?"

Jolie smeared the grease on Alex's fair skin. "Duncan's an old friend, Alex, and a good one too, so I know he's a man of honor. Just as I know he's told you he has the sexual appetite of a wild boar. He'll hop on anything that's moving and slam it with that supertool of his. He's been doing it for years and there's no end in sight."

"I know all that, but—"

"But what?"

"I can't help having some feelings for the guy. I mean I've fantasized about him for years but never dreamed this could happen."

"Mmmm."

Alex sighed and stretched out on his belly "I'm telling you Duncan is the best damned sex I've ever had."

Jolie ignored the remark. "Do you want me to do your legs?"

"Please."

Jolie chose his words carefully as he massaged the sunscreen into the backs of Alex's calves. "Please don't read this wrong, Alex, but just last night you said the same thing about Chandler."

Alex swallowed hard as memories of Chandler washed over him like the hot Louisiana sun. Jolie was right, but Alex felt he had to defend himself. "Well, when I said it I meant it. Chandler was wonderful. Duncan was fantastic."

"And Chandler is in Key West and Duncan is married with an eternally roving eye." Alex's leg tensed beneath Jolie's fingers. "Sorry. Am I rubbing too hard?"

"No. But you're hitting below the belt."

"Easy, Alex."

"I mean it's not like I'm in love with these guys."

"No one said you were, darling boy, but I saw the look in your eyes and heard that vulnerable tone when you said you didn't care what you and Duncan did as long as you were together. Those aren't the actions of a guy saying good-bye to last night's trick, and, like it or not, that's all Duncan will ever be. He's smooth and charming and obviously a heavy hitter in the meat department, but that's it."

Alex grunted. "If you weren't right I'd be pissed. Really pissed."

Jolie gave his thigh an affectionate pat. "There are few things I admire more than a man who can admit a difficult truth. I just don't want you to get hurt. So far you've only dabbled in the gay life. When you embrace it full-time it's a whole new ball game, and it's not much different from the straight world." He thought for a moment. "Except we don't fake orgasms."

Alex chuckled, pleased when Jolie's joke made him forget his ache for Duncan. He found further balm when he propped himself on his elbows and ogled the bouncy butt of a blond about his age. The guy gave him a long cruise when he passed, then looked over his shoulder and smiled as he leaned against the cabana bar, bikini-wrapped buns aimed in Alex's direction.

"Nice ass," Alex mouthed.

Attention focused elsewhere, Jolie was oblivious. "If I were you, dear boy, I'd forget about Duncan and—"

"Thanks for the advice, but I'll be fine. Excuse me a minute."

Jolie watched Alex head for the bar and strike up a conversation with the blond. The two laughed together for a few minutes before diving into the pool and swimming toward the shallow end. It wasn't long before they pressed close together and nuzzled shamelessly.

"How quickly the young's wounds heal," Jolie muttered to himself. "Especially with such delicious medicine."

Jolie was hardly surprised when the blond bombshell invited Alex home, and once again he assured Alex he didn't mind being left behind. Solitude was, in fact, a state he had come to cherish, having enjoyed more than his share of romps and flings from Paris to Tangier, New York to New Orleans. Besides, he'd had one helluva time last night with the booty from Boutte. Jolie's good mood evaporated, however, when he returned home and found a phone message from Alex's mother he could barely understand through a heavy rumble of traffic.

"This is Karen Sumner. I'm on my cell so you may have trouble hearing me. Please tell Alex things are terrible at home and growing worse by the minute. His father is furious that he disappeared, and since nobody ever disobeys him it's impossible to know his next move. Of course Alex can come home and deal with it, but my advice is to stay away and keep a very low profile. I've never seen his father so angry and I'm worried that he's going to—" That part of the message was drowned out by what sounded like an eighteen-wheeler. When the racket stopped, Karen promised she would "call again tomorrow."

Jolie hit the "save" button. "Hmmm. I wonder if smooching naked in the swimming pool of a gay club is considered low profile."

He poured a glass of Evian and wandered to the second-floor gallery, drowsing on a chaise longue as he enjoyed the final moments of the day. Dusk always unleashed flocks of purple martins that swooped and dived in graceful flight as they gorged on mosquitoes. It also brought dazzling sunsets and fantastic cloud formations inspiring Tennessee Williams to proclaim New Orleans the best city in the world for skylights. Jolie had shared many similar twilights with Tennessee and lofted his glass toward a sky streaked with high-flying, heliotrope-tinged cirrus.

"Miss you, Tenn," he murmured. He sipped the mineral water and added, "Yeah, I know. It oughta be bourbon!"

Jolie lost himself in memories of Tennessee, concern over Karen Summer's phone call, and thoughts of Alex, the poor lost lamb whose future was about to be disrupted by angry ghosts from the past. The day's cocktail consumption crept over him, as inevitable as the dusk, and Jolie dozed until Alex came looking for him.

"What're you doing up here?"

"Just napping and waiting for you. You had a call from home and—"

"Daddy?!" A cold shudder rippled down Alex's spine.

"Calm down, baby doll. It was your mother. She was on her cell. I couldn't understand everything, but I saved it so you could hear it too."

Alex replayed the muffled message three times, listening as though his life depended on it, which, in a way, it did. He shook his head. "I still can't figure out what she was saying over that damned traffic."

"Call her."

"Are you kidding? Jedediah will be monitoring the phones and reporting all caller IDs to Daddy."

"I assume Jedediah is the faithful family retainer."

Alex nodded. "More like Daddy's faithful family spy."

"What about your mom's cell?"

"That's risky too because Daddy might be around. In fact, I wouldn't be surprised if he had her phone with him. Especially after she defended me." He paced the kitchen. "There's really nothing I can do except wait to hear from her again."

"Sounds like you were living under a benevolent reign of terror," Jolie ventured.

Alex looked drawn. "I honestly didn't realize how bad things were until I left and put things into some kind of perspective. You're right. Mother and I are like prisoners in our own home. Free to come and go but with strict parameters and curfews." He pounded his fist on the counter top. "If only I knew what she meant by 'I'm worried he's going to.'"

"You don't have a clue?"

"Not when it comes to my father. The night we met you said he had too much power for his own good, remember? You're right. I've seen him use it and I'm telling you that bastard can be ruthless when it comes to getting what he wants."

"So you're worried that it'll be aimed in your direction?"

Alex nodded. "It's my guess that Daddy will do just about anything to find me and make me marry Camilla."

"You're a grown man," Jolie reminded him. "He can't *make* you do anything."

"You don't know my father," Alex muttered glumly.

"Maybe not," Jolie conceded. "But I do know that my stomach is growling and that I have a million details to attend to for tomorrow night's cotillion."

"Who's coming out?"

"*You* are, my pet. It's a gay cotillion in your honor. Your official unofficial debut. Not that you haven't been debuting your charms all over the place these past thirty-six hours. Which reminds me. How was Blondy?"

"Disappointing."

"What happened?"

"Oh, he was hot all right. A hungry little bottom if I ever met one, but . . . well, I'd never been with a blond before."

"And?"

"Still haven't."

"I just knew that kid was a bottle blond," Jolie chuckled.

"That's not what I meant. He shaves his crotch!"

"Eeeew!"

"I think he shaves his chest too because it was stubbly. Why do guys do that? Man, if I had a hairy chest I'd be thrilled. I hate being hairless almost as much as being short."

"Supposedly bodybuilders started the trend because it shows their definition better. When the gay boys turned into gym freaks a couple of decades back, some of them followed suit, and as the eternal gay quest for trendiness continues, the rest is *histoire!*"

"Chests are one thing. But pubes?"

"The gay boys will do anything to look youthful, but that's definitely going too far. It's so creepy, so weird, so . . . so Jacksonian!"

Alex frowned. "What the hell has Andrew Jackson got to do with it?"

"Not Andy, you goofball! Michael!" When Alex stopped laughing, Jolie said, "Now be an angel and see if there's anything in the fridge besides champas and that tired jambalaya. *Maman* is absolutely famished."

❧ 9 ❧

Alex in Wonderland

"Well, well. Looks like we're off to see the wizard!"

Jolie sipped his champagne and scanned the courtyard with pride. After discovering all the party stores were closed on Sundays, and knowing there were no such things as cotillion decorations anyway, he made a half dozen calls to friends and begged anything appropriate for a gay coming-out party. Naturally that meant total immersion in the rainbow theme. Rainbow beads hung from palms, hibiscus, jasmine, and camellia. Rainbow candles shaped like water lilies floated alongside the real thing in the lotus pool, totally freaking out the koi, which Jolie announced could get over it. Rainbow lights twinkled in the bamboo groves and sweet olive trees, and a series of rainbow flags fluttered from tiki lights that had been resurrected from the gardening shed and pressed into service as Polynesian flagpoles. Thanks to some hastily painted cardboard strips, garden paths were turned into the yellow brick road.

"I hope you like it, baby doll," Jolie told Alex. "Even if it does look like Judy Garland came back here and puked."

Alex laughed. "Everything but the pot of gold."

"Oh, ye, of little faith," Jolie said. "Come along to see the *pièce de résistance*. Mother of Jefferson Davis! You have no idea what I went through to get this thing!"

Alex trailed him through the multicolored madness to a gazebo in a far corner of the garden. Tucked discreetly behind, at the base of a ten-foot-high, crepe-paper rainbow was a portable toilet. Alex didn't get the joke until he saw the logo emblazoned on the door: Pot O' Gold.

"A gay outhouse!" Alex roared with laughter.

"Of course it's for decorative use only since no self-respecting fairy would dream of using a portable potty." He reconsidered. "Well, maybe at a Madonna concert."

"Then why is it locked?"

"Well, we all know booze can erode one's self-respect, and I'm taking no chances on some drunken queen mistaking it for the real deal."

"You've gone to an awful lot of trouble, Jolie." Alex gave him an affectionate peck on the cheek. "I'm really touched."

"You're very welcome, but you may have second thoughts when you get a load of the guest list. This freak show would give old P. T. Barnum a boner."

New Orleans is famous for loving a good time, and nobody parties heartier than the gay population. Alex's "cotillion" proved they were ready to celebrate at the drop of a handkerchief, thanks to Jolie's simple but fail-safe party planning. He called half a dozen men and told each to call half a dozen more, and by eight o'clock his courtyard was packed with guys eager to meet Alex. And one another of course.

"It's a system that never fails," Jolie said with some pride. "If you want the word to get out, telephone, telegraph, and telex, but by all means, tell-a-fairy!" He surveyed the crowd and shook his head. "Although I must say the theme of this party is skewing off the yellow brick road and slipping down the rabbit hole."

"What do you mean?" Alex asked.

Jolie scanned the noisy crowd. "It's turning into *Alice in Wonderland* right before my world-weary eyes!"

Alex looked at his glass. "How much champagne have you had?"

"Not nearly enough." Jolie flagged the cocktail waiter and swapped his empty flute for a full one. He took a deep sip, sighed something about "mother's milk," and pointed to a tall, slender guy with a buzz cut, voluptuous lips, and enormous, very glassy eyes. "It all began with him. Josh Bergman. One afternoon, I forget where we were, but a bunch of us did a few tokes and started making up drag names. You know. Kitty Litter. Ramona Clay. Beth Israel. Terry Dactyl. Rosetta Stone. Gloria Hole. The usual tired queen stuff. Then someone said he thought Josh looked like a cartoon character. It took a while before we figured out he's the caterpillar in *Alice in Wonderland*. See, he's got that huge head and that lanky body and that perpetual cloud of smoke around him. A total pothead. I absolutely adore him, but he hasn't drawn a grass-free breath in decades."

The more Alex studied the guy, the more he was reminded of Alice's hookah-sucking caterpillar. When Josh caught his eye, he smiled, inhaled deeply, and blew a perfect smoke ring in his direction.

Alex broke up. "You're right!"

"Of course I am," Jolie said. "Now shall I point out the Mad Hatter?" Alex scanned the crowd and came up with no candidates. "Over there. By the lotus pool. Ken Calhoun. The poor man has been through every twelve-step program in the state. And a few in Mississippi and Texas too."

"What's the matter with him?"

"He's addicted to those damned programs," Jolie said with a shrug and a sip. "He goes to Alcoholics Anonymous, Sexaholics Anonymous, Shopaholic's Anonymous, EST Addicts Anonymous, Gamblers Anonymous, Chocaholics Anonymous—you name it and he's hooked on it. His doctors have given him all sorts of medication for his addictive personality, but he won't take anything because he's afraid he'll get addicted to the meds too." Jolie shook his head. "Whew! That's probably the most convoluted thing I've ever said."

Alex laughed. "I'm not too thrilled that I understood it either."

"The sad thing is that Ken's really a very sweet boy and great fun in the boudoir. He can even do himself. It's deliciously kinky, but it's a bit like a snake swallowing his own tail. Ohmigod! It just occurred to me!"

"What?"

"Ken's even addicted to himself!"

Alex didn't pursue that. "Any other Wonderland folks?"

"Well, there's your dormouse. Tim Boyd. He doesn't really look mousy and it's not really polite of me to label him because he's a narcoleptic."

Alex was horrified. "He screws corpses?!"

"No, *bébé*. That's a necrophiliac. A narcoleptic is someone who falls asleep all the time. Can't help himself. Didn't you see—?"

"My Own Private Idaho," Alex finished. "Of course. Poor River Phoenix was always nodding off, just like the dormouse at the mad tea party."

"Very good. Now you're getting it." Jolie steered him past the lotus pool and a thicket of bamboo where he found just what he was looking for. Standing between two much younger men with an arm around each was a pudgy, balding, rather nondescript man his late forties. His friends seemed to be hanging on his every word, smiling and laughing and obviously enjoying themselves. "Make a guess."

"The White Rabbit?"

Jolie chuckled. "He's not here yet. Always late, remember?"

Alex noted the guy's nonexistent neck. "The Mock Turtle?"

"Try again." Alex thought a minute and gave up. "That's Rodney Milliken, the Queen of Hearts."

"I'd never have guessed. I mean, he's not even good-looking."

"Not really."

"Rich?"

"Comfortable maybe. He's a pharmacist."

"Horse cock?"

"Nope."

Alex was totally buffaloed. "I don't get it."

"Well, you may get your chance before the night's out. Rodney has had almost every man here, including yours truly, and he gets them the old-fashioned way. He *earns* them. Wins them over is probably a better way to put it."

"How?"

"Nothing but pure old-fashioned charm, darling boy. When he turns it on full tilt, there are damned few who can resist. I can't be more specific than that, but if the guy could ever bottle and sell it he'd be set for life."

Alex watched as one of the younger guys, a dark-haired hottie with perfect pecs, ground his crotch against Rodney's thigh. "I'll be damned."

"Come along," Jolie said. "There's one more. Or rather two more. I think I saw them near the carriage way."

"A pair? Must be Tweedle Dee and Tweedle Dum."

"Indeed. Actually, I think they were in *Through the Looking Glass,* but exceptions must be made. Ah! There they are." Jolie nodded toward two thirtysomethings dressed exactly alike. Khaki shorts. Tight white tank tops. Even the same Adidas sneaks. "René and Claude Prejean. Before you get all freaked out, they're not brothers, just cousins. From Thibodaux I believe."

"Lovers?"

"Since high school they claim," Jolie said. "But they've been, shall we say, sharing their relationship for years. I'm sure their poor farm families got rid of two scandals at once when *les hommes Prejean* decided to relocate to New Orleans and bring their incestuous dabbling with them. They have a very successful little interior design firm across the lake, decorating for all the white flight folks. Which brings me to a most unusual feature of their condo in the Warehouse District."

"Oh?" Alex watched the cousins as Jolie continued.

"It's beautifully appointed but on the small side. So the boys have managed to maximize space in a most inspired way. Or maybe I should say they make their living room do double duty. At first you see only a tasteful room dominated by two oversized sofas facing each other across a cocktail table. Very deceptive, you see, because when the table is moved and those sofas are folded out into beds, they come together to form a football field's worth of mattress, perfect for those group sleepovers the Prejean boys are so famous for." Alex had barely digested that novelty when Jolie added, "And there's our Cheshire Cat, big grin and all."

"Who? Him?" Alex asked, eyeing a guy about his height with short chestnut hair and a compact body showcased in snug jeans and a Lafitte's T-shirt. "Oh, yeah. I remember him from last night. Tends bar at Lafitte's. Killer smile. A real cutie pie."

"Correct. Joe's the name and disappearing is the game, always with someone in tow."

"Really?"

"I guarantee he'll leave tonight with someone's trick, date, or boyfriend. It never fails. Ah, look! Our last guest has arrived and Wonderland is now complete."

"The white rabbit?"

"With hair and whiskers to match," Jolie laughed. "And a wonderfully pink nose bequeathed by the Goddess Absolut. Come meet Rex Locarno."

"Wait a minute," Alex said. "You said all your Wonderland characters are here, but I don't see Alice."

Jolie grinned. "Look in the mirror, *mon cheri!*"

🐰 10 🐰

Daddy Dearest

Wonderland crashed and burned at exactly 1:47 p.m. the next day, Monday, May 14, while Alex was treating Jolie to a leisurely lunch at Mona's, a Middle Eastern restaurant in the Faubourg Marigny, the Quarter's downriver neighbor. Alex was regaling him with tales about last night's raunchy romp with Joe the Cheshire Cat when the waitress returned his Visa card and whispered a discreet refusal.

"Perhaps you did too much partying last weekend, sir."

It was designed to amuse, but didn't. "What do you mean?" Alex asked.

"She means your card's maxed out, right, my dear?"

That's when the waitress dropped the second bomb. "Actually, the card has been canceled."

Alex's jaw dropped. "But that's impossi . . . oh, shit!" He stopped cold when an ugly thought churned his stomach. He handed the waitress an Amex card. "I'm very sorry. Would you please try this one?"

"No prob."

As soon as she was gone, Alex gave Jolie a terrified look. "Know what I think has happened?"

"Daddy dearest?"

"Bingo!"

"Then 'Oh, shit!' is right." Jolie fished out his wallet. "Don't worry about lunch, baby doll."

"Thanks, but let's not jump to conclusions."

"Then you'd better not see the look on the waitress's face. I'm afraid she just got an encore performance, and your show's definitely been closed."

"Sorry, sir."

"Here, sweetie," Jolie said, handing her the cash. "Keep the change and we're sorry for the inconvenience."

"No prob," she smiled, thrilled with the biggest tip she'd ever received. "Y'all have a nice day."

"Fat chance," Alex said, stuffing the worthless credit cards back into his wallet. "That sonovabitch has cut me off."

"Maybe that was what—"

"What Mother was trying to tell me," Alex finished. "Damn! I should've known."

"The cards aren't in your name?"

"Sumner Petroleum. Every fucking one of them."

"Don't worry about it. I'll cover you until you work something out."

"I can't let you do that."

"Reality check!" Jolie said, using his open palm like a radar scan over Alex's face. "You don't have a job and you have no assets. Except a friend who's happy to help you get through hard times."

Alex was moved, almost to the point of tears. This was truly a situation where he was looking at his only friend in the world, and he reached across the table to squeeze Jolie's hand. "Thanks. I really don't know what I'd do without you."

"As our sweet but only semievolved waitress says: 'No prob.'"

"Well, one thing's for sure. I don't have to call Daddy and tell him I'm not coming in to work today. Not that anyone would notice. My job was all title and no duties."

"Let's go home and think this through," Jolie suggested. "There might be another message from your mother, and maybe she can help."

"No way," Alex lamented. "She's as much a financial prisoner as myself."

Jolie waved a hand dismissively. "C'mon."

Alex was so distressed he didn't even notice the two bare-chested marines jogging across Esplanade, making their routine run from the naval base in The Bywater to Canal Street and back. All he could think about was being penniless, a situation truly beyond his ken.

Alex had not only been born with a silver spoon in his mouth but had never been taught how to pay for food to eat with it. His life, miserable though it had been, required nothing more than constantly passing credit cards to waiters and salesmen or sticking them in cash and gas machines. He never even saw his monthly bills, since they were handled by his secretary at Sumner Petroleum.

Compounding the problem was the reality that Alex hadn't been trained to do anything. Granted he had graduated from Tulane University with a BBA, but he had finished near the bottom of his class. In fact, his GPA was so low he would never have been hired by Sumner Petroleum if Daddy hadn't been CEO, a fact despised by far more qualified classmates forced to leave the economically depressed state of Louisiana to find work. For Alex, it was an embarrassment he had to live with on a daily basis. For his father, it was business as usual.

Alex's depression was complete when he and Jolie got home and found another message from his mother. "This is Karen Sumner again. Please tell Alex his father was irate when he didn't come in to work and that he's talking about drastic steps to get him home. I'm afraid the credit cards are just the beginning. Randolph is a man with a nasty mission and he'll stop at nothing to get his way." The tone was much more urgent in this call, a mother bear protecting her cub. "Tell Alex that I love him and to keep an eye on the six o'clock news."

"Dear Lord," Alex gasped. "What the hell can that mean?"

"Only one way to find out."

At six o'clock, the two were riveted to the small kitchen television as anchorwoman Angela Hill rattled off the lead stories with her usual out-of-control hands. A dangerous chemical spill on Interstate-10. Teachers making new demands for a pay raise. Another drug murder in the Desire projects. An oil tycoon's son is missing, feared kidnapped.

"No!" Alex yelled. "That crazy sonovabitch!"

"Shhh!" Jolie said. "Somebody screwed up. It's the lead story. Look!"

Alex's face materialized beside Angela's blonde haystack coiffure. It took him a minute to recognize the photo, one taken at the Comus ball the night he and Camilla announced their engagement.

"No wonder I look like Bambi caught in the headlights."

"Shhh!"

Angela frowned slightly, a sure sign she was about to direct her Most Sincere Reporting Look at the camera. "Alex Sumner, son of oil tycoon Randolph Sumner, has been missing since last Friday evening, and is feared the victim of foul play."

"What bullshit!" Alex cried.

"Shhh!"

Angela's frown vanished as her eyebrows rose, making the viewer wonder if she was about to ask a question. "Young Sumner, last seen at the family's uptown home on Prytania Street [fade to the Sumner Garden District manse], is an employee at his father's firm, Sumner Petroleum [fade to the Sumner Building], and the family says they are mystified by his disappearance. [Fade back to Alex/Bambi] He left Friday night for a social event with friends who report that he never showed up."

"Liars!"

"Hush!" Jolie hissed.

Alex's face disappeared again, replaced by some pertinent statistics, which Angela read aloud for the visually impaired. "Alex Sumner is a white male with blond hair and gray eyes, twenty-six years old, five foot five inches, one hundred forty pounds, with no distinguishing marks."

"I've got a strawberry birthmark on my fanny!" Alex shouted, crazed with disbelief. "Maybe that'll throw them off the scent!"

"Any persons with information should call this special number," Angela concluded with impressive authority. Alex wondered absently if she had taught kindergarten before her star soared in the TV news firmament. "On I-ten this morning, a truck belonging to Palmcorp Petrochemical Company overturned—"

Alex and Jolie nearly jumped out of their skins when the phone rang. It was the first of seven calls from people who had attended Alex's gay cotillion. They all wanted to know where Alex was. Thinking fast, Jolie delivered one long run-on sentence saying that Alex had gone out last night and not come home and that he, Jolie, was as bewildered as everyone else and that the television story obviously had the time of the disappearance wrong and we should all hope and pray

for the best and that he had to go because he had another call but
thanks very much for calling.

Alex was impressed. "What a smooth liar you are!"

"I don't think any of them would call the hotline since there's no reward being offered, but why take the chance? On second thought, I
hate to say it, but it's possible Ken Calhoun might call. He's probably
addicted to publicity too!"

"Jesus!"

"Don't worry, baby doll. If they come looking for you, they'll need
a search warrant to get past me. What's more, there's a secret passageway between the second and third floors where I can stash you if
worse comes to worse. I think they used it for runaway slaves or something."

Alex was about to ask to see the passageway when the phone rang
again. "Let the machine pick up," Jolie said. He went to the refrigera-
tor and pulled out a bottle of Stoli. "Drink?"

"Please. A double."

"Good boy. Wasn't it Auntie Mame who used to say, I'll have a
'tiny triple?'"

Alex cocked his ear toward the answering machine when Jolie's
message finished. "Hello. This is Karen Sumner again. Aren't you
people ever home?"

Alex almost collided with Jolie and the vodka bottle in his effort to
get to the phone. He grabbed the receiver, fumbled, and grabbed it
again. "Hi, Mom!"

"Darling!" Karen cried, relief flooding over the wire. "Are you all
right?"

"Fine. You?"

"A little tired I'm afraid. Your father just left for the office. He's
been working out of the house all day long. It's like a sting operation
or something. Cops. Detectives. All sorts of strange people traipsing
in and out." Alex's heart sank. "I take it you saw the news."

"Yes."

"I'm telling you, Alex, your father is a man obsessed. He's been a
maniac since he got up Saturday morning and discovered you were
gone. I haven't seen him this angry since the oil bust. I've been play-

ing dumb of course, but I don't think he believes me. After my remarks about Camilla, I'm suspect too, and Jedediah is on high alert. I had to hide in the rose bushes to make this call."

"Damn!"

There was a brief pause. "What are you going to do now, darling?"

"Get out of town I guess. My friend Jolie has offered to lend me some money. I'm thinking of driving over to—"

"No!" his mother interrupted. "That red Porsche will be a flag in front of a bull. Your father's got men watching everywhere. Highways. Airports. The train station and marinas. I even heard him say something about rental car offices. They'll pick you up in a heartbeat."

Alex was staggered. "He'd do all that?!"

Karen eyed the house warily as an unfamiliar figure peered from the library windows. She ducked lower behind her prized Queen Elizabeth floribundas. "I don't think you grasp the magnitude of what you've done, son. Nobody ever defies your father, least of all his only child and heir. He's absolutely furious and terrified that the truth will leak out and embarrass the old family name. This kind of crisis always bring out the best and worst in people, and you need to know what you're up against." Sleepless for two days, she yawned, and coughed tiredly. "Believe me when I say he'll stop at nothing to get you back, Alex. Nothing."

"I'm beginning to realize that," Alex moaned.

"You know I'd do anything to help you, but my hands are tied."

"I know, Mom," he said, wishing she were there for a hug. "I'm proud of you for standing up to him too."

"It was overdue for both of us, son. I still love your father, but things will never be the same after this." She took a tired breath. "Are you sitting down?"

Alex gulped, wondering what more ammunition his father might use. "Yes."

"He's so determined to find you he's going to offer a reward. It'll be announced on the ten o'clock news."

"Jeeze Louise!" There was a long pause as the two sensed each other's anxiety. Alex's heart raced as he felt the pervasive old weakness and began to backslide. "Look, Mom. Maybe I should just forget the whole thing and come back—"

"*No!*" she cried. Jolie did too, since he was hanging on Alex's every word.

"You've come too far to quit!" Jolie said.

"You can't back down now," his mother continued. "It's high time your father learned he can't have everything he wants."

"I'm sorry, Mom. I . . . I just feel so worn out."

"I know, darling. Me too. In fact, I should get off the phone and try to get some sleep."

"You're wonderful, Mom. I love you."

"I love you too. Thank your friend Jolie for me and tell him I'll call whenever I can to find out what you've decided." Alex heard the sound of a kiss. "Bye, darling."

"Bye, Mom."

Alex reiterated the conversation for Jolie. "Can you believe that bastard?"

Jolie sipped his vodka. "Given everything you've told me and what I've read about your father in the papers, frankly, yes."

"What the hell am I going to do?"

"First of all you've got to decide where you want to go."

Alex took a big gulp of vodka. "I guess New York is the most obvious choice."

"Know anybody up there?"

"No," Alex conceded.

"San Francisco?"

"No."

"You want some place that has a big gay population, don't you?"

"Well, now that you mention it, I guess so."

"Then let's see," Jolie said, splaying his fingers and counting off the possibilities. "Palm Springs. Provincetown. South Beach. Key West—"

The idea hit Alex like a thunderbolt. "Chandler!"

"What?"

"Chandler Wilde. I told you about him. The guy I met when I was having lunch with Camilla. Bitsy Covington's cousin."

"The hottie you banged at Chez Royale?"

"That's the one." Alex rattled his memory. "God, that seems like a million years ago!"

Jolie chuckled. "Considering all that's happened since then, it should!"

"He's a really nice guy. I told him a little about my father, and he said to call if I ever needed a place to hide out or just wanted to talk."

"And what's his psychic hotline number, mon?" Jolie asked, using the worst Jamaican accent Alex had ever heard.

"His card's here somewhere." Alex dug into his wallet, found the card and punched a number into his cell phone. He redialed twice before snapping it shut. "It's dead!"

"Daddy Dearest strikes again? Guess he's too pissed to realize your cell could be a tracking device."

Alex shook his head sadly and reached for Jolie's phone. "Better start running a tab, my friend. I can't even afford to pay for a damned phone call."

Jolie's response was to refill Alex's glass.

"Hello, Chandler? It's Alex Sumner from New Orleans. We met last Friday . . . yeah. Good to hear your voice too. How are you?" He sipped the vodka and nodded thanks to Jolie. "Me? Well, not so good. I've been wondering if your offer's still good to come down. The truth is, I'm in a jam."

"The understatement of the millennia," Jolie muttered, wandering into the garden to give Alex some privacy.

Alex quickly brought Chandler up to date and was relieved when Chandler assured him he was welcome. "How will you get here, Alex?"

"Don't know yet," Alex confessed. "Right now I feel like a condemned prisoner with the noose tightening around my neck. All I know is I need to get out of town fast. When they splatter my face all over the news again with a reward attached, I won't be able to go anywhere."

"Just let me know what you decide," Chandler soothed. "You're welcome to stay as long as you like. And Alex?"

"Yes?"

"I meant what I said. No strings attached."

"You're an angel, Chandler. Thanks a million."

"Anytime," Chandler said. *"Ciao."*

Alex followed Jolie into the garden and perched alongside him on the rim of the lotus pool. He touched a burned-out water lily candle and sent it bobbing away. "Everything's cool with Chandler. Now I just have to figure out how to get to Key West." Jolie seemed off in his own little world, softly humming as he stared at some leftover party lights twinkling in the bamboo thicket. "What's that tune?"

"An old Bacharach/David hit. 'Trains and Boats and Planes.'"

"Well, that's appropriate enough, but it doesn't solve my problem." He shook his head. "Man, I feel like a criminal about to go on the lam."

Jolie let out a whoop. "Damn, Alex, that's it! You're brilliant!"

"Oh, yeah? You want to let me in on the big effing secret?"

⚞ 11 ⚟

Showtime

Jolie's enthusiasm was electrifying. "Don't you see, Alex? You know old movies inside and out. This is just like Tony Curtis and Jack Lemmon in *Some Like It Hot*. After they witnessed the St. Valentine's Day massacre they had to go on the lam, remember?"

"Sure, but what does that have to do with—"

"Gangsters were looking all over Chicago for them, so they dressed in drag and hooked up with an all-girl band on a train bound for Miami."

Alex frowned. "Don't tell me you're going to suggest I do drag!"

"Just hear me out, baby doll, and remember, drastic predicaments call for drastic resolutions. The way I see it you only have one option."

"Go on."

"The bus."

Alex was horrified. "The *what?!*"

"The bus. You know. Those big smoky things with lots of wheels and wheezing brakes and anorexic dogs painted on the sides. To put it in terms you understand: Marilyn Monroe rode one in *Bus Stop*."

"I don't do buses," Alex announced flatly.

"Well, neither do I, darling, but like I said, drastic predicaments—"

"You heard me, dammit! I'm not climbing aboard some filthy cattle car packed to the gills with the Great Unwashed, and that's the end of the discussion!"

Jolie was disgusted and disappointed by a side of Alex he hadn't seen. Clearly this was Randolph Sumner's son talking, and the picture wasn't pretty. It was time for another reality check, and some foul-tasting medicine as well.

"Well, excuse me, Mr. Born-with-a-Silver-Spoon-up-Your-Ass!"

Alex was surprised by Jolie's harsh tone. "Huh?"

"You heard me, Alex. Now is not the time to get pissy and strut your uptown pedigree. Now is the time to get down and dirty and do everything you can to beat your father at his own game. Otherwise you're no better than he is."

Alex backed off. "I only meant—"

"I know damned well what you meant. That you're only used to traveling first class in your shiny little Porsche, and that it's beneath your dignity to plop your fucking aristocratic ass on a public bus. Fine. You come up with a better solution, sweetheart, and I'll be happy to discuss it."

The unexpected outburst reminded Alex that Jolie had done nothing but help since he sent his SOS. He'd been taught another valuable lesson.

"Sorry, Jolie. I guess I deserved that."

"Yes, you did. And there's more where that came from if you don't shape up. Don't you see that's exactly the kind of response your father would have and that's exactly why this will work? He'd never expect you to ride a bus in a million years. It's perfect!"

Alex felt like an idiot when the truth dawned on him. "God, you're brilliant!"

"Of course I am, darling. Now get your ass to the phone and see what kind of covered wagon Greyhound has heading for Key West."

"Okay."

"And bring me back a fresh drink, will you, please?"

"Sure." Alex was only a few steps away when Jolie's words stopped him dead.

"And then we can talk about wigs."

"Wigs?"

"Well, sure, baby doll. We just hatched an absolutely fabulous escape plot, but that doesn't mean we can't make it even more fabulous. Now we need a disguise. I mean, how many men in this city have Harpo Marx hair like yours? Believe me, once that business about the reward airs on TV, your head will be a curly blond beacon, and it won't be just Daddy Dearest and his cronies hunting you down."

"Look, Jolie. The bus is bad enough, but the idea of riding it in drag—"

"Is absolutely inspired!" Jolie finished. "Think about the movie!"

"No drag," Alex said.

"I'm not suggesting you dress up all slinky like Marilyn, for God's sake. Just something tasteless and mundane to throw the blood-hounds off the scent."

Alex ignored him. "I'm gonna call Greyhound." He winced. "Damn! That's something I never thought I'd say."

Jolie gave up. "I'll take that drink outside."

Alex took a deep breath, called information, and asked for the unthinkable. "The number for Greyhound please." He groaned. "This is getting more surreal by the moment!"

Alex wasn't thrilled to learn the bus ride would take almost twenty-eight hours and required changing buses in Mobile, Jacksonville, and Miami. As if that wasn't bad enough, the next one left at 6:50 in the morning. Still worse, since he couldn't pay for it with a credit card, he had to be there an hour early with cash.

"I'll just bet the bus station is a real vision at that hour," he muttered. "Drunks and druggies and homeless people stinking up the joint." Then Alex remembered Jolie's on-target comment about his condescending attitude and stayed focused by conjuring images of his scowling father and the cloying Camilla. Then he envisioned his mother's sweet face, Jolie's too, glowing with love and encouragement. "A man does what a man's gotta do," he told himself. Then, "Jesus! I sound like John Fucking Wayne!"

He freshened Jolie's drink and took it outside along with the news about the bus schedule. "Well, look at the bright side," Jolie chirped. "It takes those poor Cubans days to make Key West, and they have to deal with dehydration, sunburn, and sharks."

"I didn't say a word," Alex sighed.

"No, darling, but you were thinking it. I know because I was thinking the same thing. As the jet pelican flies, Key West is only a couple hours away. What a shame Daddy's watching the airport."

"Don't remind me," Alex grumbled.

"Sorry. How about something to pass the time until the ten o'clock news?"

"You want to show me that secret compartment?" Alex asked.

"No. I want to show you my private wig collection."

"I told you I'm not doing drag! The idea disgusts me!" When Jolie looked offended, Alex hurriedly apologized. "It's different for you, Jolie. You've got lots more to work with. I on the other hand would make one helluva ugly broad."

"But don't you see? That definitely works in your favor. No one looks at an ugly woman."

"Not interested," Alex said.

Jolie tried another tack. "Fine. We'll think of something later. For now, I'll order dinner from Verti Mart and we'll watch *Some Like It Hot*. I have the DVD somewhere."

Alex brightened. "Great. It's one of my all-time faves."

They were aching from laughter as Jack, Marilyn, Tony, and Joe E. Brown boated off into the sunset when Jolie noticed the time. "It's witching hour, baby doll." He switched the DVD player to television just in time to catch Marvin Robertson's opening line on the ten o'clock news.

"In an effort to find his missing son, Randolph Sumner called a press conference this afternoon and made a surprising announcement."

Coanchor Jolinda Bulessi picked up the thread. "The CEO of Sumner Petroleum is offering $25,000 to anyone with information on his son's whereabouts."

The phone rang. "Ignore it," Jolie said, riveted to the television. Once again he was amazed by the audacity of Alex's father.

Alex couldn't help hurrying into the kitchen on the off chance that it might be his mother again. Instead he heard the Mad Hatter leaving a message.

"Hi, Jolie. Ken Calhoun here. Did you see the news about Alex Sumner disappearing? His old man's offering twenty five thousand bucks for information so I'm wondering if I tell him I saw Alex last night and—"

"Shit!" Alex grabbed the phone. "Hey, Ken. It's Alex."

Ken sounded totally befuddled. "Oh, hey, man! What's up with your old man?"

"It's a publicity stunt," Alex said, thinking fast. "His company's in trouble and he's trying to win the sympathy of the stockholders."

"Huh?" Ken sounded skeptical.

"I know it sounds off-the-wall, but that's the kind of shit my old man pulls. That's why I'm holed up at Jolie's house for a few days."

"That's fucking twisted!" Ken grunted.

"Yeah, well, welcome to the wild and wacky world of corporate America. Whoops! Got another call!" Alex hung up and listened to the next message. He smiled when he heard Duncan's husky tones.

"Hi, Jolie. Just saw the news and was wondering what the hell's going on with Alex and his father."

Alex quickly picked up. "Hey, Duncan. I'm fine. It's just Daddy's master plan to get me back home."

"So what're you going to do?"

"Nothing," Alex said, deciding not to tell anyone except his mother about Key West. "Just lay low and see how much Daddy will up the ante."

"It sounds like a bad version of *Survivor*."

"Yeah. This whole thing gets crazier by the minute."

"Well, I say hang in there and don't worry about me blowing any whistles. Believe me I know the importance of keeping secrets."

"It never crossed my mind," Alex said, thinking how good Duncan's voice sounded and how much he'd like to be snuggling against that wonderfully furry chest. "I'm glad you called."

"Me too. G'night, babe."

"Good night." Alex had barely cradled the receiver when it rang again. "Damn!" This time it was Rex Locarno, the perennially late and sloshed White Rabbit. He was so drunk Alex could barely understand him.

"Reward . . . Alex . . . gonna call that number on the—"

Alex intercepted and used the same tale he'd used on Ken. He needn't have bothered because Rex passed out and dropped the phone, leaving only drunken snores.

"At least that will tie up the phone for a while," Alex muttered. He'd barely said the words when Jolie's cell phone rang. "Holy shit!"

For the next twenty minutes, Jolie fielded phone calls from half the people at the party. Most were genuinely concerned for Alex's safety, but a couple of guys were actually after the reward. Adding to the nightmare, Rex finally hung up so the other phone started ringing off the wall. Alex and Jolie listened with alarm. Some were people Jolie knew, some he only vaguely remembered, still others he didn't know at all.

"Damn, Alex! Everybody in New Orleans is looking for you. Talk about tell-a-fairy!"

"Shit," Alex groaned. He paced the kitchen like a caged animal, but just as abruptly he stopped. "I'd better grab a quick shave."

Jolie threw his hands up. "You haven't got time for that! For all we know, someone's already called about the reward and the cops are on their way here. Maybe your father too!"

Alex tossed down the last of the vodka and rubbed his chin. "If I'm going to travel as Alexandra Yusuppov," he sniffed, "I have no intention of showing any blond stubble, much less my Harpo Marx curls."

"Who the hell is Alexandra—?" Jolie beamed when he saw the twinkle in Alex's eye. "Wig and all?"

"Wig and all."

Jolie beamed. "You go, girl!"

PART TWO

"Will you, won't you, will you, won't you, will you join the dance?"
"Will you, won't you, will you, won't you, won't you join the dance?

Lewis Carroll,
Alice's Adventures in Wonderland

✍ 12 ✍

Hit the Road, Jack!

At five in the morning, the New Orleans Greyhound Station was everything Alex feared and then some. As he entered the terminal, his nostrils reacted to an acrid, very potent amalgam of industrial cleaner, sour sweat, and stray odors he didn't want to think about. Jolie had dismissed it as "a momentary descent down the Dantean ladder" and Alex agreed, looking the other way when a street person chose that moment to change her soiled drawers.

He scanned the noisy room, found the counter for picking up tickets, and took his place in line. He tried to remain inconspicuous and ignore what swirled around him—no easy feat since he was repulsed everywhere he looked. Alex had never noticed how fat Americans were, and was appalled by the avalanche of enormous tits, bellies, and butts that threatened to crush him from every direction, most encased in clothing that was way too tight. The woman in front of him pulled a half-eaten drumstick from her purse and gnawed away. In a line to the right, a gaggle of runaway teens in filthy shorts and jeans flaunted so many piercings their heads looked like pin cushions. One pimply girl's especially large nose ring was, for Alex, the revolting *piece de resistance.*

Jeez Louise, he thought. *This is like a casting call for a Fellini movie!*

Desperation to flee New Orleans was all that kept Alex centered. He closed his eyes and conjured his father's angry face, then dissolved to the swaying coconut palms of Key West. Alex was so good at self-detachment that he only vaguely remembered buying his ticket and climbing aboard the bus marked MOBILE. In fact, he didn't recall much of anything until an elderly woman across the aisle struggled to stow her bag overhead. Without hesitation he jumped up to help, then was brought back to reality by the old lady's heartfelt response.

"Why, thank you, miss."

Miss?!

Alex had ventured so far into his detached mode that he'd forgotten his disguise. Shortly before midnight, Jolie raided his vast costume closet for something forgettable. "Always remember that unobtrusiveness is your best weapon, *cheri!* The tackier, the better!"

The frenzied search yielded a pair of capri pants left over from last winter's Trailer Trash Party. "The length is weird because you're shorter," he conceded, "but you're hardly strutting your stuff on a Paris runway." He tossed Alex a huge gray sweatshirt. "That thing's so baggy you won't need fake boobs."

The blond curls disappeared beneath a shaggy brunette wig hiding much of Alex's face, and a light touch of lipstick to the full, Brendan Fraser lips was his only concession to makeup. Alex agreed to everything until Jolie suggested replacing his Prada shoulder bag with a cheap imitation.

"People don't carry designer luggage on buses," Jolie insisted.

"You're right," Alex agreed. "They carry fakes. Trust me, they'll think this cost twenty dollars on the street and not six-hundred dollars at Saks."

Jolie conceded and, with the addition of a pair of unfashionable, low-heeled sandals and horn-rimmed glasses with smoky lenses, Alex's ensemble was complete. Jolie had proclaimed it "White Trash Chic *par excellence!*" and pretended to weep as he kissed Alex on both cheeks.

"Oh, dear!" he wailed. "My little girl's all grown up and leaving the nest!"

The close encounter with the old woman on the bus reminded Alex his mannerisms had to match his clothes. He smiled, elevated his voice an octave and said, "You're welcome, ma'am."

He took a seat by the window and looked outside, recoiling when he saw Fried Chicken Lady lining up to board. She was still munching away as she waddled her three hundred plus pounds toward the bus. Alex slunk lower in his seat, and was praying she wouldn't plop her space-devouring ass beside him when something else caught his eye. It was a dream and a nightmare rolled into one.

"Damn!" he breathed.

Glimpsed periodically behind the woman's monstrous bulk was a man a few years older wearing a white tee so tight Alex saw prominent nipples. He also saw heavy pecs and biceps, flat abs, and beefy thighs in faded, well-worn jeans. The rest of the package was impressive too, although the guy was hardly matinee idol handsome. He had dark, close-cropped hair, pretty eyes, and a firm jawline, but his nose looked like it had been broken, and a nasty scar marred his stubbly left cheek. A baseball cap with a small rainbow flag announced his sexual preference to those who read the code. Scar and all, Alex was strongly attracted, but knew the guy was potential trouble. He remembered Jolie's warning that most gay men had an innate skill at spotting drag, bad as well as good, and he couldn't risk anyone blowing his cover. At least not until he was well out of Louisiana.

Alex closed his eyes and feigned sleep as the boarding continued. To his relief, the bus was only about three-quarters full, and no one sat beside him. Mr. Beefy Tee sat up front while Chicken Woman roosted toward the rear near the Human Pincushions. Alex actually managed to sleep as the bus hummed across the Pearl River and into the dark Mississippi night. His last memory before going under was the rattle of plastic and the smell of fried chicken grease.

"Mobile, Alabama, ladies and gentlemen! Mobile!"

Alex was startled awake when the driver's voice boomed through a speaker just above his head. He looked at his watch. It was 10:15 in the morning. He didn't know how he had slept through over three hours of bus stops but was grateful to have missed a chunk of the trip. He rubbed his eyes, remembering Mobile was where he transferred to a bus for Jacksonville. He had another important change to make too.

Alex bade a secret farewell to Chicken Lady and reeled sleepily off the bus, wandering into the terminal with a handful of other passengers. A growling stomach reminded him he was famished, but first things first. He headed for the restrooms and stopped dead in his tracks.

"Shit!"

Safely in Alabama, Alex planned to ditch the drag and change into his own clothes, but he faced a critical dilemma. As a woman he couldn't walk into the men's room, but he also risked pandemonium if he emerged from a ladies room stall as a man.

"Double shit!"

He had only forty-five minutes to have some breakfast and formulate a plan before the bus left for Jacksonville, and hoped a hearty Southern breakfast would feed brain as well as body. More self-conscious than ever in the brightly lit coffee shop, he took a seat in a far corner and ordered ham, eggs, grits, and black coffee from a bubbly waitress who was, poor thing, even homelier than himself. Alex was oddly flattered when he realized the woman was flirting, and, even more surprising, he flirted back.

"Thank you, darlin'," he chirped, purposely brushing fingertips with the waitress as he passed back the menu.

Alex's patronizing smiles brought the food with amazing speed. He nibbled in the most ladylike manner he could manage, oblivious to being watched by someone besides the lonely lesbian waitress. As he finished eating, he stayed focused on the need to change clothes before boarding another bus, and when no plan emerged, he resigned himself to continuing the trip in drag.

The solution hit like a lightning bolt.

"Of course!"

Alex dabbed his mouth with a napkin, reapplied his lipstick, overtipped the lovestruck waitress, and hurried out of the restaurant. He found what he was looking for on the other side of the terminal and eagerly tried the door, relieved to find the room empty.

"Thank God for handicapped restrooms," he muttered.

In the privacy of the unisex bathroom, Alex chucked his wig, wiped off the new coat of lipstick, kicked off the sandals, and stripped to his briefs. He tucked the drag in his bag before tugging on Calvin jeans, Gucci loafers, and a navy Polo shirt. A quick brush through his tangled curls and he was ready to face the world.

As he strode through the terminal, liberated at last, Alex remained unaware that his strange metamorphosis was not going unnoticed.

☙ 13 ☙

The Long and Winding Road

Alex headed for the back of the Jacksonville bus and heaved his bag onto the overhead rack. He'd barely settled into his seat when he spotted Mr. Beefy Tee heading down the aisle along with several other New Orleans passengers. Now that Alexandra Yussupov was only a lonely lesbian memory, Alex didn't shy away from dispatching a long cruise as the guy approached and eyed the empty seat. He felt a familiar tingle when he heard the deep voice.

"Anybody sitting there?"

"Help yourself."

The stranger nodded but didn't return Alex's smile. "Thanks."

Biceps bulged as he tossed a heavy duffle bag onto the overhead. He stretched and plopped down beside Alex, then leaned forward to pull a paperback from his hip pocket. Alex couldn't make out the title.

"Going all the way to Jacksonville?" Alex asked.

"Sugarloaf Key." He didn't look up from his book.

"Yeah? I'm going to Key West. Is it close?"

"'Bout twenty minutes."

Noncommittal, aren't we? Alex thought. They sat in silence until the bus swept through the long tunnel under Mobile Bay and emerged in the bright Alabama sunlight. Alex found the quietness awkward.

"If we're spending the next eleven hours together I guess we ought to introduce ourselves." He held out his hand. "I'm Alex."

"I'm Cord Foster." The grip was bone-crushing and brief. "You got a last name?"

"Yussupov," Alex blurted, wondering if his lie was necessary since he'd completed his New Orleans escape. When he got a curious look, he added, "It's Russian."

Cord grunted and went back to his book. Alex glimpsed the title when they shook hands and caught himself before reading it aloud. *The Zen of Deep Sea Fishing.*

Jeez Louise, he thought. *Maybe the guy plans to bore himself to sleep.* After a few more minutes he decided to make another overture

"You like fishing?" He nodded at the book, hoping his question wasn't as dumb as it sounded.

"My old man's the fisherman," Cord said. "Got a boat down in Sugarloaf. Takes the tourists deep sea fishing."

"Sounds like interesting work."

"I'm about to find out firsthand, and not by choice."

"Oh, yeah?"

"Yeah."

When Cord went back to his book, Alex was frustrated by the abrupt dismissal and wondered how someone could make a remark that tantalizing and leave it hanging. He tried again.

"What do you mean?"

Cord closed the book and faced Alex. "Look, man. I appreciate your efforts to be friendly but I'm not in a very chummy mood. In fact, I haven't been since I lost my job as a personal trainer in Houston three months ago."

That explains the muscles, Alex thought.

"I went through my savings and am now on the verge of bankruptcy. At the ripe old age of thirty-two I'm having to crawl home and beg my old man for a job, and I'm stuck on a fucking Greyhound bus for the next twenty-four hours."

"With some chatty asshole who won't leave you alone," Alex finished. He was tempted to add, "PS, your cat is dead!" but figured Cord wouldn't get the reference to an old gay play.

His stab at humor worked. Cord's lips slowly curled into a smile and he said, "Yeah. PS, my cat is dead."

Alex burst out laughing. "I was just about to say that myself. Great play, wasn't it?"

"I didn't know it was a play," Cord said. "It's just something I heard my brother say." He took off the baseball cap with the tiny rainbow flag and rubbed his forehead. "This is his hat. He left it last time he visited."

"Oh."

Alex swallowed and looked away. *Your brother's cap, huh? Maybe you're not gay after all, and that's why you're ignoring my overtures. Shit! So now I'm sitting next to Mr. Texas Angler all the way to Jacksonville. Double shit!*

"You live in Key West?" Cord asked.

Alex was surprised by the question, assuming the guy would go back to his book after that woeful diatribe. "No," he replied. "I'm visiting a friend."

"Ever been before?"

"No."

"Interesting old town. Lotsa drunks and queers but some damned good seafood."

Queers, huh? Alex decided things had just gone from bad to worse. So now he had Mr. Homophobic Texas Angler as a traveling companion. He felt like his cat had died too and decided to bury his misery in the thriller he'd filched from Jolie's bookshelf.

"Can I get by?" he asked, nodding at the overhead rack. "I need to get in my bag."

"I'll get it." Cord stood up and inadvertently shoved his crotch in Alex's face as he retrieved the heavy bag with ease. He propped it on the armrest while Alex unzipped the appropriate compartment and pulled out his book. "Nice bag."

"Thanks," Alex said as Cord shoved it back overhead.

"I never could afford Prada."

"It's a fake," Alex said.

"Bullshit."

"Excuse me?"

"I worked at the Houston Galleria once, selling luggage at Neiman's. I know the real deal when I see it."

"Oh."

Cord frowned. "Why'd you lie?"

Alex wished he hadn't ignored Jolie's warning. "Because it's probably not smart to carry Prada on a bus trip."

"So why'd you do it?"

"I . . . I was in a hurry."

"What's that supposed to mean?"

"Fine!" Alex snapped, irked by the sudden interrogation. "It's the only luggage I have, all right?"

"And I guess the only watches you have are Rolexes." Cord nodded the $2,000 chunk of metal gripping Alex's wrist. "Huh?"

"No," he shot back. "I've got a Movado and a couple of Guccis stashed in my bag too. So what?!"

"Take it easy, man," Cord said. "You were giving me the third degree back there. I was just returning the favor."

Alex's cherubic cheeks flamed. "I'm . . . I'm sorry. I guess we're both a little edgy right now."

"I guess," Cord agreed. After a moment he said, "After weighing the evidence, I'd say my problem is not enough money and yours is too much."

Alex knew he was drifting toward troubled waters, but a combination of fear and loneliness made him encourage this perfect stranger. *As long as I'm careful what I say, maybe it's a good idea to have an ally during this interminable ride through hell. Someone to talk to might even help pass the time.*

"What do you mean?"

Cord faced Alex and the blurred Alabama countryside before dropping the bomb. "Because you've got all the signs of a poor little rich boy running away from home."

Alex's cheeks reddened even more. "Why do you say that?"

"How old are you? Twenty-two?"

"Twenty-six."

"Whatever." Cord shrugged. "Anyway, how many dudes dripping with authentic designer shit haul their ass on a Greyhound bus?"

Those troubled waters Alex had feared suddenly swirled around his neck. If this conversation stayed on course, he worried Cord might learn much too much. He thought fast.

"You're very observant, Cord. Let's just say I'm doing undercover work."

"Who for? Or is it a secret?"

"Not really," Alex said stalling. He started to claim he was a travel writer, then reconsidered. "A rival bus company. I'm supposed to report on everything from on-time performance to seat comfort, clean restrooms, stuff like that. You know. See what the competition is doing." He knew it sounded stupid and wished he'd stuck with his first impulse, especially when he heard Cord's next question.

"Who do you think's going to recognize you?"

"Well, you never know," Alex said. "Besides, I'm just doing as I was told."

Cord leaned closer and spoke in a conspiratorial tone. "With all due respect, Mr. Yussupov, bullshit!"

Alarmed as well as annoyed, Alex beat a hasty retreat. "Believe what you like," he said, opening his book. "I'm going to read awhile."

"Go right ahead," Cord said. "Me too."

Alex opened his novel but couldn't concentrate. The words swam as he evaluated his situation and worried about Cord's on-target observation. A rich kid on the lam, he thought. Bingo! Then there was the business about the designer stuff, especially the watches. This perfect stranger had confessed that he was desperate for money and was now within reach of thousands of dollars worth of jewelry. Alex flashed back to a train trip through Hungary when a gang of Gypsies burst into his first-class compartment and menaced him until the conductor threw them off the train. For all he knew, Cord might wait until he dozed off, grab his bag, and hop off at the next stop. Alex retrieved his itinerary and counted the stops between Mobile and Jacksonville.

"Eleven stops," he muttered.

Cord was staring right at him. "Yeah. It's gonna be a damned long day, buddy."

No shit, Alex thought.

∽ 14 ∽

What a Drag!

Alex tossed and moaned. Like Scarlett in *Gone with the Wind,* he was running blindly through the fog, toward an unknown, elusive destination. He knew he'd never find what he was looking for, and that terrible reality worsened when hands emerged through the fog to impede his flight. When they grabbed and shook him, he tried to scream.

"Easy, Alex!"

Alex woke up, gasping for breath. He was staring into Cord's dark eyes and felt a powerful grip on his shoulders. "What's—"

"You were having a nightmare," Cord explained. "You yelled so loud you scared the bejesus out of those old ladies across the aisle. They thought you were having some kind of seizure, and frankly, I wondered myself."

Alex blinked like an owl in the sunlight, then rubbed his eyes. "Wow. That was a little too real."

"What was?"

"I was dreaming that . . . oh, it doesn't matter." He looked through the window, as though searching for a recognizable landmark. He saw a blur of piney woods, scrub palmetto, and Spanish dagger: the monotonous landscape of panhandle Florida. "Where are we?"

"Coming into Tallahassee," Cord replied.

Alex frowned. "The last place I remember was Chattahoochee."

"That was over an hour ago. You had quite a snooze, man."

Alex sat up as he came fully awake. He remembered his concerns about Cord being a thief and chided his paranoia. He'd slept through two bus stops, giving Cord ample opportunity to abscond with his bag, and the guy had been nothing but helpful. He felt sheepish.

"Thanks for waking me up."

"No problem." Cord chuckled, making Alex think he was more relaxed too. "I'm surprised you didn't wake yourself up from the snoring."

Alex was embarrassed. "I was snoring?"

"A little," Cord reported. "But nothing like last night. Man, you sounded like a buzz saw."

"What're you talking about?"

Alex's question earned a consequential stare, and as the last of his sleep cobwebs disintegrated, the terrible truth dawned. Cord had seen through his disguise!

"You knew that was me?"

"Not right away. I got suspicious when I went to the lavatory and heard you snoring. I didn't know women snored like that, and was still thinking about it when I went back to my seat. As I passed by I noticed your Adam's apple."

Alex gulped. "Oh."

Cord winked. "And your wig was crooked."

"Oh, shit!"

"Then there was that quick change act you pulled in Mobile. In the handicapped toilet."

"You don't miss much, do you?"

"Just part of what I learned at the police academy."

Alex's heart leapt. "I thought you said you were a personal trainer."

"I am. I found out I wasn't cut out to be a cop so I never finished the training. I remember a lot of stuff though."

"Did you think you were witnessing . . . uh, criminal behavior?"

"Let's see. A man carrying super-expensive luggage dressed as a trailer trash woman? Nah." When Alex gaped, Cord added, "Hey, who am I to be judgmental? I'm on a fucking Greyhound bus too, for God's sake."

For the first time in his life, Alex was at a loss for words.

"Relax, man. What you do is your business. If you want to tell me the story, fine. If not, well, that's okay too."

Alex felt relieved, and more than a little ashamed for his earlier suspicions. "You're an awfully trusting soul."

"Something else I learned at the academy. I'm a pretty good judge of character. Not always, but usually. When I guessed you were a rich kid running away, the look on your face told me plenty."

"I guess there's no point in denying it."

"Nope."

Both looked up as the driver bawled, "Tallahassee, folks. This is Tallahassee. You have forty-five minutes for dinner. Tallahassee!"

"Wanna hear the gory details over dinner?" Alex remembered Cord was broke. "My treat."

"You trying to bribe me?"

"Sort of," Alex said. "Although I assure you I haven't committed a crime."

"Just one," Cord said as the bus turned into the terminal parking lot and lurched to a stop with a loud sneezing of air brakes.

"What's that?"

"That tacky drag you were wearing last night. Honey, you're lucky you didn't get nailed by the fashion police."

Alex considered that loaded sentence. Straight men didn't use words like "tacky drag" or talk about the fashion police, and they sure didn't call each other "honey."

Alex decided to bite the bullet. "May I ask you something?"

"Hmmm. *May* and not *can?* Somebody's gone to the right schools."

Alex ignored the jibe. "Well?"

"Shoot."

Alex took a deep breath. "Are you a friend of Dorothy's?"

Cord let out a whoop, but no one paid attention in the chaos of people scrambling off the bus, eager to grab a quick bite before the long haul to Jacksonville. "Man, I haven't heard that old chestnut in years. I didn't think guys your age knew what it meant."

"Just because I'm in my twenties doesn't mean I'm a gay-illiterate," Alex declared. "So I guess the answer is yes."

Cord leaned close. "In keeping with the Oz theme, let's just say I'm about as straight as the yellow brick road." He chuckled and moved into the aisle, motioning for Alex to step in front. "Now c'mon. Let's eat."

They were halfway down the aisle when he grabbed Alex's shoulder. "You gonna leave your bag onboard?"

"Why not? Everybody else is."

"Man, I hope you got a big bank account because you sure got shortchanged in the brains department." He leaned close again. "Everybody else doesn't have a shitload of expensive watches in their bag. Now grab it and come on."

Alex's feelings were hurt, but he knew Cord was right as he slung the bag over his shoulder and followed the crowd. He still couldn't quite process what had happened, couldn't believe that a perfect stranger would befriend him after witnessing such peculiar behavior. *Oh, well,* he thought. *Jolie warned me this bus ride would be like falling down the rabbit hole, and at least Cord is keeping my mind off Daddy.*

Alex was further distracted, happily so, as he trailed Cord into the bus station. He hadn't seen the guy from behind and had to admit he was quite a package from this angle. Cord's broad shoulders made his narrow hips seem even more so, and after enjoying the view, Alex quickened his step and caught up.

"Sorry about the blond moment back there."

"You just need to be more careful," Cord said. "You're obviously out of your element."

"Not by choice, I assure you."

"Tell me later," Cord said, picking up the pace. "They don't give us much time to eat."

Alex paused outside the restaurant. "Order me a cheeseburger and fries, will you? I'll be right back."

"Where are you going?"

"To the men's room."

"Why didn't you go on the bus?"

"I couldn't pee in there," Alex confided. "It creeps me out. Aw, don't look at me like I'm a spoiled brat, Cord. I'm pee shy, okay? We all have our peculiarities."

"Just hurry up," Cord grunted.

Cord found an empty table and idly studied a television monitor in a far corner of the restaurant. He couldn't hear what the CNN newscaster was saying, but there was no mistaking the image that popped up behind him. Or the title of his story.

"Holy shit!" Cord muttered, half rising from his seat. Alex was midway across the terminal when Cord ambushed him. "C'mon!"

"What's wrong? You look like you've seen a ghost."

"Yours, kiddo," Cord hissed. "Now keep walking. We're getting back on the bus."

"But I'm starving, man!"

"Just do it!"

The steely grip on his elbow gave Alex little choice and in minutes they were back on the deserted bus. "Thank God everybody's stretching their legs," Cord said. "You didn't throw away that wig and god awful drag did you?"

"It's in my bag," Alex replied, more confused than ever.

"You're about to experience your first bus lavatory." Cord gave him a shove. "Now get in there and put it back on! And plenty of lipstick too."

Alex jerked away, wondering why Cord had freaked. "Not until you tell me why!"

"Because I just saw your face on CNN!"

Alex's jaw dropped as realization sank in. "What—"

"And that mop of blond curls will be a fucking magnet for fortune hunters. Now git!"

Shock and fear propelled Alex down the aisle and into the lavatory. No doubt his father had pulled strings and expanded his search. Randolph Sumner had direct connections to some of the most powerful men in industry, communication, and politics. Alex once heard him talking to the vice president of the United States, an experience he found both humbling and scary. Alex was no authority on his father's wheeling and dealing, but he knew the man owed and was owed plenty of expensive favors. This gave him a terrifying amount of clout, extending his greedy reach into the most distant, unlikeliest of places.

Even, Alex thought grimly, *the Tallahassee bus station!*

"Damn!"

The confines of the bus lavatory forced Alex into a contortionist's moves as he stripped and struggled into the capri pants and sweatshirt. Worst were securing the sandals and wig, but he finally managed, and emerged to find the bus filling up again. His quick-change act had taken a lot longer than he thought.

"C'mon," he whispered, crawling over Cord and settling into the window seat. "Give me some details."

Cord leaned close. "I couldn't hear anything but the words KIDNAPPED and TWENTY-FIVE THOUSAND DOLLAR REWARD were right above your curly head. I figured if I recognized your face from thirty feet, somebody else could do the same thing and turn you in."

Alex slid lower in the seat and tugged more synthetic tendrils over his face. "How come you didn't?"

"I might," Cord said. When he saw Alex's face turn ashen, he said, "I'm just kidding, man. That wouldn't even pay off my creditors!"

"How   how do I know that?"

"You don't," Cord snapped. "Now stop with the damn questions and answer one for me."

"Okay."

"So you *are* a rich kid on the lam." Alex nodded. "Do you know who's offering the reward?"

"My father," Alex muttered, relieved when the driver revved the engine and the bus careened out of the parking lot.

"He's sure as hell determined to find you."

"Desperate to control my life you mean." Alex grunted. Disgust gave way to anger, then loathing. "Running away is the only way to stop him."

"He obviously cares about you."

"Yeah? Well, he's got some damned weird ways of showing it." It took Alex a few miles of silence to realize Cord had revealed something of himself. He remembered the guy's father was taking him in and giving him a job. "You and your father must be very close."

"Get real," Cord grunted. "I'll hate the sonovabitch until the day I die."

"Then why are you going to stay with him?"

"I already told you, Alex. I've got no choice. I'm flat broke and I've got no prospects. Personal trainers are a luxury, not a necessity, and in today's greedy Bush economy—"

"But there must be other ways to earn a living."

"Believe me, I've thought of everything and came up with zip." He slid lower in the seat. "Every mile disappearing between me and my old man makes me hate my life even more."

"Jesus, Cord. What did he do to you?"

"It's what he did to all of us," Cord replied, absently touching the scar on his cheek. "I probably should have killed him."

The ugly admission iced Alex's heart. The man beside him suddenly radiated danger but intrigued him at the same time.

"You want to talk about it?"

Cord muttered something unintelligible. Then, "How much time you got?"

Alex glanced at his watch, then quickly tugged a sleeve over the gleaming Gucci he'd forgotten to remove when he changed clothes. "Almost four hours to Jacksonville."

"It's a start."

⟋ 15 ⟍

Daddy Dearest Revisited

For the next 163 miles Alex hung on every word of a story that was alternately heroic and horrifying. Cord's childhood was spent on a small Alabama farm, and, for as long as he could remember, he, his younger brother Darcy, and their mother had been punished for no other crime than keeping company with Frank Foster. Cord and Darcy grew up believing it was the lot of every child to be beaten or berated for the pettiest of matters, so they never questioned their father's actions.

"I've been to lots of support groups," Cord confessed, "and that kind of behavior is usually fueled by booze or drugs, or maybe the abuser is mentally unhinged. In my Dad's case, the guy was nothing but a born bully, a bad-to-the bone sonovabitch who took pleasure in tormenting those he should have loved most."

"Jesus," Alex breathed.

This was difficult for Alex to process because it was the sort of thing that happened to "other people," those poor, tortured souls exposed daily on talk shows and television newscasts. Granted, his own father was manipulative and a bona fide control freak, but Randolph Sumner had never laid a hand on his wife or only child. As Alex was about to discover, however, abuse assumed more insidious guises than he realized.

"The worst thing," Cord continued, "was that it was so damned unpredictable. Dad was like a volcano waiting to erupt. He could simmer for days at a time and then explode without warning. Once we were eating dinner in silence and staring at our plates, because that's how Dad wanted it. I felt something in my gut and risked a glance in his direction. When I saw him glaring at Darcy, I braced myself."

"For what?"

"When Dad stared at you, it meant trouble, plain and simple. No one ever knew what was inside his head, what prompted him to attack suddenly, like a wild animal. That particular time he leapt across the table, sending food and dishes flying everywhere as he lunged for Darcy's throat. My brother toppled over backward with Dad on top, beating the daylights out of him."

"But why?"

Cord's terse response was chilling. "They never give reasons."

Alex swallowed hard. "Your mother didn't do anything?"

Cord's smile was heartbreaking. "What could she do? Dad was a powerful guy, and she had endured so many years of abuse she was only the shell of a human being. She was worn down to nothing, with no strength or will to protect her children. If she had said anything she would've just gotten a worse beating. Those were the simple rules."

"I can't imagine something like that."

Cord nodded. "I appreciate your honesty, Alex. Most people just nod their heads and say 'that's terrible' or 'I understand' when they don't have a fucking clue." He rubbed his cheek.

"Did your father give you that scar?"

"Yeah, but it's nothing compared to the scars inside."

Alex's sympathy swelled. "Maybe you shouldn't talk about it."

Cord looked up as someone lurched down the aisle and knocked his elbow from the armrest. He whirled, then caught himself, but not before Alex saw rage flare in his eyes. He settled back and folded arms cross his chest.

"Don't worry," he said. "I've learned anger management. It's all part of breaking the cycle, of letting go of the hatred my father instilled in me. Believe it or not, I had to learn it wasn't okay to hit someone else. After all, that's how I'd been raised and assumed it was the norm."

Alex thought Cord had forgotten about the scar. He hadn't.

"One night, Dad pulled one of his surprise attacks on Mom. To this day, I'm not sure why I fought back but somehow I got on his back, kicking like crazy and beating him with my fists. I screamed for him to get off my mother, and next thing I knew I was flying across the room. My face hit a picture hanging on the wall. The glass broke and cut my cheek open." The painful memory made the scar turn red. "I don't remember going to the doctor but somehow I got stitched up."

"Surely the doctor asked what happened."

Cord shrugged. "We lived on a farm. Accidents are a daily hazard. I'm sure Dad made up some crap and that was the end of it until I started first grade. You know how kids are. They all asked about the scar."

Alex shuddered at the thought of a grown man hurling a six-year-old against a wall. "What did you say?"

"I don't remember. Some fanciful lie I suppose. What else could I do? Tell them my old man was beating me and my brother and my mom? Dad knew just what he was doing. He had us so terrified, so intimidated that we didn't dare open our mouths."

"Sweet Jesus. What a way to live." Alex reflected on his own father-son relationship and what Jolie had called a "benevolent reign of terror." It paled beside Cord's ongoing horror stories.

"It's a lot more common than you know," Cord muttered. "Anyway, things changed when I hit puberty. I shot up like a beanpole and was suddenly as tall as my father. He still outweighed me by a good forty pounds, but that changed too once I joined the wrestling team. By my sophomore year I was solid muscle, and, man did I love the feeling of power. Pretty soon Dad noticed the difference and started leaving me alone. Darcy too once he bulked out. We thought it was all over, but we were wrong."

Alex groaned inside. He wasn't sure he wanted to hear the rest, but reminded himself he had asked. In any case, Cord didn't seem about to stop.

"The summer after I graduated high school, Darcy and I went to visit our grandparents in Birmingham. When we came home, Dad was out in the fields somewhere, and Mom was in bed. He had beaten her real bad, just this side of needing medical attention. That bastard really knew what he was doing, just when to quit, you know?"

"Jesus."

"Darcy and I tore across the fields and caught Dad just as he was climbing off the tractor. I butted him in the stomach to take him down, with my brother right behind me."

If Alex hadn't known Cord was on the way to see his father he would've asked, with good reason, if the Foster brothers had killed the man. He swallowed and found his mouth was almost painfully dry. A growling stomach reminded him they had missed supper.

"Did you and Darcy. . . ?"

"We showed him the same lack of mercy he had shown us as children."

Alex didn't press for details. "Were . . . criminal charges filed?"

Cord gave him a lopsided grin. "Against Dad? Or Darcy and me?"

Alex held up his hands. "Either one I guess."

"Nope. After telling Mom good-bye, Darcy and I got the hell out of Dodge. There was no reason to stay behind."

"Is your Mom . . . is she still—"

"Alive? No." Cord's mood darkened further. "We begged her to leave with us, but like a lot of battered women, she lived in such denial and shame she refused. She even told us if we forced her she'd find a way to come back. She died about a year later, emotionally and spiritually wrecked. Dad killed her as surely as if he'd put a bullet in her brain."

"God, that's horrible."

"You think so?" Cord attempt at humor was strained. "Man, that's just the G-rated version."

"After all that's happened," Alex ventured, "why would you want to see him again?"

"You don't understand abusive relationships," Cord said. He reconsidered. "Maybe you do. I mean, what your father does is a form of abuse, and emotional beatings are often worse than the physical ones. As I said, the cycle is very hard to break, and underneath it all the man is still my father. I know there's a shitload of denial in that statement, but I can't help it."

"How do you feel toward him now?" Alex asked slowly. "Emotionally I mean."

Cord coughed, cleared his throat, and faced Alex squarely. "He's seventy-one now but tells me he's still fit. There's a reason he made a point of telling me that. Like he's inviting me to a final showdown. A sort of winner-take-all proposition."

An icy dart tingled in the small of Alex's back. "What do you mean?"

"It's a no-brainer," Cord replied. He stretched and yawned. "If he lays a hand on me I'll fucking kill him."

16

The Odd Couple

By the time the bus pulled into Jacksonville, it was nearly 10:00 p.m. Alex had never been so hungry, and as he followed Cord into the station, he had never been so scared either. He was now the subject of a national manhunt and he didn't need Cord's police training to know the importance of a low profile. Afraid of being recognized if he sat in the restaurant, he went to the farthest, emptiest corner of the station and waited for Cord to bring him something to eat. They were an odd couple indeed, the bodybuilder and the homely dark-haired woman, but no one seemed to notice. As the son of Randolph Sumner, Alex was used to plenty of attention, but now he welcomed being ignored.

"Know what?" he said as Cord handed him a chili dog. "I have new respect for ugly women. People look right through me, like I'm invisible or something."

"Count your blessings," Cord grunted. "And come outside. We're gonna eat in the dark."

His edgy tone alerted Alex. "You just heard something, didn't you?"

"Yup. Your old man just turned up the heat a couple of notches."

They hurried outside and found a spot in the shadows of an idling bus. Alex was so hungry he scarcely noticed the noxious fumes as he gobbled his chili dog and waited for Cord's news. "Well?"

"He's offering fifty thousand dollars for anyone with information—"

Alex whistled. "Fifty grand?! Jeez Louise! He's really getting desperate."

"So will a lot of people who'd like that fat reward." Cord shook his head. "You can't trust anyone, man."

Does that include you? Alex wondered. *Sure, you blew off hocking a bunch of designer watches and even ignored $25,000, but with Daddy upping* *the ante, is $50,000 too much to resist?* Didn't every man have a price? Alex nervously gnawed his hot dog as the earlier uncertainty returned in a harsh rush. This was, after all, someone he hardly knew, even if Cord had confided the facts about a brutalized childhood. That wasn't really so surprising. Alex knew people told perfect strangers things they wouldn't tell their best friend. On the other hand, he felt less confident when he remembered Cord's upbringing included values so skewed he could consider killing his own father.

"Shit," he muttered.

Cord swilled down the last of his cola. "I know what you're thinking, Alex."

"I'm not thinking anything," Alex lied. "I'm too damned scared."

"Sure you are. You're wondering if I'd turn you in for the reward money." He chuckled at Alex's feigned shock. "Man, it's a good thing you didn't try acting because you'd be terrible." His straw made a noise when he sucked air instead of cola. "Relax, man. Your secret's safe with me."

"Why should you be any different, especially when you're dead broke?"

"Who knows?" Cord waved his hand dismissively. "Maybe I'm a sucker for a hard-luck tale, even one as lame as yours."

"Why is it lame?" Alex bristled. "I can't help who my father is, any more than you can. It's all the luck of the draw."

"You're right. That was a shitty thing to say. I guess I just get fed up with rich people's sob stories. All this woe-is-me business. I've had to work for every nickel I ever got. Nobody never gave me nothing." He snorted. "The bad English was intentional by the way."

Alex ignored it. "Put yourself in my position, Cord. What was I supposed to do? Insist on going to those godawful New Orleans public schools instead of private schools where I'd learn something? Tell him I didn't want a car and trip to Paris for graduation? Tell him I preferred Sear's to Brooks Brothers and—"

"You got a car *and* a trip to France?"

Alex resented the accusatory tone. "Yes, I did, and I'm not apologizing because I didn't ask for either one. They were offered and I accepted. Only an idiot would say no."

"I always wanted to go to Paris, but I was too busy struggling to make the rent."

Alex's resentment turned into annoyance. "Give me a break. That sounds like some damned Joan Crawford movie."

Cord gave him a strange look. "That better be a joke or I'm gonna be pissed."

"It's a joke," Alex said quickly, hoping he sounded believable. He reminded himself he couldn't afford to offend his only ally.

"I'm not so sure," Cord muttered.

Alex was scrambling for some sort of self-defense when Cord grabbed him hard and kissed him on the mouth. He was sputtering for an explanation when he looked over Cord's broad shoulder and saw a glowering security guard. Alex wondered how long he'd been standing there and if he'd heard Alex's baritone.

"What's going on here?" the guard demanded, crossing his arms over a belly big as an inner tube. "Well? You two deaf or something?"

"Just telling my wife good-bye," Cord explained, mussing Alex's wig to cover more of his face. "She hates public displays."

The guard looked dubious, chilling Alex as he waddled over for a closer look. Alex told himself he was being paranoid, that the guard couldn't possibly know his identity, and prayed he was as stupid as he looked. He held his breath as the guy leaned in.

"What's your name, young lady?"

Alex inhaled, making his voice as high and breathy as possible. "Dorothy Gale."

The guard got closer still, close enough for Alex to smell onions on his breath. "You sure look familiar." He frowned, and Alex's heart pounded as he waited for recognition to flood the fat face. After what seemed like an interminable pause, the man said, "You related to the Gales down in Clay County?"

"Oh, no, sir," Alex whispered. "I'm from Kansas."

"Umm." The guard grunted, scratched his inflated stomach and stepped back. "Well, this bus is getting ready to board, so you two better move on."

"Yes, sir," Cord said. He positioned himself between Alex and the guard as he hustled Alex toward the terminal. "C'mon, honey." His affectionate tone changed as the minute they were out of earshot. "Are you fucking crazy, man?"

"What do you mean?"

"Dorothy Gale from Kansas?! What if he'd seen *The Wizard of Oz?*"

"I was scared," Alex said. "It was the first name I thought of. Actually it was the second."

"What was the first?"

"Cindy Birdsong."

"Jesus!" Cord shook his head.

"For God's sake, Cord. Nobody remembers Dorothy's last name. In any case, the guy was an idiot."

"Maybe so, but you've got to stop doing stupid things." Cord glowered. "We can't take any more chances. Understand?"

Alex nodded. "Thanks, Cord."

"For what? Telling you something any fool ought to know?"

"No. For saving my ass back there."

Cord ignored the praise, grateful to hear an announcement for the 10:50 for Miami. "Well, that's us. C'mon."

"I'll tell you something else," Alex said, taking Cord's arm as they headed for the gate.

"What's that, I'm afraid to ask?"

"You're not a bad kisser."

"Aw, shut up, Dorothy."

~ 17 ~

Miami Vice

Seven hours and five stops later, the bus finally rolled into Miami. For most of the trip, Alex had slept, although fitfully, and looked out the window toward a faint gleam over the Atlantic. The sun wasn't up yet but it was burnishing the sky like a pale topaz. Alex had only a glimpse before buildings obscured the ocean view and, except for the occasional coconut palm, the bus could've been rumbling into Anywhere USA. He sat up and stretched, careful not to waken his traveling companion.

Cord was sound asleep, lips parted slightly with a soft, steady snore. He looked peaceful under the first pale fingers of dawn, features softened, guard down. Alex studied his slumbering savior, deciding the guy was handsome despite the broken nose and ugly scar. He thought about the first moment he had seen Mr. Beefy Tee and figured fear and flight had kept him from realizing Cord oozed a natural sex appeal that could never be cultivated. And that body! Alex felt the familiar stirring as his eyes roved over biceps and thighs, wondering if the rest of Cord was as well developed. Then, just as quickly, he chided himself.

Keep your eyes on the prize, he thought—the prize being Key West and the man next to him the escort to safely get there. He felt new gratitude for Cord, for quick thinking that had bailed him out more than once, and then shuddered when he considered what might have happened if he had wandered the Tallahassee bus station without knowing his face was all over the television monitors. Thanks to Cord, he was right where he should be, and if things stayed on schedule, they would have a forty-minute layover in Miami, catch another bus at 6:20, and be in Key West by 10:45. *Key West,* he thought. *And*

Chandler Wilde. He felt the erotic stirring again, but forgot about the gorgeous Mr. Wilde when Cord opened sleep-slit eyes.

Alex smiled. "Good morning." Cord barely grunted. Alex raised his voice when more passengers awoke and started tugging belongings from the overhead rack. "Sleep okay?"

"No. The usual bad dreams about the old man." He yawned and closed his eyes again.

Alex gave him a nudge. "C'mon, Cord. We're pulling into Miami and we've only got forty minutes to grab breakfast before the next bus. I'm starved!"

"Hope I can stay awake that long," Cord muttered. He was still half-asleep when they ordered breakfast, but woke up fast when he took inventory of their fellow diners. "Shit, Alex! Check it out!"

Alex had been so hungry he hadn't paid attention to anything but the menu. Until he followed Cord's gaze, he hadn't noticed half the men in the restaurant wore tank tops or T-shirts stretched to the max by pumped up chests. They were surrounded by bodybuilders, and it took them a nanosecond to determine they were all gay.

Cord leaned toward the adjacent table and grinned. "What the hell is this, man? A gay bodybuilding convention?"

"Sort of." The beefcake returned his smile. "We're headed for the Mr. Gay Key West Contest."

"I'll be damned!"

The stranger's smile broadened, his lusty gaze evaluating Cord's prominent pecs while totally ignoring the plain woman at his table. "Maybe you ought to enter too."

"I'm no bodybuilder, man. Just a personal trainer."

"No shit?" The guy scooted his chair closer. "What diet do you do?"

Alex resented the stranger's intrusion and was rankled further when he and Cord had an intense discussion about workouts and diet, steroids and discipline. Alex didn't give a damn how much Cord could press or how many carbs he didn't eat. All he cared about was somebody intruding on the private bubble he shared with his protector. The situation worsened when Cord's new friend insisted on dragging him from table to table and introduced him to the other bodybuilders.

Alex was so thoroughly ignored he decided he might as well be alone. When breakfast came, he wolfed down his food, growing angrier with each bite until he finally decided he'd had enough.

Fuck him, Alex thought. *I don't need him any more. All I have to do is get on the bus, keep to myself, and coast down to Key West. If Cord wants to fraternize with his new beefcake buddies, fine. I'm outta here.*

It never occurred to Alex that he was being driven by pure, old-fashioned jealousy as he downed the last of his coffee, slung his bag over his shoulder with mock drama nobody noticed and stomped out of the restaurant. He didn't give Cord the satisfaction of looking back, but loud laughter prompted him to glance at the glass door. His resolve to go it alone was complete when Cord sat down with a table of complete strangers.

Alex hurried through the station, surprised at how busy it was at such an ungodly hour. He glanced at his watch and checked the monitors, grimacing when he saw the bus to Key West was half an hour late.

"Shit!"

Needing to kill time and wanting to get as far from Cord as possible, Alex headed outside. As he walked away from the terminal, he reviewed what had happened in the restaurant and was as angry with himself as with Cord. He realized he had behaved like a jealous lover, petty and petulant just because other men fawned over Cord and he had been left alone. Alex reminded himself he'd known the guy less than twenty-four hours and had no claims, emotional or otherwise. Sure Cord had been helpful during this insane flight from Daddy, but only the last leg of the bizarre odyssey remained, and he could finish it by himself just fine, thank you.

Alex felt more confident as he continued his stroll, even chuckling when he caught his ridiculous reflection in a storefront window. It was not quite light, so he used the glow of streetlights to adjust his wig and touch up his lipstick. He thought he heard something but ignored it until it grew more pronounced, and he realized too late that he had wandered down a deserted street.

"Gimme the bag, bitch!"

In a flash, Alex was knocked hard to the ground, banging his head against the sidewalk. He looked up just in time to see a shadowy figure flee with the Prada bag and everything in it. Seconds later another blurry form sped by.

"Cord!"

Alex watched Cord pursue the mugger around a corner, then got shakily to his feet. He leaned against the building, heart in his throat as he waited for the rest of the ugly scenario to unfold. He felt like it was forever before Cord reappeared, gasping for breath and, unfortunately, empty-handed.

"Couldn't catch the bastard," Cord said. "You okay?"

"I guess so." Alex rubbed his head where a knot was already rising after his collision with the sidewalk. "Except for losing my last cent."

Cord glared. "Your cash was in the bag?"

"Jolie said it would look suspicious for a woman to carry money in her hip pocket, so my wallet was in the bag. Jolie's never wrong about that kind of stuff."

Cord didn't ask who Jolie was. "What about credit cards?"

"Nope."

"ID?"

"Gone." Alex thought for a moment "I'm fucked now. I sure as hell can't go to the police. What am I going to do?"

"Well, you're just a few hours from Key West. When you get there call someone for money."

"I don't even have a quarter for the phone."

"I think I can spare a quarter or two."

"I can't take your money," Alex sniffed.

"It's a fucking quarter, for God's sake. Stop being such a drama queen and act like a man. And use your head once in a while. I swear every time you wander off alone you get into trouble. That's why I came looking for you as soon as I knew you'd left the restaurant. When I couldn't find you in the terminal, I figured you were just stupid enough to stomp off into the dark. Don't you know Miami's a fucking dangerous town?"

"I'm not stupid," Alex said peevishly. "I just made an error in judgment."

"One that could've cost you your life," Cord grumbled.

Alex fought tears. He was embarrassed as well as broke and scared, but he was damned if he was going to cry. He tried hiding behind anger. "Fuck you!"

Cord blew it off. "Fuck you too. Now c'mon. We got a bus to catch." He took Alex's arm and steered him toward the brightly lit terminal. "Promise me something, will you?"

"What?"

"Promise you won't wander off alone again."

Alex took a deep breath to control his trembling lower lip. He was furious with this man, for nothing other than being right all the time. At the same time, he was more attracted than ever and wondered how this lunacy would finally play out. To keep from going crazy, he pushed it from his mind.

"Okay."

"And another thing."

"What?"

"Straighten that damned wig!"

~ 18 ~

Stormy Weather

"This should make you feel better," Cord said as the bus finally left the Florida mainland and rumbled onto the Overseas Highway. "We're now on Key Largo and it's a straight shot right to Key West."

Cord was right. Alex's mood improved as one island after another melted beneath the wheels, and for the first time since fleeing New Orleans he believed escape was within reach. He even stopped worrying about bring broke, sure Chandler would stake him a few bucks until he found some kind of work.

He also revised his opinion about the seven bodybuilders. They commandeered the rear seats on the half-empty bus, and once Cord introduced him as his half-sister, Alexis, Alex discovered they weren't the egotistical boneheads he thought. Thinking him a hopelessly plain Jane with no tits, they adopted him as their mascot and made him promise to attend the contest. Alex soon joined the fun, joking and camping and dismissing his earlier jealousy as childish. He was especially drawn to a boisterous redhead named Larry, but was glad Cord laughed off Larry's suggestion to switch seats. Cord whispered to Alex that the guy could be bi with a penchant for mercy fucks and decided Larry didn't need a closer look.

"We'd better stay away from those two rednecks too," Alex added, nodding toward the front of the bus. "They were on the bus from Jacksonville and they've been staring at me ever since we left Miami."

"You mean that backwoods version of Laurel and Hardy?" Cord returned the pair's attention with a pointed glare. "I wouldn't worry about those inbred homophobes. Even they're not stupid enough to fuck with a bunch of bodybuilders."

While Cord resumed joking with his new friends, Alex forgot about the rednecks and admired infinite stretches of blue-green on both sides of the Overseas Highway. Rodriguez Key, Plantation Key, Islamorada, and Long Key glided by in an aquamarine rush, but by midmorning he noticed clouds piling high toward the south and west. He was surprised by how fast they swept toward the chain of tiny islands. They reminded him of gigantic jack o' lanterns, dark, menacing monsters lit from within by lightning. By the time the bus left Marathon Key, huge drops of water pelted the windows, and within minutes a fierce thunderstorm crashed across the highway. The turquoise waters turned an ugly gray as visibility plummeted.

"How can the driver see in this?"

"Dunno," Cord said. "Looks pretty nasty."

Larry leaned over the back of their seat. "That asshole should've pulled over back there. He's got us on the Seven Mile Bridge."

"What does that mean?" Alex asked.

"We're driving through seven miles of open sea, that's what," Larry grunted. "We'll get slammed in all directions."

"You know this area?" Cord asked.

Larry nodded. "I grew up on Boca Chica. The last stop before Key West."

Talk stopped as the driver plowed into the heart of the storm. Howling winds made conversation impossible anyway, as did a numbing fear when the bus rocked and skidded under increasingly powerful gusts.

"Why doesn't he pull over?" Alex yelled.

Nobody answered, just held tight as the bus slipped and slid across the bridge. By following taillights, barely visible in the driving rain, the driver miraculously managed to negotiate the seven treacherous miles of causeway and get the bus to Big Pine Key. As they reached solid ground, however, relief was short-lived as the bus skidded hard right, veered off the highway and plowed into a pothole-riddled vacant lot. Bags and packages flew from the overhead racks, pelting passengers who screamed and held tight as the bus careened out of control. It finally bounced to a halt just fifteen feet from a trailer park. No one was thrown from their seats, but the driver slammed into the steering wheel and was knocked cold. A fast-thinking passenger at the front of the bus leapt up to hit the brake and turn off the ignition.

When it was all over, Alex realized he had grabbed Cord and was tight in the man's embrace. People looked around, making sure no one was hurt and wondering aloud what to do next. Larry was the first to grab his cell phone and call 911. He reported their location and the injured driver and shouted over the storm in an attempt to reassure the other passengers.

"They'll send someone as soon as the storm passes, folks," he yelled. "We're supposed to sit tight."

"When are they coming?" asked a woman on the verge of hysteria.

"Shouldn't be too long, lady. If anyone needs help, we've got a nurse aboard!" Larry motioned to his partner. "Better take a look at the driver, Jeff."

By the time they located the first aid kit, the driver regained consciousness. Jeff bandaged his forehead and announced it was only a mild concussion. He confided to Cord that he was bluffing in an attempt to maintain calm while the winds continued to howl. Another hour dragged by and then, as fast as it had risen, the storm blew north toward the Everglades, and skies cleared to a glorious blue. Everyone sighed with relief, and spirits rose further when an ambulance pulled into the lot and paramedics scrambled aboard. Alex admired their professionalism as the chief paramedic hustled the driver into the ambulance and checked to make sure no one else was hurt.

"We'll ask you to wait here until we contact the bus company to find out what to do with you people," he said. "If you want to stretch your legs, there's a diner on the other side of that trailer park sign. Please don't wander any further."

"You sure you're okay?" Cord asked Alex as he continued to cling tight.

"Fine." Alex was disappointed when Cord moved his arm away. "But I'm starved."

"Danger sometimes does that." Cord got up and retrieved a fallen bag for the woman across the aisle. "Let's grab a bite while we're waiting."

Alex blushed and motioned him close. "I don't have any money."

"I think I can spring for a sandwich." Cord chuckled. "And maybe a lipstick too. You could sure use a touch-up." Alex reddened even more, prompting Cord to reassure him. "C'mon, kid. You're with me."

Alex wasn't sure what had happened, why Cord was suddenly so protective, attentive even, but he reveled in the feeling. Since he still wore the wig, he risked taking his "half brother's" arm as they walked the twenty yards to the diner. It felt good, and he was pleased when Cord grinned.

Everything about the Blue Marlin Diner was left over from the 1950s, including the menu. Alex couldn't remember the last time he saw banana splits on the menu, not to mention blue plate specials served on dishes with dividers. Old enough to be everyone's mother, the waitresses peppered their conversations with "dearie" and "sugar" and were as retro as the food with their pink uniforms, name tags, and immobile beehive hairdos. The one named Rayette flirted shamelessly with Jeff until he put his arm around Larry and told her they were lovers.

Rayette rolled her eyes in mock shock, leaving no doubt this was not her first brush with gay men. "Not again! Why is it always the pretty ones?" She blew kisses to Larry and Jeff before going to place their orders.

"Are people in the Keys always so friendly?" Alex asked.

"I wish they were," Larry lamented. "Everything's built up now, and mom-and-pop places like this are disappearing. We used to drive up here especially for the conch fritters. Better than anything in Key West. Lots cheaper too." He nodded at a television over the cash register. "That's new since I was here."

"Maybe we should turn it on," Jeff said. "Might find something about the storm."

Alex shot Cord a look of panic, terrified the waitress would tune into CNN. Larry unwittingly saved the moment. "Aw, those storms are nothing special. They blow up all the time and are gone before you know it."

Although nobody admitted it, the four were still a little shaky after the accident. All were thinking it could've been much worse, especially Larry who'd seen terrible accidents on the rain-slicked Seven Mile Bridge. Conversation was spotty as they ate an early lunch, mostly of speculation about when they'd get a replacement driver and halfhearted efforts to make the best of a bad situation. An hour and a half later, they wandered back to the bus and joined the others awaiting further instructions. The storm had dumped high humidity atop ninety-degree temperatures, but everyone was outside since there was no air conditioning without the motor running. It wasn't long before Alex's wig began to itch.

"How do people wear these damned things?" he grumbled. "My scalp's burning up."

"Cool it, Alexis," Cord said, hoping Jeff didn't overhear the remark.

"I can't help it," Alex hissed back. "It's like having an itch you can't scratch, and what's more those damned rednecks are staring again."

"I told you to forget about those jerks. Besides, it looks like help has arrived."

A dark sedan dislodged a man with Greyhound insignia stitched on his shirt. He approached the disgruntled group confidently, broad smile aimed at defusing bad news. "We're sure sorry for the inconvenience, folks. We've been in touch with the Miami office and they'll have a new bus and driver here by five o'clock." He raised his voice over the chorus of complaints over the additional six-hour delay. "I'm afraid that's the best we can do. The storm flooded part of the highway on Key Largo and we're waiting for that to clear. In the meantime, if there's anything we can do to make you folks more comfortable—"

Cord had heard enough. "Let's go, Alexis."

"Where are we going?"

"To use the phone back at the diner. I hate to ask him, but I'll call my old man and tell him to come pick us up. Sugarloaf Key's only twenty-five miles away. After that I'll drive you down to Key West."

"You'd do that for me?" Alex said, surprised again.

"I got to keep tabs on you somehow," Cord said. "After all, you owe me for a grilled cheese sandwich and a lipstick."

"Aren't you ever serious?"

"Too much of the time," Cord replied.

Alex followed him back to the Blue Marlin and went into the ladies room while Cord used the phone. He was readjusting his wig in the mirror when images sharpened behind him that iced his heart. He kicked his voice as high as it would go without cracking.

"I'm afraid you gentlemen are in the wrong restroom."

"We ain't the only ones!"

~ 19 ~

Thumbs Up!

Alex smelled them as soon as he saw them. The two rednecks radiated stale body odor, and the skinny one's grin revealed a row of randomly missing teeth. His porcine buddy was even more repulsive, with bits of food stuck in his scraggly beard. Alex could almost hear Jolie asking if this was an open call for *Deliverance II*.

"Quint here recognized you back in Jacksonville," the fat one said. "What with that wig and all, I wasn't so sure until I seen you myself on the TV back in Miami."

"I don't know what you're talking about—"

He grunted and scratched his left nipple. "Cut the crap, Mr. Sumner. We know who you are."

"And we know what you're worth," Quint added. His scowl and beady eyes reminded Alex of a snake. "Don't we, Burt?"

"Yup. According to CNN, that's about one hundred grand."

Alex sagged against the basin, barely feeling the cold porcelain against his butt as he learned his father had upped the reward to $100,000. Just when Key West had loomed close it was about to be yanked out of reach. His mind raced with what to do next but came up empty. The pair was squarely between him and the only door.

"Okay then. What do you want?"

Quint sneered. "The fucking money, that's what. And if you play nice, nobody will get hurt." He moved closer. "You can start by taking off the wig."

"Get away from me!"

"Gimme that fucking wig!" Quint demanded, snatching at Alex's head.

Alex dodged and bolted sideways into the restroom's only stall. It was an old metal model with a firm lock, and Alex quickly slid the bolt. He squatted low on the toilet when Quint overturned the waste can and climbed on top in an effort to grab him.

"Fucking faggot!" he snarled, reaching over the stall. "C'mere!"

Alex's response was to scream at the top of his lungs. "Help! Rape! Someone help me! Help! Rape!!"

"Shut the fuck up!"

While Quint angled from above, Burt hit the floor with a fat plop and was groping under the stall when the restroom door burst open. Cord led the rescue effort, followed by Larry, Jeff, and two more bodybuilders, and suddenly the small ladies room overflowed with bulging biceps and flying fists. Larry and Jeff yanked Quint from the wastebasket and jammed him in a corner while their buddies rolled Burt over and pinned him on his back, helpless as a turtle. No match for so much brute strength, the rednecks struggled and cursed but couldn't break free. Jeff took special glee in turning the waste can upside down and planting it on Quint's head, while Larry silenced Burt with a wad of dirty paper towels in the mouth.

Body surging with adrenaline, Cord barely controlled the urge to kick in the last of Burt's teeth. "Put those assholes in the stall and keep them there while I call the cops!" He pounded fiercely on the stall door. "C'mon, Alex! Let's go! Now!"

Alex flattened himself against the sink as the rednecks were shoved into the stall. "You okay, girlfriend?" Jeff asked.

"Fine!" Alex called as Cord herded him out the restroom door. "Thanks guys!"

"Yeah, thanks!" Cord yelled. Back in the restaurant, he paused just long enough to scoop his duffle bag and calm the terrified waitresses. Rayette and Charlene had heard Alex's cries of rape and were white with fear. "Everything's under control, ladies. We've called the cops, and until they get here I'm afraid the ladies room is *occupado*." He bowed low and blew them a collective kiss. "Adios!"

Alex pondered this bizarre Zorro behavior and struggled to keep up as Cord jogged a hundred yards past the restaurant. He followed him behind a tractor trailer, bewildered when Cord tossed him the rainbow cap. "Ditch the wig and tuck your curls under this."

"But what—"

"The sweatshirt too." When Alex stared dumbly, Cord grabbed the sweatshirt and tugged it over his head. Alex was so scared and confused he barely heard Cord's praise. "Hey, you got a nice chest, kid. A few months with me and you'd buff up just fine."

Alex was still gaping when Cord tossed off his tight tee and tucked it in his back pants pocket. This was the first time Alex had seen his bare chest, and the sight took his breath away. Cord was even more ripped than he thought, and he couldn't help wanting to see the rest of the package. Cord's orders snapped him back to reality.

"C'mon, baby. Time to get the hell outta Dodge."

Alex followed with a barrage of questions. "Why did we take our shirts off? And what's this about calling the cops? What if those rednecks tell everyone—"

"Just shut up and stick out your thumb!"

Alex was incredulous. "You mean hitchhike?"

"You guessed it!" Cord flexed his big biceps and made his pecs dance. "Didn't you see that old movie where Claudette Colbert stops traffic by pulling up her skirt?"

"Sure. *It Happened One Night.*"

"Well, this is the gay version and what better place to work it than Key West?"

While Cord faced the oncoming traffic and flashed his best grin, Alex wavered behind and wondered if this was all a crazy dream. Nothing had made much sense since the bus skidded off the highway, and the bizarre cast of bodybuilders, rednecks, and big-haired waitresses made him feel like he'd tumbled down another rabbit hole. It was unsettling to think that everything he'd done in his life had led him to this moment, standing half naked on a Florida highway with his thumb stuck out and a future as uncertain as the Gulf weather. He took a deep breath and tried to focus, grateful when a cool ocean breeze cleared some of the mental cobwebs. The sun felt good too, kissing his bare chest and shoulders, and he felt better still when a truck pulled over and the driver motioned them to climb aboard.

"Jackpot!" Cord said, flashing the driver a thumbs up. "C'mon, Alex!"

The driver leaned out of the window as they approached. "Where you guys headed?"

"Sugarloaf," Cord said.

The guy jerked his head. "Get in."

Once Alex was sandwiched between the driver and Cord, the driver introduced himself as Ramón and said he was headed for the festivities in Key West. Alex started to ask if he could ride the whole distance but had second thoughts when Ramón's fingers snaked onto his knee and squeezed.

"You guys want to hook up tonight? I'd be glad to come back up to Sugarloaf."

Cord thought fast, not wanting to piss the guy off and lose their ride. "Man, a week ago I'd have jumped at the chance, but Kevin and I are on our honeymoon." He gave Alex a peck on the cheek and winked at Ramón. "You know how it is."

"Sure." Alex was relieved when Ramón moved his hand away. "I gotta admit I'm disappointed, but, hey! Congratulations!"

The rest of the drive was spent discussing the gay scene in Key West, but Alex couldn't stop thinking about Cord's timely lie about their honeymoon. Since leaving home, his new world overflowed with men available for his personal pleasure, delicious packages to be unwrapped and sampled. Until that moment, he had never considered anything more permanent, but Cord's impromptu declaration rattled his thinking. He gave Cord a sidelong glance, pretending to look out the window as they slowed for some congestion on Little Torch Key. The rugged profile flickering under bright sunlight was only one of many different faces. In the past twenty-four hours, Cord had appeared as battered child, avenger, savior, tough guy, soft touch, and Good Samaritan. The man might have been down and out, but he had unhesitatingly bought lunch for a perfect stranger, not to mention lipstick. Of all the things Cord had done for him, Alex considered that simple, unselfish act the most touching of all.

Flushed with a rush of gratitude, it seemed the most natural thing in the world to reach over and take Cord's hand.

❧ 20 ❧

Torrid Zone

Cord crumpled his father's note and tucked it in his jeans. "Well, this explains why my old man didn't answer the phone. He's out on a fishing boat until next week." He tried the door. "Unlocked, just like he said."

"Hard to believe unlocked doors this day and age," Alex observed.

He followed Cord into the cottage. He didn't know how he expected a child beater to live, but it was a place so clean and tidy it bordered on fussiness. Almost everything was covered with plastic—sofa, chairs, lampshades, even pillows and a small ottoman. Cord wasn't surprised.

"Looks like the old bastard still has Joan Crawford's dirt phobia. Used to beat the hell out of all of us if things weren't spotless." He rubbed a chair back until it squeaked. "Hope you're not allergic to plastic because you're stuck here until he gets back with the car."

Alex rolled his eyes. "Oh, my God! I can't believe I forgot to call Chandler. He'll be worried when he hears about the accident. I'd better call and get him to come pick me up and . . . Cord? Why are you looking at me that way?"

Cord said nothing, just pulled Alex into his arms and gave him the sort of kiss to make his head swim. Alex didn't know what to think as Cord pressed their bodies together. Because they were still shirtless, Cord's firm flesh burned against Alex's chest, igniting an erotic electricity that shot low in Alex's body and smoldered. It seemed forever before Cord released him, and when the two came up for air Alex stepped back, surprised and a little embarrassed by the unsteadiness in his knees. Not to mention a physical excitement impossible to hide.

"What . . . what was all that about?"

"First tell me why you took my hand in the truck."

Alex shrugged. "I'm not really sure, Cord. It just seemed the thing to do at the time."

"I think it's more than that."

"You're right," Alex conceded. "After you told that Ramón character about the honeymoon, I started thinking about everything you've done for me. I mean, you really came to my rescue and—"

"It's more than that," Cord repeated.

Alex's knees were so weak he sank onto the couch. He remembered his earlier suspicions that he felt something for Cord he'd not experienced before, and that possibility unnerved him even more. For a moment he thought he might hyperventilate.

"May I have a glass of water?"

"Sure. But don't even think about changing the subject."

Alex leaned back, then sat upright when his bare shoulders stuck to the plastic. When Cord returned with the water, he sipped slowly to prolong what he had to say. He passed the empty glass back to Cord.

"Well?" Cord asked.

Alex took a deep breath, reaching into unchartered territory for his response. "There's no way I can explain the emotional roller coaster I've been riding the past few days, Cord. I've broken from my family, walked away from an engagement—"

"An engagement! I guess another piece of the puzzle falls into place."

"I guess. Anyway, my nerves were about as raw as they could get, and I admit I was scared to death when I got on that bus in New Orleans. Not just because I was going it alone for the first time in my life but also because I had a price on my head. I've faced one calamity after another, and every time you were there to bail me out. That was quite a surprise considering how rude you were at the beginning." He thought a minute. "And I guess I wasn't exactly Mr. Warmth either, telling all those lies, trying to keep my head above water." He took another deep breath. "Okay. Here goes nothing. Somewhere along the line, I started feeling something, Cord, and that's why I took your hand."

"What were you feeling?"

"I'm still not sure. It's all . . . so strange and different."

"Then maybe we should stop talking and do something about it."

Cord stood and pulled Alex to his feet. When they kissed this time, Alex found himself in a full-body press that took his breath away. As his lips were parted by Cord's insistent tongue, Alex thought of the promiscuous path he'd blazed through the French Quarter, of Chandler and Duncan, of Joe the Cheshire Cat and the blond bottom whose name he couldn't remember. None of them had a fraction of the allure Cord radiated, an attraction that swelled and totally enveloped him once they slipped into bed. Clothing evaporated, bodies merged, and time stopped as it often does when people make love for the first time. A second romp an hour later debunked that old myth that the first time is always the best, and Alex curled happily against Cord's shoulder as he considered the new erotic plateaus he'd explored and transcended. His cheek rested only an inch from Cord's furry left nipple, and he yielded to the temptation to give it a lick.

"Whoa!" Cord protested. "You're wearing me out."

"I'm wearing *myself* out," Alex confessed. He sighed and traced a finger across the ripped pecs and washboard abs. "You're absolutely incredible, Cord, like a marble statue. I've never been with a man so physically perfect."

"You're pretty special yourself," Cord said with a contented smile. "I don't remember when I enjoyed myself so much."

"Same here."

They cuddled a while, each lost in their own thoughts. Alex even dozed a bit, and when he awoke he inhaled the pungent smell of bacon and eggs. He tugged on his briefs and padded into the kitchen where Cord stood over the stove, naked except for an apron. Alex ogled the bare buns.

"Ohmigod! I'm having a vision!"

Cord smiled and nodded at the skillet. "Hot grease is serious business, kid."

Alex nuzzled the nape of his neck. "Be extra careful there. I don't want you injuring any vital parts."

"I was about to say the same thing, baby. I didn't hurt you back there, did I? I mean, I'm kind of big and—"

"Are you kidding? We're a perfect fit!"

"That's a relief."

Alex got another glass of water and sat at the kitchen table, wondering why the chairs were plastic-free. He shuddered to think what Cord's father would say if he knew someone in their underwear was sullying his chair.

"I still haven't called Chandler."

"He won't go for the reward, will he?"

"No way. His family's really loaded. Besides, he's a friend and knows all about Daddy."

"Good." Cord nodded at the phone. "Tell this guy you're all right, thank him for his hospitality, and say you're staying on Sugarloaf for a few days with your new boyfriend."

Alex grinned. "New boyfriend?"

"Sure." Cord blew him a kiss and dished up breakfast. "Why not?"

Why not indeed, Alex thought. "Okay."

"Atta boy. Now how do you like your coffee? With cream? Sugar?"

"With you," Alex said.

~ 21 ~

Paradise Found

Alex and Cord spent the next few days exploring Sugarloaf Key, and each other. Insisting that Alex remain incognito after his near exposure at the Blue Marlin, Cord bought him a pair of oversized, very dark sunglasses and made him keep his telltale blond curls tucked under a baseball cap. With Alex's face mostly obscured, they felt free to wander the tiny town, mingle with the tourists, and enjoy colorful tropical sunsets reminding Alex of a kaleidoscope he had as a child. At home, they sunned naked in the small backyard, drank endless glasses of iced tea with lime, and bared their souls. Alex felt a closeness he'd never experienced with anyone, not even Jolie, and that bond left him both exhilarated and exhausted.

So did the sex. Alex was thrilled to feel like a lovesick teenager, and his libido responded accordingly. He couldn't get enough of this guy, and Cord gave as good as he got. The delicious discovery that they were sexual soul mates was something they savored again and again, once getting so carried away in the front yard they nearly put on a show for some nosy neighbors.

Only one thing marred their emotional and spiritual journey to paradise: money. Alex had none and Cord's funds had dwindled to $27. Unexpected help came one morning when Cord was making pancakes and discovered the flour canister contained a wad of bills inside a plastic bag.

"I'd forgotten Pop was always squirreling money away," he said gleefully. He joined Alex at the kitchen table and made a quick tally of the crumpled bills. "Almost three hundred dollars!"

"You're not gonna take it, are you?"

"Believe me, he'll never miss it. It was a family joke that he stashed so much money when he was drunk that he forgot what he put where. That's how Mom got extra money for Darcy and me." He counted out a hundred and replaced the rest. "How about surf and turf for dinner? We'll pick up some steaks at Murray's and then hit the Freshwater Market for some gulf shrimp."

"You're spoiling me," Alex sighed.

Cord's voice softened as he tucked the bills in his jeans and folded Alex in his arms. "I wish I really could spoil you, Alex. I know you're used to having pretty much whatever you wanted and wish I could buy—"

"You're giving me something money can't buy," Alex interrupted, suddenly serious. "Believe me, I know."

Cord kissed the top of Alex's head, then knelt to look him in the eye. "I hope so."

Alex took a deep breath and addressed what they'd both danced around for days. "Are we falling in love?"

"I don't know, Alex, but just when things couldn't possibly get worse, you plopped right in my lap!"

"I feel the same way, Cord. I still can't believe the way you rescued me over and over again. If I didn't believe in guardian angels, I do now."

"Believe me I'm no angel," Cord insisted. He thought for a moment. "Although my little brother used to call me that because I was always trying to protect him. With Dad around, danger was everywhere and came without warning. I was always on the alert as a kid, and I guess I still am."

"Thank God," Alex sighed. There was a heavy moment of silence before he continued. "We're not being totally honest, are we?"

"What do you mean?"

"Well, I asked if we were falling in love and we talked about it but no one—"

Cord pulled Alex to his feet and gathered him in his strong arms. Then he looked deep into the heartbreaking blue eyes. "I'm not one of those people who won't say it because they're afraid they won't hear it in return. I love you, Alex. With all my heart."

The words rushed from Alex's soul. They were strong and unstoppable, finding freedom before he realized it. "I love you too."

Their kiss was brief. It was, Alex reflected, more a gesture of confirmation than passion, and that made it especially meaningful. A smile grew gradually, then bloomed as he was consumed by bliss.

"You sure you know what you're getting into, Cord? I mean, you pretty much pegged me right off: a spoiled little rich kid feeling sorry for myself."

"I'm sure." Cord held him closer. "Besides, we both know I've got serious issues too. We'll be a lot more successful working on them as a team."

"I like the sound of that." Alex tingled pleasantly and then grew aroused as Cord's embrace intensified. "Suppose we talk more tonight?"

"Why not now?" Cord asked. His answer was an insistent stiffness against his thigh.

"Uh, okay, honey, but what about our pancakes?"

"They'll taste better after we've worked up an appetite."

The rest of the day was a glorious repetition of those before it. Alex and Cord made love, showered, had breakfast, went for a walk along the water, laid in the sun, made love, ate lunch, walked into town and bought steaks and seafood, took naps, made love, and showered. By six o'clock they were on a nearby beach, deserted except for an old die-hard fisherman. They sat on the sand, sipping chardonnay while the sun shimmered and vanished through a grove of feathery coconut palms. Sated and relaxed, Alex remembered a game he and Jolie used to play.

"Movie cliché number one," he said. "'I wish this moment could last forever.'"

"Movie cliché number two," Cord said, quickly catching on. "'Love means never having to say you're sorry.'"

"Number three. 'I love you more than my luggage.'" When Cord looked blank, Alex added, *Steel Magnolias.*

"How about, 'I never knew it could be like this.'"

"*From Here to Eternity,* right?" Alex sipped thoughtfully. "Want to hear the real kicker, Cord? I really *didn't* know it could be like this, and I'm not quoting some old movie either."

"I know, Alex. Me too." He held his wineglass against the sunset and watched it turn molten gold. "But I'm worried."

"About what?"

"How we're going to support ourselves. I've gotten used to a hand-to-mouth existence but—"

"Don't worry about me, Cord. I'll be fine if we're together."

Cord tugged off Alex's cap and mussed his curls as he often did. "That's sweet, and I know you mean it, but I've got to be honest. It's rough for any two people starting out. There are so damned many un-avoidable obstacles, and lack of money is the worst. People probably argue over that more than anything."

Alex knew Cord was only being realistic but his feelings were still hurt. "That's not very supportive."

"Please don't misunderstand me. I'm just trying to head off prob-lems at the pass. You've got to admit, we're a pretty odd couple."

"That's part of the excitement," Alex said. He slipped a hand over Cord's knee and for a moment considered sliding it higher. Cord's words stopped him.

"I know we had a pact not to watch television, but I turned it on this morning while you were still asleep."

Alex was disappointed. "Why?"

"Well, it's been almost a week since we saw CNN and I wanted to know if you were still big news. After all, if we're going to start a life together we need to know what we're up against."

"A stone wall," Alex sighed. "If I know my father, he'll never give up."

"You're right." He took Alex's hand and squeezed. "He's raised the reward to a quarter-million bucks."

Alex sagged backward, sloshing half his wine onto the sand. "Jeez Louise!"

"With that kind of fortune at stake, it'll be like being in the witness protection program, Alex. We'll have to watch our step every day, more than we do now, and we'll never know who we can trust."

Alex hated it when the demons of doubt fluttered inside his head. He told himself that this man had professed love and wanted to build a life together, yet he still couldn't stop thinking that Cord could be swayed by the small fortune at stake. Especially now that it had swelled to such an outrageous level. He believed in Cord's love but was worried it might erode when the reward money increased, which it no doubt would. His fears deepened when he put himself in Cord's place and saw an unbelievably heady chance to grab the golden ring. It was a dizzying merry-go-round he was ill equipped to handle.

"Damn," Alex moaned. "I can feel my father tightening the noose. Even down here."

"Don't you realize that's exactly what he wants? Your father wants to wear you down like an Al Qaeda terrorist and make you think your only choice is surrender. Fight fire with fire, honey, and beat him at his own game." Cord made a face. "God, enough with the clichés!"

"No, no! You just gave me a great idea!" Alex's mind raced and he sat up so fast he finally spilled his wine. "I just thought of a way out."

Cord's eyebrows rose. "Go on."

"Well, suppose you turn me in and collect the reward money?"

"What?!"

"Just hear me out. I'll go back to New Orleans and pretend to play along with Daddy Dearest while you bank the funds. Then, you disappear, and after a certain period of time, I do too. We'll hook up and live happily ever after, courtesy of Daddy's generosity."

"You've got to be kidding!"

"I was never more serious in my life," Alex insisted. "What could be simpler?"

"From what you've told me, your father's a force to be reckoned with and that means he's probably considered that angle and plenty more as well."

Alex was confident. "I think that's the one angle he *hasn't* considered! Daddy would never suspect me of doing something so underhanded. Rebellious, yes. Vengeful, no. I'm sure of it, Cord."

"I love you, man, but you're crazy as a bedbug."

"So what? Everything about us is crazy. That's why my idea is so perfect!"

Cord retrieved the wine bottle and poured new drinks. He weighed the proposition again and shook his head. "I can't do it, Alex."

"For God's sake, why not? It's our one-way ticket to happiness!"

"It's also extortion."

"Only if we get caught."

"You just said you felt your father's noose tightening all the way down here. What's to keep him from finding us and sending us to jail?" He paused. "Well, me anyway."

Alex was stunned. "That's an awful thing to say."

"Maybe so but you know it's true. He might know we're in cahoots but he'll accuse me of tricking or unduly influencing you. There's no point in telling him we're in love. The gay thing will never be worth anything because he doesn't want to hear it."

"Cord, don't—"

"Bottom line, my love, is that he'll never send his only son and heir to prison."

"You don't think I'd insist on going with you?"

"I think you'd be a fool if you did."

"Answer my question."

"Honestly?"

"Honestly."

"No, Alex. I don't think you'd insist on going to prison."

Alex was hurt but he was also seething. "Why not?"

"It's not your fault, honey. It's just not in your makeup. Not the way you were raised."

"'Reared,'" Alex amended loftily. "Animals are raised."

Cord ignored the snotty correction. "The point is if you had to choose between a stretch in the slammer and returning to your cushy lifestyle . . . well, you're only human."

Alex was even angrier with himself because he knew what Cord said was true. Crippled since birth by his father's calculated amalgam of indulgence and control, he wasn't equipped to cope with the real world. Proof lay in the harsh fact that he would never have made it this far without Cord's timely interference. Still, he struggled to defend himself.

"And what would you do if you were in my shoes?"

Cord held out his hands, palms up. "Probably the same thing."

"How fucking patronizing is that?" Alex got to his feet, voice shaking. "Obviously this whole love business is one-sided."

Cord rose too. "If you really believe that, then you don't know me at all."

"So all of a sudden I'm a poor judge of character."

"I didn't say that, Alex."

"You may as well have!"

"Stop shouting. That old fisherman is staring."

"Fuck him!" Alex yelled. "And fuck you too! I came up with a perfect solution and you blew it off!"

Cord tried desperately to calm Alex, to show him the truth. "Don't you see? This is what I was talking about at breakfast. Money is already causing problems."

"It's a problem I can solve if you'll help me."

Cord was tired of arguing, a painful reminder of his turbulent childhood. "You haven't thought this through, Alex. Anybody can see it's a half-baked idea that—"

"So now I'm stupid too. Is that it?"

Now it was Cord whose patience was running out. "Once again you're putting words in my mouth."

"I'm stupid and immature and—"

Cord's temper blew. "All right then, yes! Spoiled and selfish too! What's more, I don't think your love is strong enough to hold us together when the going gets rough!" He made a fist and pounded his head. "Dammit, Alex! Why do you make me say things like that?"

"So everything's my fault, is it?"

Cord knew to keep his mouth closed, to hold in his rage before matters worsened. It was a trap taught by his father and he refused to fall into it.

Alex misread Cord's silence. "Fine," he said, dumping his wine on the beach. "I've had enough of this cheap shit."

That was one revelation Cord couldn't ignore. "I'm sorry it's not Cristal."

Alex forced himself to calm down, determined to display maturity and control. "I'll call Chandler and ask him to pick me up."

"Do whatever you like," Cord muttered, thoroughly exasperated. "You always do."

"Because somebody's got to know what they're doing!" Alex snapped.

A tear trickled across Cord's scar as he watched Alex walk away. He waved at the old fisherman and said, "I've got a phone call to make too, along with the biggest damned gamble of my life."

22

Paradise Lost

Alex sat on the cottage's front steps, feeling like he had lost his last friend in the world. It had only been half an hour since he and Cord argued, but the minutes dragged with a painful slowness. He started to swallow his pride and walk back to the beach but decided the best plan was to stay put. He knew in his heart of hearts that Cord would come back and he could apologize then.

"Cord!" He jumped to his feet when a familiar silhouette emerged from the shadows "I'm so sorry!"

Alex threw himself in Cord's powerful arms but they remained hanging at his sides. He stepped back, frightened and bewildered.

"What's wrong?"

Cord's husky tone was unreadable. "Have you forgotten what just happened?"

"Of course not," Alex replied anxiously, "but I said I was sorry. Can't we just forget about it and have our nice surf and turf dinner? Let's open another bottle of chardonnay."

Cord grunted. "I remember how much you liked the first one."

"I said I was sorry."

"Poor baby," Cord said. "You think that by just apologizing everything goes back to normal? It doesn't work that way. I wish it did; but it doesn't."

Alex was confused. Cord kept changing the rules, kept doing things he didn't anticipate and certainly didn't understand. This was the man he loved, yet he didn't comprehend his behavior at all. He stared into the night, helpless and lost.

"When is Chandler coming?"

"He's . . . he's not. I didn't call him."

Cord looked stricken. "What?!"

"Well, I started thinking about what I said and did and decided you were right. I was stupid and had no business storming into the night." Cord backed away when Alex tried to embrace him. "What's wrong?"

"I hope with all my heart you'll understand what I'm about to say, Alex. I truly do."

An icy pain slashed Alex's heart. "Please don't say you don't love me, Cord. Please don't say this is some terrible fag joke and that I'm just another notch on your belt. You're my first real love and I can't handle knowing I was a fool."

"I meant it when I said I loved you, Alex. You can be sure of that."

"Then what are you trying to tell me? And why do you look like a damned deer in the headlights?"

"I only did it because I thought you were going to keep running. I—"

"No!" Alex knew what was coming and covered his ears as though he could block the terrible truth. "You didn't! You couldn't have!"

Cord nodded slowly. "I called your father."

The rest of Cord's words were buried in a dull roar originating somewhere deep in Alex's guts and radiating outward until his fingers and toes tingled. He was emotionally unmoored, like the night he witnessed a drive-by shooting outside a seedy jazz club on Rampart Street. A black youth lay dead on the sidewalk, blood running toward Alex's feet, and Alex didn't know whether to look or look away. That same sensation of loss and confusion gripped him now, turning his insides to jelly.

He jerked his head toward town. Riding a soft gulf breeze were the sounds of screeching tires and high-pitched female laughter. Was calamity averted? Was someone amused and thrilled by near-tragedy? Nothing made sense!

When Alex remained mute, Cord said, "I did it for your own good, Alex. You're not equipped to keep running away, mentally, emotionally, any way you look at it. You've got to go back and face your father with the truth. Otherwise you'll never find peace of mind and we'll never find a future together. Anything built on lies is doomed to failure."

Alex heard only what he wanted to hear. "Spare me the platitudes, man. You're going after the money aren't you?"

"No," Cord said softly.

"Liar!"

Alex had never wanted to hit anyone in his life, but for a moment he thought of beating Cord's chest hard with his fist. He was oddly comforted when the urge passed, telling himself it wouldn't have done any good. He was no match for that mass of muscle, but he delivered a verbal barb he hoped would sting.

"I just hope that some day someone hurts you as much as you've hurt me."

"Damn, Alex! Why can't I make you understand this is the best thing I could do, for you, for me. For *us?*"

"Bullshit!" Alex snarled. "Now get the hell out of my way. I'm going to Key West if I have to walk every fucking step of the way."

"You'll never make it," Cord said wearily. "The police will be here any minute."

As if choreographed, a siren wailed in the distance and grew with alarming speed. While Alex's feet remained rooted to the ground, a patrol car screeched to a halt not twenty feet away. Its blue lights remained flashing as a pair of middle-aged cops got out and strode toward the cottage. To Alex they seemed to move in slow motion.

"Alex Sumner?"

A wave of nausea swept through Alex, and for a moment he thought he would be sick. He wobbled toward the porch, but when Cord rushed to help he shoved him away. Propelled by anger, his composure flooded back.

"Yeah, I'm Alex Sumner."

"Your father's looking for you, son."

Alex sighed tiredly. "Along with the rest of America I suspect." He looked from one policeman to the other. "Well? You going to handcuff me or something?"

"Not if you cooperate," the cop replied.

His buddy opened the car door. "Get in please."

Alex started for the car but paused to face Cord a final time.

"A while back you said my love for you wasn't strong enough, but you're wrong. It's your love that's weak, not mine." He looked the man hard in the eyes. "I didn't make a phone call and run away, Cord. *You* did."

"Alex, I swear—"

"But you were sure right about one thing. I *am* stupid. You were after the money all along, weren't you?"

"Sure," Cord grunted. "It was always about the money."

PART THREE

"Let's all move one place on."

Lewis Carroll,
Alice's Adventures in Wonderland

✒ 23 ✒

You Can't Go Home Again

"You were kidnapped, understand?"

Randolph Sumner paced the library, double bourbon in one hand, advance copy of the New Orleans *Times-Picayune* in the other. He shook the newspaper in his son's face and scowled.

"Look at these headlines, Alex. It's all right here in black and white, and I've kept it very, very simple. You were kidnapped at gunpoint in the parking garage at Canal Place after shopping at Brooks Brothers. Your abductors took you to the Florida Keys where you managed to escape and call the police." When Alex barely glanced at the paper, Sumner leaned in his face. "Are you listening to me?!"

"Yes, sir," Alex muttered. He turned his head, repulsed by the smell of bourbon. He had never seen his father drink so early in the day.

"I'm not so sure. Since you got home this morning it's like you were on something." The elder Sumner sipped his drink and studied his son. "Damn, boy! Is that it? Are you on some kind of drugs?"

"No, Daddy."

Sumner frowned. "I think maybe you need to see Dr. Marlow."

"I'm just tired, Daddy. It was a very long night."

He doesn't have a clue, Alex thought. *As usual he's blind to all crises and needs except his own. If anyone ever deserved an IT'S ALL ABOUT ME T-shirt, it's Daddy.*

As his father's rant continued, Alex studied his bedroom slippers and thought about last night's flight from Key West. Alone aboard Sumner Petroleum's corporate jet, he had been overwhelmed by the emotional debris of his desperate escape attempt. The combination of two shattering events had rendered him almost catatonic. First was the defeat of returning to live under his father's thumb, and second was discovering that Cord, the first great love of his life, was a fortune hunter. By the time he shuffled into the Garden District house at four in the morning, Alex felt like he was phoning in his life. The powerless sensation intensified when he heard his father's latest series of dictates, and he doubted if a Parris Island recruit could feel more debased.

"Like everyone else, Camilla knows only what she's been told," Sumner continued. "Your mother phoned her last night right after the Florida police called. We told her you'd call as soon as you could. I'm sure she's home right now, waiting to hear from you."

Just what I need, Alex thought glumly. *More lies, more spiderwebs of deceit, more of Daddy's endless bullshit. God, help me! I'm so exhausted I just want to sleep for the rest of my so-called life.*

"Fine."

Alex barely looked up as the phone was shoved at him. "For the love of God, boy! Do I have to call for you?"

With his father standing over him, berating him like a child, Alex was so unnerved he called a wrong number. Sumner grabbed the phone, punched in the proper digits, and thrust the phone back in his son's face. When he heard Camilla's chirpy hello, Alex felt sick to his stomach.

"Hello, Camilla."

"Alex, honey! Thank the good Lord you're home safe and sound. I've been worried sick of course and, well, I was so thrilled and relieved last night when your darling mama called with the wonderful news."

The receiver seemed to grow heavy with the weight of Camilla's syrupy diatribe. Conversational details failed to penetrate Alex's fog, rendering him incapable of responses requiring more than an occasional "Mmm-hmmm." A long silence made him realize he was supposed to say something.

"What's that?"

"Poor baby. You sound so stressed out. I was just asking if you were up for dinner tonight at Galatoire's. If you're not, I totally understand. I mean, after all you've been though I wouldn't blame you if you crawled back into bed and—"

"Maybe lunch tomorrow," Alex managed. "I . . . I didn't sleep very well last night."

"Then you just stay home and rest up," Camilla gushed. "And you call me first thing in the morning. We have so much to talk about and, well, you know the wedding's less than a month away now."

"I know," he muttered. He listened to Camilla's treacly good-bye and put the phone back on the hook. He looked at his father. "We'll have lunch tomorrow."

"Good." Another sip and more pacing. "You'll stay home today and come into the office tomorrow. I'll organize a little 'welcome back' party, so be prepared. The media wants an interview, but I told them you're too distraught and issued a press release instead." He held out a piece of paper. "Read it."

Alex only pretended to peruse the pack of self-serving lies before handing it back. "Okay, Daddy."

"Then you think we've covered all our bases?"

Don't you mean all of your *bases?* Alex thought. "You always do, Daddy."

"Somebody's got to know what they're doing," Sumner grunted.

Alex shuddered inside. The rude declaration was exactly what he'd said to Cord last night, a time and space that now seemed light years away. The more he thought about Cord, the more the man seemed to be only a fantasy, a dream that had morphed into a nightmare from which there was no waking. He closed his eyes, then opened them again in hopes he would find his memory of Cord erased. Instead he faced his scowling father.

"Damn!" Alex muttered.

"What did you say?"

"Just talking to myself, Daddy."

"That does it. You'll see Marlow today."

"I don't need a doctor, Daddy. I just need some sleep."

"All right then." His father downed the whiskey and set the glass aside. "I'd better get to work. Lots to do today and I know the phone will be ringing off the hook. It'll be just as bad here, but I don't want you talking to anyone except close friends. I've put a major spin on things and I don't want you undoing it. Understand?"

"Yes, sir."

"That reminds me," Sumner muttered. "I'd better call Turner and thank him again for all his help. CNN's coverage was amazing, wasn't it?"

As usual, Randolph Sumner didn't wait for a reply and rushed away on his own cloud of self-importance. That was fine with Alex. The less he saw of his father, the better. He looked at the empty glass and considered a shot of whiskey. The idea disgusted him, not so much at the idea of alcohol at nine in the morning but that he would be imitating his father. *No,* he thought. *I need to work on clearing my mind and getting a hold on reality.* He closed his eyes and drifted again, smiling when he replayed his father's absurd, utterly predictable performance.

The most amazing, yet least surprising, thing was that Sumner never once asked why his son ran away from home.

✺ 24 ✺

Revelations

"Oh, darling. I'm so sorry. I feel like it's all my fault."

"Don't say that, Mama," Alex chided sweetly. "Everything that's happened is a result of my decisions and actions. Both my running away and my coming home."

Alex was rejuvenated after a two-hour nap, the last of his mental cobwebs swept away as he and his mother shared a late breakfast. He was further rejuvenated by the richness of *pain perdu,* the Creole version of French toast he'd loved since boyhood. The day was so inviting that they dined on the terrace, and Alex tried not to think about Key West as a warm breeze stirred some nearby palms.

"Maybe I shouldn't have encouraged you to run off like that," Karen persisted.

Alex smiled. "To the contrary. You should've kicked me out years ago."

Karen touched her lips, a sign to be silent while Jedediah refreshed their coffee. The old man had been the Sumner butler and driver for years, and when Karen married into that family she quickly learned his loyalties lay with her husband, and that everything she said and did was duly reported. She continued after Jedediah was gone.

"What exactly happened down in Florida, son? Can't you tell me anything?"

"There's really not much to tell," Alex said, couching the truth as always and wondering if he could ever be totally truthful with his mother. "I took the bus as far as Sugarloaf Key, just this side of Key West. Some guy recognized me from Daddy's CNN blitz and blew the whistle. Last night Daddy's jet swooped in to pick me up and *voila!*" He sipped his coffee. "Here I am."

Karen slid aside the magnolia centerpiece so she could see him better. She squinted in the bright light "You look different to me, darling. As though something profound happened during that hiatus. Was it a learning experience of some sort?"

Her intuition was uncanny, Alex thought, and not a little unnerving.

"Oh, I learned something all right. I learned that whether I travel to Tibet or Timbuktu, Daddy's going to find a way to drag me back home." He forked a piece of yellow toast. "Do you know he hasn't asked what happened, or even why I left? All he cares about is putting things back the way they were. He even made me call Camilla this morning, as though he never heard me say I don't want to marry her."

Karen leveled a provocative gaze. "Why don't you tell her yourself?"

"Oh, Mom!" Alex laughed. "If I broke the engagement Daddy would make good his threat and cut me off without a cent."

"Would that really be so bad?"

Alex's spirits sank. "If you'd asked that the night I left this house, I would've said no. Something else I learned when I ran off is that I'm not too good at taking care of myself. I never got the chance to find out if I could earn a living without Daddy's help, but considering all that happened, I probably couldn't."

Karen reached across the table and took his hand. "For heaven's sake, son. Something *did* happen to you!"

"Yes, it did," Alex confessed. "As a result, I've got a lot of soul-searching to do and as much as I'd like to confide in you, there's only one person in the world I can talk to."

"Jolie?"

Alex's eyebrows rose. "Well, well! My mom, the mind reader!"

"He's a very nice man. We managed to sneak a couple of chats while you were gone, and he was as concerned for your welfare as myself." She took his hand. "It's all right, Alex. I think I understand why you need to talk to him. Jolie's a good friend, and I'd very much like to meet him sometime."

"I promise I'll arrange it." Alex wondered what his mother would say if he told her she'd already met Jolie as Tatiana Yussupov.

"I called Jolie right after Daddy left for work. I'm going down to the Quarter after lunch."

"Easier said than done," Karen warned.

"Why not? Daddy sent his goons home last night, and—"

"After you went back to bed, a half dozen news teams camped on the front lawn. You'll never get past them without an interview, and I know you're not up for that."

Alex's spirits sank. "You're right."

She squeezed his hand. "But that doesn't mean we can't run the gauntlet."

"What do you mean?"

"The trunk in my Caddy can't be too uncomfortable, for a short period of time anyway. I'll drop you off at Jolie's house and do some shopping in the Quarter while you two are talking." She rolled her eyes. "If you're truly going through with this sham of a wedding, I want a shamefully outrageous hat for the occasion. What better place than Fleur de Paris on Royal Street?"

Alex knew his mother disapproved of Camilla but hadn't expected such a potent indictment of the marriage, not to mention a plan to smuggle him through the army of reporters. "You're sure full of surprises this morning!"

"*Moi?*" She chuckled. "My poor darling, I've got so many surprises bottled up inside of me that . . . well, one of these days you'll see."

He rose and hugged her close. "Mom, you're the best."

An hour later, Alex experienced a welcome rush of déjà vu as he perched on Jolie's gallery and related details of his bizarre Florida odyssey. His tale came in a torrent, and when he finished the last of his intimate revelations, Jolie was exhausted.

"My God, Alex! I'm worn out just hearing all that. Who knew when I dropped you off at the bus station that you'd have such a wild teacup ride? I mean, intrigue and conspiracy, love and betrayal, sex and violence. Wow! To paraphrase dear Birdie Coonan, 'Everything but the bloodhounds yapping at your heels!'"

Alex rolled his eyes. "Skip the theatrics, Jolie. Now that Alex is back in wonderland, what am I going to do?"

"Well, first of all, you should be very grateful that I'm not berating you for falling back into the trap that sent you packing in the first place. As the French say, '*Plus ça change, plus c'est la même chose.*'"

"The more things change, the more they stay the same," Alex translated tiredly. "I know. Now how about less platitudes and more advice?"

Jolie pursed his lips. "The way I see it is you only have two choices. You can get the facts from Cord or you can go on living a lie."

Alex was humiliated by the pronouncement but pressed the issue. "What facts?"

"Oh, come on, dear boy! I did some intense reading between the lines, and do you honestly think the man's a fortune hunter?"

"He called Daddy, didn't he?"

Jolie was incredulous. "Alex, I know you're naive about life in general, and the gay lifestyle in particular, but can't you see what Cord was trying to do? He knew you two could never make it unless you learned to be independent, and that meant standing up to your father. The only way he could make that happen was to force you back here to face the music. Oh, your little scheme to cheat Daddy out of the money was amusing, but Cord is right. It would never have worked and was just another way of dodging the real issue. Like it or not, Alex, you've spent your life avoiding responsibility, and at some point it became convenient to do what Daddy said. You've used that as a crutch, and in this case running home is much easier than working on a relationship."

"Ouch."

"Remember, I told you the first sign of recovery is admitting there's a problem."

Alex thought a moment. "You really believe Cord loves me?"

"Judging from everything you've told me, yes. And that's taking into account that absolutely everything I know about Cord is from someone who's furious with him."

"I wish I could be sure. I wish I'd get some kind of sign."

"For God's sake, Alex. A sign?! You sound like Dolly Levi waiting to hear from her late husband Ephraim. Why not give Cord a sign instead?"

"You think I should call him?"

"Among other things."

"Such as?"

"Breaking your engagement and telling your parents you're gay."

Alex caught himself just before blurting that he was afraid of being disinherited, but Jolie was too quick.

"Granted it's a huge risk, but if you don't take it how can you live with yourself? And, no, that's not a rhetorical question."

"I know." Alex looked away, seeking comfort in the tranquil courtyard and splashing fountain. He found none. "It took every bit of courage I had to run away, but you're right as usual. I'm right back where I started from, doomed to marry some damned tight-ass Junior Leaguing, garden clubbing, opera guilding, Bryn Mawr perfect post-debutante who . . . aw, shit, Jolie! I'm more confused than ever."

"Confusion is not the issue here. Honesty is."

"I know that, and I want to be honest but . . . oh, my God! I sound like such a coward." Alex blinked away tears. "Is that the real problem, Jolie? Am I a coward?"

"You're just afraid, *bébé*. All gay people are afraid in the beginning. When we learn we're different, told day in and day out that what we're feeling is sick and sinful, it's only natural to deny it and pray it will go away. Most of us eventually struggle out of the closet, some even kick the damned door down, but others endure lonely lives pretending they're something they're not."

Alex immediately thought of Duncan.

"We all seek self-truths in our own ways. Lord knows my own journey was fraught with anxiety and wrong turns, including an ill-conceived marriage at a very young age, but I finally figured out who I was. Or, more accurately, who I *wasn't*."

Jolie took Alex's face in his hands and looked him hard in the eyes.

"If you don't remember or believe anything else I tell you, understand that being honest about who and what you are is the greatest present you'll ever give yourself. You're the only one who can make it happen, and when you do, I promise you'll feel like the world's burdens have been lifted from your shoulders. It's really that simple." He kissed Alex's forehead. "End of sermonette. Cue Star Spangled Banner. Fade to black."

Alex whispered a barely audible, "Thanks."

"De rien." Jolie kissed Alex again and glanced across the courtyard, eye caught by a glimmer of sunlight in the bamboo thicket. He got up slowly, bones aching from being in the same position so long. "The sun may not be under the yardarm but I sure as hell need a drink."

Alex rubbed his eyes, dizzy and a bit overwhelmed by all Jolie had said. "Me too."

"Name your poison."

"Surprise me."

"Coming right up." Jolie was halfway down the gallery when he stopped and did a very slow turn. "Did you say Bryn Mawr?"

"Huh?"

"Did you say Camilla went to Bryn Mawr?"

"Yes. Why?"

"My God, where is my effing brain these days and why didn't I think of it before?! It's absolutely inspired!"

"Jeez Louise, Jolie! You look like you've seen a ghost!"

"Resurrected a ghost is more like it, and it's sure as hell not Christmas Past!" He grinned and fluttered back to his chair. "More like Carnival Last!"

"What on earth are you babbling about?"

Jolie's face was flushed with evil excitement. "I have this fabulous friend named Angelique Poché who lives in the one thousand block of Burgundy, and she knows absolutely everyone. More important, she has all the dirt on them."

"So?"

"So I remember hoisting more than a few with dear Angelique at the Bombay Club last Mardi Gras and I just recalled something *trés* naughty she said about an uptown girl who went to Bryn Mawr."

"How do you know it was Camilla?"

"Do the math, sweetie pie. How many uptown girls go to Bryn Mawr? Besides, her name has always dogged me just like it dogged poor Princess Diana. It was just too, too familiar, and now I know why."

"But Camilla's a saint."

"Says who?"

"Everyone." Alex reconsidered. "Well, mostly Camilla now that I think about it."

"*Exactemente!* And as our beloved Oscar Wilde once said, 'Every saint has a past and every sinner has a future.'" He frowned. "Or something like that."

"Go on."

"Well, unlike most coeds, our little Miss Round Heels disdained collegiate types and had a unquenchable thirst for the common man."

"Meaning?"

"Meaning, my dear, that she loved to fuck the Great Unwashed. Angelique said she slummed in bars frequented by factory workers and eventually became high on their list of local scenic attractions and fun things to do. Only one way to find out if Camilla's our gal." He retrieved a tiny cell phone from his shirt pocket and punched a recall number. "In the meantime, how about whipping up some appletinis while *maman* does her homework?"

"Sure."

"There's a good lad!" He grinned into the telephone. "Angelique? It's Jolie. I know, my darling. It's been absolute eons!"

With the French doors to the kitchen flung wide, Alex heard snatches of conversation while he mixed the drinks. Jolie's chuckles were interspersed by long periods of silence, and when Alex returned to the gallery, cocktails in hand, he was just in time for the wickedest, most vitriolic cackle yet.

Jolie looked at Alex and nodded furiously. "A UPS man? *Two* UPS men? No!" Another loud cackle plus a snort. "At the same time? Darling, no! Tell me you're making this up! What? Oh, good Lord!"

Alex gave Jolie his drink, wishing he could hear the other half of the conversation. The cell phone was turned up just loud enough to dispense tantalizing snippets. "Local scandal . . . hushed up . . . probation . . . rich Daddy . . ."

Alex thought Jolie would never get off the phone. "Well?"

"Honey chile, this is the hottest thing since Emeril's cayenne chicken!" Jolie lofted his appletini and clinked Alex's glass. "Here's to Angelique Poché, our source for all things dark and beautiful!"

Alex sipped quickly, bursting with curiosity. "Are you going to tell me what you found out or what?"

"Oh, not I!" Jolie said, pressing a hand to his chest. "These naughty pearls of wisdom must come from Angelique's lips alone."

"Damn, Jolie! After all I've been through, I don't think my nerves can stand any more waiting."

"Not even ten minutes?"

"Huh?"

"You're about to pay a visit to Chez Poché, *bébé,* so drink up!"

~ 25 ~

Ah, Sweet Mystery of Life

Alex gave his mom a quick call and with instructions to pick him up at Angelique's house in half an hour. He was relieved but not surprised when she didn't ask for an explanation. More and more Alex realized that he was cursed by one parent and blessed with the other.

As he and Jolie walked the three short blocks to Burgundy Street, Alex felt oddly apprehensive. At first he told himself it was the potent appletini, but he admitted it was really the ugly suspicions about his fiancée. Despite being engaged to Camilla, he didn't know her very well, but he certainly understood she was her father's daughter, meaning power and privilege were all that mattered. That hardly justified her lying about her chastity, however, and the more he thought about it, the more upset he became. By the time they reached Angelique's house, that apprehension had metamorphosed into full-fledged anger.

"That lying bitch!" he muttered.

Jolie grinned. "You haven't even heard the evidence and already you're pronouncing a verdict?"

"I think I've heard enough," Alex grumbled.

"Oh, but you haven't heard the juiciest parts!" Jolie rang Angelique's bell and grinned as the first few bars of "Ah, Sweet Mystery of Life" pealed forth. "I've absolutely begged Angelique to tell me where she found that damned doorbell, but she insists one in the French Quarter is enough. I suppose she's right." His smile bloomed into a toothy grin when the door swung open. "Darling!"

Alex's first glimpse of Angelique Poché made him feel as if he'd fallen back down the rabbit hole. Swathed in antique clothing appropriate for a silent-screen siren, complete with turban concealing all but a few platinum tendrils, she could have been channeling Theda

Bara or Alla Nazimova. Jolie had declared Angelique a knockout for a woman in her fifties, and he hadn't exaggerated. Curvy, voluptuous, and unashamedly bottle blonde, Angelique was what his mother would call "a handful."

"So you're the celebrated Alex Sumner everyone in the country was looking for." Angelique delivered a dazzling smile and offered both rouged cheeks for a kiss. "It's a real honor, and of course any friend of Jolie's is always welcome." Copious turquoise bracelets clanked and jangled as she swept an arm across the entry hall. "The parlor is through there. What are you gentlemen drinking?"

"Appletinis," Jolie said.

"I'd better have water," Alex said. "I'm really feeling that last drink."

Angelique looked skeptical. "I always say more is better, but suit yourself, my dear."

While she mixed drinks, Alex ventured through antique portieres into a parlor dominated by theatrical gloom. Once his eyes adjusted, he saw that the early nineteenth century antiques usually found in Creole town houses had been vanquished by furnishings providing an ideal backdrop for his exotic hostess. Late Victorian collided with arts nouveau and deco in overstuffed chairs, settees, and a chaise lounge swarming with tasseled pillows. Fringe was epidemic, dangling everywhere from lampshades to piano shawls, and vases of peacock feathers and pampas grass were tucked alongside stereopticons and globed gaslights. Presiding over all above a Carrara marble mantle was a painting of Angelique as Pauline Borghese, breasts boldly bared, like the original. A blue Amazon macaw perched on the chandelier, but Alex didn't notice until an earsplitting shriek announced Angelique's return.

"Dear God!" Alex nearly jumped out of his skin.

"Say hello to Sazerac," Angelique said as the bird descended to her shoulder with a great fluttering of wings. "I'd say she won't bite, but forewarned is forearmed. Some might even accuse her of being an attack parrot, but that would be an exaggeration."

"Not according to Margarita Bishop," Jolie said with a wicked chuckle.

"Nonsense. Margarita only got a petite peck on her overly rouged cheek. Believe you me, if I'd wanted Sazerac to attack, Margarita would be missing one of her chins." She clinked glasses with her guests. "On that note, chin chin!" She drank deeply and got right down to business. "So, Alex, Jolie tells me you need a little dish on your fiancée."

"I'm afraid so."

"Oh, you mustn't be afraid, darling. Getting even with someone who has badly wronged you is delicious indeed, and I guarantee by the time I'm finished you'll have all the ammunition you need."

Alex liked Angelique at once. "How do you know Camilla?"

"Back in the Stoned Age, I was in school at Ole Miss with a gal named Celia Christmas of all things. She was as antisorority and antiestablishment as myself, so of course we became fast friends. We remain so to this day."

Angelique lit a cigarette tucked in a wire holder affixed to her finger. Alex remembered Gloria Swanson sporting one in *Sunset Boulevard,* a film Jolie described as "essential to any conscientious gay man's filmography." When she noticed his stare, Angelique waved it in the air.

"Yes, I copied it from *Sunset Boulevard* and tried to market it back in the seventies. I actually sold a few dozen until I got a cease and desist letter from Swanson's attorneys. As Jolie will tell you, just one of my many failed endeavors. Alas, the only thing I was ever any good at was marrying up."

"Which you do better than anyone, even the Gabors," Jolie offered.

"Well, Daddy used to say you only have to do one thing well in life." Angelique blew a stream of bluish smoke, prompting Sazerac to sneeze and, thoroughly offended, flee to its crystal perch. "Anyway, Celia and I eventually put rebellious things away and she went on to join the faculty at Bryn Mawr. Over the years she worked her way up to Dean of Women, so when she told me about this wild child from New Orleans I paid attention. Now don't get me wrong, darling boy. I'm all for kicking up one's heels as long as one is honest about it."

Alex squirmed as those last words hit home, especially since he knew Jolie recognized his discomfort. Angelique continued, oblivious.

"I'm afraid Camilla Spivey is anything but honest." Another elegant toke and exhale. "She was, according to Celia, problematic from day one—willful, headstrong, and most of all horny. Our gal misbehaved mightily, in ways putting poor Celia and me to shame. Time and again she was reprimanded, then disciplined for missing curfew and other infractions, but her luck ran out when she was seen climbing into a delivery truck parked on campus. An investigation exposed Miss Camilla in *flagrante delicto* with two deliverymen, accommodating both gentlemen at the same time no less. Celia said that was the last straw. Daddy was summarily summoned by college officials and he hushed the affair with a hefty endowment. Excepting her family and present company, New Orleans remains unaware of Camilla's perverse peccadilloes."

"But that was a long time ago," Alex blurted.

"Mais non, ma petit!" Angelique dispensed a sympathetic smile. "I'm afraid some things don't change."

Alex was reeling. "But how is this possible? The Garden District's so damned incestuous, everyone knows everyone else's business."

"That's where Camilla's smart," Angelique explained. "She never strays with her friends. It's always men from out of town. She picks them up in bars in Slidell and Covington and takes them to her father's fishing camp across the lake. She has a special penchant for farmhands and shrimpers. Aside from being plebian, their only common denominator seems to be residing well outside New Orleans."

"Oh."

Alex's obvious pain brought intervention from Jolie. "You know I would never doubt you, Angelique, but Alex needs proof. Especially considering the magnitude of what I'm planning. Lives and futures are hanging in the balance here."

Angelique crushed her cigarette in a gilded art nouveau ashtray. "That's perfectly understandable, *mon cheri.* I'd demand exactly the same thing were I in your shoes. The fact is, with one exception, I learned about Camilla's outrageous didoes from the lady herself." When Alex frowned, she said, "That's *didoes,* not *dildoes,* darling. Although those figure prominently as well."

"Jeez Louise."

"What's the one exception?" Jolie pressed.

Angelique crossed herself with mock humility and said, "Forgive me, father, for I have shared. Yes, gentlemen. I had the dubious pleasure of sharing one of Camilla's half-witted, horse-hung studs at the family fishing camp."

"How in the world did you and Camilla connect?" Alex asked.

"Last summer she was slumming down in the Quarter at one of Eulalie Butler's Sunday salons on Esplanade. When we were introduced, I recognized the name instantly and told her I was close friends with Celia. As you can well imagine, that really shook her up, but, well, one thing led to another and we soon discovered we had more in common than knowledge of her checkered past. When I admitted I too had a certain predilection for the proletariat, well-endowed of course, Camilla invited me across the lake for some fun and games with a couple of studs from her regular stable. The rest is *histoire*." She patted Alex's shoulder. "I hope this isn't too painful for you, my dear."

Alex had a strange look in his eyes. "It's funny, but the more I hear the less pain I feel. Like you say, revenge is sweet, but one needs the right weapons to succeed. Thanks to you, I feel very well armed."

"*Bon!*"

He thought for a moment as pieces of the ugly puzzle began falling into place. "It makes sense now, when I think about Camilla insisting she needed all those solitary drives in the country to clear her head. I always thought it peculiar that she demanded so much time to herself since she's such a social thoroughbred and prefers big dinners and cocktail parties to quiet evenings alone with me. Now I know why. Shit! What an idiot!"

"Remember, cuckolding is a two-way street," Jolie said.

Angelique burst into laughter. "Now *there's* a sentence you don't hear every day."

"But he's right," Alex conceded. "I'm guilty of the same thing."

"Cut yourself some slack," Jolie said. "Camilla made a conscious choice to pursue a life of hypocrisy and duplicity, whereas you're trying to make peace with a difficult lifestyle not of your choosing and to be honest with yourself and those around you. Besides," he winked at Angelique, "the good, old double standard dictates that the groom-to-be is entitled to kick up his heels while the bride-to-be languishes at home with virginity intact. With those ancient parameters in place, I suggest we find a way to reveal Camilla's indiscretions to the person who'll be most offended."

Alex's pulse quickened. "You're not suggesting we—"

"Daddy Dearest!" Jolie finished triumphantly. "We'll get Camilla to admit her guilt and let *him* break the engagement. Thus you're off the hook and free to come clean about . . . well, all those things we were talking about on the gallery."

Angelique was as skilled at resisting questions as asking them and knew when something was none of her business. She feigned distraction by blowing kisses at Sazerac.

"I'll take your advice," Alex promised, "but I have to pick the time."

"That's fine, my pet, but right now time is the thing we're running out of. Fast!"

"I agree, but how on earth can we make Camilla confess?"

"Oh, ye of little faith," Jolie said, using one of his pet phrases. "Don't you know gays aren't the only people who can be outed?"

26

Truth or Dare?

Alex hadn't seen Camilla since the "kidnapping," and as he drove to her home he thought of nothing but Angelique's raunchy revelations. By the time he wheeled the Porsche into the Spivey driveway and saw Camilla wave from the veranda, he was almost delirious with a desire for vengeance. He wanted to confront her but stayed focused, reminding himself he'd been given just one assignment—to have her in Galatoire's at one, sharp—and he mustn't drop the ball. Especially with the wedding only sixteen days away.

"Darling!" she called. "Welcome home!"

What a phony, he thought, disgusted by her fluttering handkerchief as he climbed out of the car. *Well, two can play this game.*

"Sweetheart!" he called back. "I've missed you so much!"

As he took Camilla in his arms, Alex wondered how many other men had done plenty more than embrace his fiancée. He had to admit he'd never seen sullied goods so sweetly packaged. In a peach frock showcasing her creamy complexion, Camilla was as pretty as a bouquet of oleander. And, Alex thought, just as poisonous.

"Was it just too dreadful?" she asked.

"Most kidnappings are, I suspect."

She hugged him again. "Oh, my poor baby! You've no idea how scared I was. I cried into my pillow every night!"

Spare me the Scarlett O'Hara theatrics, he thought. "I worried about you too. More than you can imagine."

Camilla practically purred. "I want to hear everything that happened to you, honey. Every last detail."

Sure, you do, Alex thought. *I wonder what part you'd like best. My coming-out party in the Quarter or my romp with Duncan Stone. Or maybe the*

151

first time Cord and I made love and kept each other up half the night with instant replays.

"I'll tell you anything you want to know."

"I'm so glad. I don't believe in secrets you know."

"Perish the thought."

She stood on tiptoes and offered her lips for a kiss. "I love you, sweetie pie!"

"Me too."

Camilla finally dispensed with the ridiculous hanky prop and took Alex's arm as they walked back to the car. "I've asked Bitsy and Puddin' to meet us at Galatoire's. Is that all right, honey?"

"Your wish is my command," he said, slopping the sugar right back.

This is so typical, Alex thought. While insisting she wanted to hear all about his ordeal, Camilla had instead orchestrated a crowd scene where she was sure to be the center of attention. As they drove downtown, he groaned just thinking about Bitsy and Puddin' and decided a genuine kidnapping was preferable to lunch with those airheads. Puddin's voice was so high every dog in the Quarter would start circling the restaurant, while Bitsy's repertoire consisted of girl talk, girl gossip, and more of the same. He had no choice since the maitre d' wasn't the only one expecting them for lunch.

Alex was halfway through the restaurant's signature crabmeat Sardou, mind numbed by Puddin's squeals, when the mystery player appeared from stage left. She was a knockout in a red Balenciaga suit and black straw hat swarming with red cabbage roses complete with faux dew. An oversized ruby brooch grabbed overhead light and shot it laserlike through the crowded dining room. Alex glanced at his watch. One o'clock sharp.

Right on cue, he thought.

Angelique Poché negotiated Galatoire's like Dolly Levi revisiting Harmonia Gardens. There didn't seem to be a head she didn't turn, and as she simultaneously smiled, nodded, and blew kisses, she reminded Alex of a one-woman crowd scene. Her destination was Camilla's table, and she wasted precious little time getting there.

"Ma chers!"

Alex politely rose as a dizzying round of air kisses threatened to suck all oxygen from his table. Once Angelique greeted Camilla, Puddin', and Bitsy, all of whom paled against her worldly exuberance, she turned her full attentions in his direction.

"So you're Alex!" she gushed, convincingly pretending this was their first encounter. She offered both cheeks for kisses before delivering a dazzling smile. "I'm Angelique Poché, but my friends call me Contessa."

"Am I considered a friend?" Alex asked, playing smoothly along.

"Absolutment!" Angelique mock-glared at Camilla. "Shame on you for keeping him all to yourself." She licked her lips. "He's so scrumptious I could just spread him on toast!"

"Angelique!" Camilla gasped. She blushed so fetchingly Alex almost bought it. "You shouldn't say such things!"

"Well, that's one thing about being a world-weary old broad," Angelique said. "You get to speak your mind and not give a damn who cares." Everyone laughed, especially Puddin', who continued calling all dogs.

"You're way too hard on yourself," Alex said.

Angelique fluttered her eyelashes and swooned against his lapel. "You're just too, too divine, and you, Camilla, are the luckiest thing since the new Mrs. Trump!"

"Thank you," Camilla said. "You're very . . . uh, sweet."

Alex smiled as Camilla stumbled over her words. He considered her a cool customer, impossible to ruffle, but Angelique's flamboyant and unexpected appearance clearly did the trick. Alex took perverse pleasure from the chink in Camilla's cosmetic armor, especially the fine froth of perspiration on her upper lip as she struggled uncharacteristically to shift attention away from herself.

"Who's your lunch partner today, Angelique?"

"My old chum Mimi Collingsworth. I'm glad she's late because I want to ask you about something." Her tone was purely conspiratorial.

Camilla's eyebrows rose in response. "Really?"

"Yes, darling. I remember you telling me about some sweet little nature trail out by your father's fishing camp and I wondered if I might come out and explore it with a friend."

"Anyone we know?" Bitsy asked.

"I don't think so. Jacques lives across the lake you see."

Bitsy and Puddin' swapped looks of ill-concealed disgust. It was beyond their ken that anyone could live across the lake, on the West Bank or, God forbid, downriver from Jackson Street.

Angelique couldn't have ignored them more obviously as she continued. "I must confess, Jacques is just the teensiest bit younger than I and a serious exercise fanatic. In fact, he's absolutely inexhaustible." She looked right at Camilla. "Darling, are you sure this isn't an imposition?"

"Not at all," Camilla said, quickly taking the bait.

Alex couldn't resist a tweak. "You never mentioned a nature trail at your daddy's place, sweetheart."

"Oh, I go there sometimes when I want to be alone. You remember."

She leaned close and bussed his cheek. Ordinarily Alex would have welcomed it as an affectionate gesture. Now it was as phony as Angelique's platinum rinse.

"Of course, I remember," he said.

"Daddy's in Venezuela and won't be up there for weeks," Camilla assured Angelique. "It's yours whenever you like."

"You're a doll!" Angelique gushed. "Call me after the honeymoon and we'll make arrangements for the key."

Alex's knees weakened at Angelique's gamble since the fishing camp rendezvous had to happen before the wedding. He needn't have worried. Camilla was chomping at the bit.

"Oh, I'd better do it now while I'm thinking about it," she insisted. "I've got so much on my mind with the wedding plans. Swing by tomorrow afternoon around two and pick up the key."

"Fabulous!" Angelique smiled at Alex. "Perhaps sometime you and this handsome lad can join Jacques and me and make it a fourway."

Puddin's squeal pierced all ears within twenty paces. "You mean foursome!"

"Of course. Silly me!"

Camilla hurried to smoothe the awkward moment. "Perhaps indeed."

Angelique turned toward the door. "Oh, look! There's Miss Mimi! Woo-hoo!" She blew kisses all around, patted Alex's fanny in full view of everyone and vanished in a cloud of Jean Patou's Joy. "*A bientot,* everyone. See you in church!"

"Wow!" Alex said. "What a character!"

"Angelique's a little over the top," Camilla confided, "but she's fun in small doses."

Alex wanted to slug her.

"She's so unlike your other friends," he said, pushing the envelope a smidgen. "How do you know her, sweetheart?"

"She and mother went to school together."

Camilla's fast, slick lie made Alex more anxious than ever to put Jolie's plan into play. He devoured his crab as eagerly as the girls swallowed Angelique's outrageous performance, then used his old cell phone ploy.

"Excuse me, ladies," he said, rising. "I have to return this call."

"Oh, pooh!" Camilla pouted. "What could be more important than this?"

"Wedding secrets, honey!" he teased. "I'll be back in a flash."

Alex blew her a kiss and rushed outside to tell Jolie the stage was set for Act Two in their perverse little play. He wasn't yet privy to the details, but knowing Jolie and Angelique, it was sure to be a humdinger.

✺ 27 ✺

The Games People Play

The Sumner Petroleum Building rose forty-eight floors in the New Orleans CBD, dwarfing all surrounding skyscrapers except One Shell Square. Even though his position was all title and no real responsibility, Alex's penthouse office commanded an imperial view including the grand curve of the Mississippi that earned New Orleans the nickname "Crescent City." He truly loved his hometown, never more than today when he looked out the window and felt like the entire city was at his feet. He was still enjoying the natural rush when he called Jolie. They hadn't spoken since yesterday's phone conversation outside the restaurant.

"Any new developments?"

"Oh, *bébé!*" Jolie said. "When Angelique got home from Galatoire's there was a message from Camilla waiting on her machine. She wants to rendezvous at the camp at one o'clock tomorrow afternoon."

"Right after the bridal shower Heidi Perrin's giving her," Alex said with a chuckle. "There's a twisted irony in there somewhere. Hey! Maybe one of the girls will give her condoms."

"Never mind the jokes. Angelique told Camilla she wanted to go early so she's got keys to the house for us. While Camilla's at Heidi's shower, Angel will call to claim a headache and explain that not one but two horse-hung studs will be there for Camilla's pleasure. She'll probably get a ticket for speeding across the lake!"

"Oh, what tangled webs we weave," Alex said.

"You're not kidding, kiddo. And I've barely got time to coach the supporting cast on getting Camilla's antics on videotape."

"What supporting cast?" Alex asked. "I mean, who are these alleged studs anyway?"

"I'll explain everything when I see you tomorrow. The heat is on!"

Alex digressed for a moment. "Talk about heat. Angelique scared the hell out of me when she told Camilla the fishing camp rendezvous could wait until after the wedding. If Camilla had agreed, that would've ruined everything."

"Angelique didn't want to sound too pushy, Alex. She knows Camilla thinks about dick more than gay men, if that's possible, and was positive she'd take the bait. Did she ever!"

"She was practically salivating," Alex reported. "You should have seen her face when Angelique said her boyfriend was insatiable. Not to mention the intentional gaffe about a foursome."

"Angel told me, but never mind about all that. We need to be at the fishing camp by noon to set things up. Can you pick me up at eleven?"

"Sure. In fact I can do anything I damned well please. I've been studiously playing by Daddy's rules since I got back and it's working, because last night I overheard him call off the last of his bloodhounds."

"Great. We sure as hell don't need them sticking their noses in what's going down tomorrow."

"Hang on a second." Alex put Jolie on hold while he took an interoffice call. He clicked back to Jolie. "Daddy's summoned me to the inner sanctum. Hope I didn't speak too soon about the bloodhounds."

"Good luck!"

"I'll need it. See you tomorrow at eleven."

"Eleven it is. *Ciao* for now!"

Alex hung up and took a deep breath as he headed down the hall. Randolph Sumner's suite of offices was legendary in New Orleans. They were designed to intimidate the visitor, and with their luxurious Southern Empire furnishings, complete with authentic antebellum paintings, they usually succeeded. Alex felt like he was visiting a museum whenever he entered the towering double doors with intricate marquetry and fine veneers and passed through a lavish waiting room before reaching his final destination. The CEO of Sumner Petroleum reigned from a heavy oak desk that once belonged to Stonewall Jackson himself. Alex always thought the calculated setup spoke volumes about his father's drive to succeed where others had failed.

"Hi, Daddy."

Sumner's outstretched palm told his son to sit. "How was lunch with Camilla yesterday?"

"Very nice. Bitsy and Puddin' joined us."

"Everything's all right with you two?"

Alex nodded. "As good as it gets." He knew his father despised small talk and wasn't surprised when he got right to the point.

"So whatever burr you had up your butt is gone?"

"I won't run off again, Daddy. I promise."

Sumner frowned. "I'm no fool, Alexander. You must've been pretty unhappy to run away from home, and I figure it's because I ran your life the way I ran my company. That probably seems cold and calculating, but it's the only way I knew. It's how my father raised me, and his father before him. I went to school where I was told, married a woman that was handpicked, and went to work for my father straight out of college. I'm proud to say I've expanded Sumner Petroleum into a bona fide empire. It's the kind of inheritance people steal and kill for, and it's being handed to you on a silver platter."

Dear God, Alex thought grimly. *You sound more like Big Daddy Pollitt every day. Pretty soon you'll be bragging about your "twenty-eight thousand acres of the richest land this side of the valley Nile."*

Alex began tuning him out, but Sumner grabbed his attention with an abrupt change of tone. The uncharacteristic softness in Sumner's voice put Alex on high alert.

"Son?"

"Yes, sir?"

"I want you to have it all. Every dollar and cent, every oil well and plantation. And I want you to have it with my blessing."

Sumner's unctuous sincerity was the biggest red flag of all. Alex had heard it all before, many times, and braced himself for the facade to drop. He wasn't disappointed as Sumner stood and gripped his desk with both hands as he leaned toward his son.

"But if you run off again, I won't come looking for you. And this . . ." He swept his arm around the opulent office and indicated the infinite Louisiana horizon behind him. "I swear to God all this will be gone forever. Do I make myself clear?"

Alex tried not to smile. *You're so damned predictable, Daddy. You pulled that train into the station right on schedule.*

"Yes, sir."

"Good." Sumner leaned back. "Now tell me something, son. Man to man."

Uh-oh, Alex thought. *Is this the moment of truth? Did Daddy's investigators uncover my French Quarter double life? Do they know what was going on in that little cottage on Sugarloaf Key? Have they interrogated Cord?*

"Yes, sir?"

"Is marriage to Camilla really such a terrible thing?"

Heartily relieved, Alex seized the moment and emoted with a flair he knew would make Jolie proud. "No, sir. I've done a lot of thinking since I got back and, well, I guess being gone made me realize how much I loved and missed Camilla. After seeing her again yesterday, I'm counting the days until the wedding."

Sumner beamed. "Son, I can't tell you how happy that makes me."

Along with Camilla and her money-grubbing parents, Alex thought. *Not to mention the stockholders in Sumner Petroleum and Gulf South Oil. Well, I suppose one good crock deserves another.*

"Don't worry, Daddy. I promise to give Camilla everything she deserves."

"That's my boy." More expansive than ever, Sumner strode around his desk and put an arm around Alex's shoulders as he ushered him out of the lavish inner sanctum. "Now I want to show you how glad I am to have you back home."

"Really?"

Whatever it was, Alex knew it would have a big price tag and watched, secretly amused, as his father reached in his pocket and withdrew a set of shiny new keys.

"It's in the garage downstairs."

Alex was disgusted by such empty extravagance as he fingered the keys to a Lamborghini Murciélago. The emptiness deepened when he recalled Cord's passion for sports cars and his near-adolescent excitement when a Lamborghini roared past their bus somewhere south of Miami. Alex remembered being shocked when he learned the price tag was over a quarter of a million dollars.

"I don't know what to say."

"'Thanks, Dad!' will be fine." Sumner said.

"Thanks, Dad!"

"You're welcome, son." Sumner flashed his best corporate-takeover smile. "And for God's sake, keep that expensive machine out of poor neighborhoods."

A car like this makes the whole world a poor neighborhood, Alex thought. "Don't worry."

Sumner's high spirits faded as he stopped short of the outermost office door. "There's one more thing, Alex."

"Yes, sir?"

"It's about the guy who turned you in."

"Oh?" Alex's insides turned to mush.

Sumner shook his head. "That's one weird sonovabitch."

Weird or queer? Alex wondered. "What do you mean?"

"First off, how'd you get hooked up with him?"

"He was on the bus," Alex said, trying to think fast and stay sane at the same time. He was certain his father's spies had supplied some pertinent details and tried to squeeze them into some plausible sequence. "The bus had an accident coming into Big Pine Key, so we hitchhiked to Sugarloaf Key. That's when he saw me on CNN and called the police."

"Well, all I can say is he's one crazy bastard. I've seen and heard some weird shit in the business world, but I couldn't believe it when my attorneys called this morning and said the guy had refused the reward."

Alex's heart clutched. "He what?!"

"Said he didn't want the money, but that's not even the strangest part."

"Oh?"

"Sent me a bill for a grilled cheese sandwich, a toothbrush, and a lipstick of all things. What the hell do you suppose that's all about?"

Alex shrugged. "No idea. Like you said, he's one weird SOB." He jangled the gleaming Lamborghini keys, so ecstatic from the news about Cord that he almost floated to the private elevator. He couldn't wait to be alone with his thoughts "Thanks again for the car."

"You're welcome. You can take the rest of the day off too. I know you're anxious to try out your new toy."

"You're reading my mind, Daddy. I'll see you and mom at dinner."

Fifteen minutes later Alex roared along I-10, not at all oblivious to the stares garnered by his outrageous toy. The windows were down, and the wind snatched at his blond curls as he raced north until Lake Pontchartrain nudged the highway from the right. Myriad whitecaps warned of an approaching storm, but Alex was consumed by far more important omens. He truly believed he had received the sign he was waiting for and was happier than he thought possible. *Jolie was right,* he thought. *Cord didn't want the money after all. He wanted me!*

"I'm in love!" he yelled into the wind. "And he's an honest man!"

ᕤ 28 ᕦ

Sex, Lies, and Home Videotapes

"Judas Priest!" Jolie looked through his parlor window and gasped at the dazzling yellow Lamborghini. It had only been parked a few minutes but was already attracting a crowd of curious locals and tourists. "I'll say one thing for your old man. When he tries to buy you off, he doesn't skimp!"

"I guess big guilt requires big bucks."

Jolie didn't know much about automobiles, but even he could see this one was built for speed as well as looks. "How fast does that thing go?"

"Zero to sixty-two in less than four seconds. It tops out at over two hundred miles an hour." Alex nodded toward the interior. "The engine's in the middle and the transmission's divided front and back. For better balance at top speed."

Jolie yawned. "Mechanics bore me, but it's a shame you didn't have it for your Key West getaway. No lawman in the world could've caught you."

"Story of my life," Alex joked. "A day late and a quarter of a million dollars short."

"Is that what that hunk of metal is worth?"

"Well, since this particular Lambo is used, I suspect Daddy Dearest got a little off the list price for a new one."

Jolie whistled. "That's a lotta moola for something that resembles a gilded suppository. It does have a trunk, doesn't it?"

"Sort of."

Jolie shoved an expensive leather satchel in Alex's arms. "Then stash this, will you?"

Alex was puzzled by the bag's lightness. "It's empty."

"Au contraire, mon cheri. You whole future's inside."

"Huh?"

"Like I told you yesterday, all will be revealed." Jolie opened the front door and, nodding toward the car, said, "Let's roll."

Despite loathing what the Lamborghini represented, Alex couldn't help preening a bit as he waded through the admiring crowd. Jolie, however, was grandeur personified as he brushed people aside. More than a touch of Tatiana colored his performance, but he regretted such showiness when Alex popped the flamboyant gull wings. Jolie balked at the treacherously low-slung interior.

"Dear God! I'll need a shoe horn to get in and out of that thing."

"You'll manage," Alex said, slipping smoothly into the body-hugging leather seat and smiling at Jolie's less than stellar maneuvers. He chuckled as his friend settled beside him with an awkward plop. "Well, maybe with a little more practice."

"Humph! I'd like to see the tsarina negotiate this sardine can!" Jolie recovered enough lost dignity to deliver a regal wave to the crowd before gliding down Royal Street. Then he made a confession. "I'm getting too old for this nonsense, Alex. I feel like I ought to be wearing goggles and a scarf." He grunted. "Or maybe a truss."

"Never mind about all that. It's exactly an hour to the Spivey fishing camp. Now fill me in on your best-laid plans."

"Well, before Angelique set the trap at Galatoire's, I telephoned Rodney Milliken. You may recall he was the Queen of Hearts at your coming-out party."

"I remember." Alex turned right on St. Peter Street and headed for Rampart. "He's had half the guys in New Orleans, right?"

"C'est vrai. Anyway, I knew if anyone was up to casting our tricky supporting players, it would be Rodney. He's an expert on scouring the Quarter's underbelly for men who need money and don't ask questions. Since he owes me a couple of favors, he didn't ask questions either."

Alex frowned and eased the Lamborghini into the light flow of traffic on I-10 west. "What are you saying? I mean, are these guys criminals or what?"

"Only peripherally," Jolie replied with a wave of the hand. "Besides, we could hardly hire upstanding citizens for such a caper. All that matters is they'll do the job for a thousand each, and that's a real bargain if you think about it. Bottom line is we have to get as down and dirty as your randy fiancée, and these are definitely the right men for the job."

"I guess," Alex conceded, "but you should've told me about the thousand bucks. I didn't bring any money."

"Not to worry. I brought cash because you never have any, and I hardly think this particular pair will honor your Visa card."

Alex remained dubious. "Man, this whole idea is crazy."

"Of course it is. That's what makes it so much fun."

"For you maybe. I'm scared to death." Jolie didn't say anything, but Alex felt his disapproving gaze. "Maybe we should just forget about the whole thing and—"

Jolie grabbed his knee. "Listen, kiddo. I've gone to a helluva lot of trouble to set you on the road to liberation once and for all. Sure, there's risk involved, but that's inevitable when you're juggling people's lives. I've done plenty of homework on these two rapscallions, and I guarantee they're capable of delivering the goods." He squeezed to the point of pain. "Are we on the same page with this, or do you want to turn this outrageous contraption around and go back to your life of lies?"

Alex felt sheepish and ashamed. In the brief but intense time they had known each other, Jolie had proven himself to be reliable and devoted, and Alex had no cause to doubt his motives or methods for helping him out of this monstrous jam. He knew the real reason for his apprehension was challenging the stale, dead-end status quo of his life, and to conjure the requisite bravery, he thought about Cord. *He loves me and he's not a fortune hunter,* Alex thought, repeating the deeply personal mantra until it was embedded in his psyche. He was exhilarated to discover it delivered the rush of courage he so desperately needed.

Even when we're apart, Alex thought happily, *Cord is here to support me.*

"You're right as usual, Jolie. I'm sorry."

Jolie patted Alex's knee and withdrew his hand. "No need to apologize for a bad case of the fantods. Now as I was saying, these two fine specimens of youthful manhood are named—promise you won't laugh!—Cletis and Dooley. According to Rodney, when they're not working the shrimp boats, adding to their tattoo collection, or boffing their white-trash girlfriends, they peddle their sausages at the Corner Pocket."

Another chunk of plot fell into place when Jolie mentioned the most notorious pay-for-play bar in the French Quarter. "They're hustlers?!"

"Oh, they're lots of things, my boy. Rodney says they're both hung like mules and have made any number of amateur porn videos. Cletis has also worked behind the cameras, which is why he's ideal for the job."

"What do you mean?"

Jolie jerked his head toward the trunk. "My little black bag back there holds a teeny tiny camera phone with video recorders and a very compact camcorder. Once the guys get Camilla in a compromising position, Cletis will suddenly get a phone call while Dooley keeps the heat turned up. With his alleged elephantine endowments, Camilla will be thoroughly distracted and you'll *both* get the footage you need."

Alex chortled. "So to speak."

"So to speak," Jolie echoed. "Angelique will be a no-show of course, so Camilla will have these two gents all to herself. Given Camilla's track record with the UPS men, double trouble is right up her alley."

"So to speak," Alex said again. He turned serious. "So once we have Camilla on videotape, it's just a matter of getting Daddy to break the engagement by sending him a copy."

"Anonymously of course."

"And in a tasteful plain brown wrapper," Alex added.

"Precisely. That ought to give the old guy a jolt."

"Now that you mention it, if Daddy sees Camilla with her ankles around her neck it could give him a heart attack. He's such a damned prude."

"So much the better. Two birds with one stone."

Alex's frowned. "For God's sake, Jolie. I just want the bastard to call off the wedding. I don't want him to die!"

"My apologies for such bad taste." They rode in silence for a few months, each lost in thought. Alex recovered first and chuckled to himself.

"What's so funny?"

"I was wondering what kind of whitewashed explanation Daddy will give Mother once he decides to call things off. He won't dare tell her the truth, although I'm sure she would be thrilled. She's almost as anxious as me to end this whole charade."

"Dear, sweet Karen doesn't need to know too many sordid details. She especially doesn't need to know that her son was one of the cameramen."

Alex's eyebrows shot up. "Huh?"

"The camera phone's for Cletis. The camcorder is for you." When Alex gaped, Jolie said, "We need you for backup camera work, *bébé*. Insurance, so to speak."

"Why me? I don't know anything about a camcorder."

"Not to worry. They're so easy a child can operate them."

"Is that the voice of experience?"

"Actually it's Rodney's voice. My dear, he has the most extensive amateur porno collection in town. It's truly amazing how many young men these days are eager to have their anatomies immortalized on videotape. No doubt because they're the gay generation of buffed bodies. Of course, I'll admit sometimes Rodney cheats and videos while they're asleep, which I don't exactly consider cricket. I mean—"

"Never mind all that. Is the camera phone his too?" He eyed Jolie suspiciously. "I know you love new gizmos. It's yours, isn't it?"

"Guilty!"

Alex was relieved. "Great. Then you'll be assistant cameraman."

"Not a chance. I adore the occasional dirty home video, but not when they're coed." He shook his head as Alex glided onto the causeway across Lake Pontchartrain, leaving a wake of stares in the toll-booth. "Just one peek at Camilla's pudendum, and I'll go screaming into the swamps."

"How can you be so squeamish after watching people eat all that disgusting crap on those reality shows?"

"Everyone has their *bete noir*," Jolie sniffed. "Alas, the labium laid bare is mine." When Alex looked skeptical, Jolie said, "Pretend you're doing undercover work. Hmmm. Just like Camilla."

Alex grimaced. "Will you please stop with the lame jokes and get serious, Jolie? I'm a nervous wreck."

"Calm down, my pet. Angelique drew me a map of the place and gave me her key so we'll be there in plenty of time to teach you how to use the camera. All you do is point and shoot through the window. There's really nothing to it."

Alex's patience was thinning. "Nothing to it?! I'm secretly photographing my fiancée screwing some redneck bisexual hustlers and, well, you know what? That's not just something I do every day!"

"Well, look at the bright side."

"What's that, pray tell?"

"You're gonna see two of the biggest dicks in the parish."

The calculated wisecrack had precisely the desired effect. Alex broke up laughing and his anxiety eased as they sailed across the causeway. "My dear Jolie. What on earth did I do for fun before I met you?"

"It's my guess you didn't have much."

Alex gave Jolie a dazzling smile. "If that wasn't true I'd be pissed."

"Feeling better?"

"Much." He thought for a moment. "Poor Camilla."

"Why 'poor Camilla'?"

"She has no idea what she's getting herself into."

"Man, oh, man!" Jolie cackled helplessly. "Considering what Rodney said about these hustlers, it's definitely the other way around. Now step on the gas and show me what *this* thing can do."

🐇 29 🐇

Close Up and Very Personal

Louisiana isn't nicknamed "Sportsman's Paradise" for nothing. The state's plentiful waterways are often dotted with thousands of fishing camps providing access to the abundant aquatic life in lakes, rivers and bayous. Typically they are rustic shacks perched atop pilings, accessible only by boat or narrow boardwalks, and often without indoor plumbing. The Spivey camp, however, was anything but typical.

Nestled alongside the picturesque if occasionally unruly Tchefuncte River, it was a handsome raised Louisiana cottage with every imaginable amenity. When Cleve Spivey gathered his buddies for a weekend of fishing, he offered much more than bait and beer. The bar was stocked with top-shelf liquors, and each of the four bedrooms boasted comfortable beds and private baths. The boathouse held a sleek Pro-Line fishing boat with the latest gadgets for finding fish, and the state-of-the-art kitchen included a chef to broil, bake, stuff, or fry it. Camilla's mother, Ivy (who had the misfortune to marry a man with the surname Spivey), had tallied the trees and one-upped Margaret Mitchell by dubbing the house Thirteen Oaks. Luckily, the rest of the family didn't share her pretensions and called it simply The Camp.

As Alex eased the car along the curving drive, he spotted a battered pickup truck and a couple of unsavory-looking characters in undershirts and worn jeans slouching beneath one of Ivy's numbered oaks. One was short and beefy, the other tall and thin, and together they boasted a collection of seventeen tattoos. They gawked as the Lamborghini hummed to a halt, and although their envious smiles revealed some missing teeth, Alex conceded these shrimpers-cum-hustlers had a certain raffish charm. He could not imagine paying them for sex, but Jolie, always the pragmatist, confessed that he'd bang the day-lights out of the shorter one.

"He's just one big hunk of andouille sausage!"

Alex ignored the obvious implication. "Which is which?" he asked.

"Your guess is as good as mine," Jolie replied as the gull wings popped up. Never shy, he beckoned assistance. "How about a helping hand, young man?"

"Sure," relied the stocky one.

"You must be Rodney's friends," Jolie said as he was pulled from the low-slung car.

"Yeah. I'm Cletis, and this here's Dooley."

"Nice to meet you I'm sure," Jolie said "This is Alex. His girl-friend's the one you two gentlemen are supposed to, uh, entertain."

Dooley chuckled. "That a polite way of saying 'fuck'?"

"Call it what you wish," Jolie conceded.

"You want a tape too, eh?" Dooley pursued. He gave Alex a lewd wink while rearranging the considerable bulge inside his jeans. "Right?"

Alex tried not to look disgusted. "Uh, right."

"Well, you've come to the right place, man. Me and Cletis are pros at this kinda stuff. Matter of fact—"

"We're well aware of your credentials," Jolie interrupted, taking charge as Alex paled. "Shall we discuss the details?"

"Yes, sir," Cletis said, clearly the brighter of the two. "I've got some questions."

"Nothing of a personal nature I trust," Jolie said.

"We don't give a shit about nobody's personal bizness," Cletis grunted. "I just wanna get the money out of the way. Mr. Milliken guaranteed a thousand up front and a thousand after you see the pic-tures, right?"

"Right." Jolie counted out ten crisp hundreds and passed them to Cletis. "Deal?"

"Deal." Cletis gave Dooley his cut and said, "Let's take a look at your equipment and then see what kind of setup we got inside."

Despite his Neanderthal demeanor, Cletis, to Alex's relief and sur-prise, proved remarkably professional. He was familiar with both camera phone and camcorder and deftly showed Alex how to use the latter. He then adjusted the lighting in the master bedroom and tilted the shutters just enough to give Alex discreet filming access.

"You shoot from there and I'll shoot from over here. That way we'll cover all the bases."

"Fine," Alex said. He relaxed a little as Cletis paced off the room again. "Anything else I should know?"

"Yeah," Cletis grunted. "Once you see us getting busy, tell your buddy here to give me a call." He rattled off his cell phone number to Jolie. "That'll be my excuse to use the camera phone and get some close-ups of Dooley and your girlfriend. What's her name again?"

"Camilla."

"Camilla," Dooley drawled, lending it an especially lascivious spin. He flicked his tongue like a lizard. "Should be a no-brainer, man."

"I hope so."

Repulsed by the prospect of debasing a woman, Alex reminded himself how Camilla had lied about her virginity while screwing untold numbers of men like these two leering, bottom-feeders. If this were not the ugly truth, he knew he wouldn't find himself in such a disgusting predicament.

"I'd better move the car before she gets here."

Cletis jerked a thumb over his shoulder. "Plenty of room behind that boathouse."

"Thanks," Alex said. "We'll wait there until she's inside the house."

"Cool." Dooley grabbed his crotch again, lewd grins and body English suggesting he'd just as soon bonk Alex as Camilla. "Maybe we can party some more after she's gone, huh? Sort of a celebration."

"Maybe so," Alex said. The idea horrified him, but he knew not to trouble the waters with so much at stake. He mustered a tired smile. "Catch you later."

Alex stashed the car and, with Jolie in tow, stayed behind the boathouse until he heard the purr of a familiar engine. He dared poke his head around the corner long enough to see Camilla scramble out of a red sportscar and wave to Cletis and Dooley.

"I'll be damned!" Alex hissed to Jolie. "Daddy gave her my old Porsche and didn't even tell me!"

"All in the family," Jolie whispered. "Now be still and watch what happens."

"Hey, y'all!" Camilla called cheerily.

"Fuck me!" Alex muttered as he aimed the camcorder and focused. "Would you look at that getup?!"

While Alex watched in shock, Camilla climbed out of the Porsche and jiggled across the driveway in skin-tight shorts, skimpy halter that barely contained ample breasts, and the kind of platform shoes none of her circle would be caught dead in. He never imagined Camilla had such items in her wardrobe, much less wore them, but he was finally seeing the naughty alter ego Angelique had described. Any and all doubts about those raunchy tales evaporated when Camilla flashed her tits before crushing them against Dooley and giving him a tongue-filled kiss. At the same time, she told Cletis to get off the phone and helped herself to his crotch.

"I'm Camilla," she said when she finally came up for air. "Angelique's not coming, but I'm sure we can have a good time by ourselves. She said you two boys really know how to party, and I can't wait to—"

The rest of Camilla's conversation was lost as she unlocked the house with Cletis and Dooley trailing like obedient puppies. When loud rock music startled an egret from Oak Number Eleven, Alex and Jolie sneaked around the house and hovered below the master bedroom window. It was only a matter of minutes before they heard Camilla's high-pitched squeals and guessed correctly that the action had shifted to the bedroom. There were more squeals and a series of lusty moans as the guys got down to business. When the erotic noise grew hot and heavy, Alex ventured a peek through the slit between the shutters. He was mesmerized by what could only be described as a live sex show.

"Damn, Jolie!" he breathed. "You won't believe this!"

"Don't talk!" Jolie hissed back. He nudged the camcorder in Alex's hand. "Get busy!"

Alex forced himself to concentrate on taping and ignore what he was seeing, especially the identities of the parties involved. Cletis and Dooley stood by the side of the bed, trousers open, endowments every bit as spectacular as Rodney Milliken promised. Naked as the day she was born and obviously enthralled by her oversized boy toys, Camilla paid them luscious and very noisy lip service while Alex, after bringing his shaking hands under control, caught the action on tape.

Cletis and Dooley were also working hard, feeding Camilla plenty of prime meat and whetting her appetite for more. Cletis glanced at the window a couple of times, assuring himself Alex was in place. At just the right moment, he urged Dooley to climb into the saddle, and as his buddy pumped away, a strong glare was Jolie's cue to phone.

To Alex's amazement, Camilla never flinched when Cletis's cell phone rang. She remained oblivious while he answered and carried on a fake conversation while clicking away with the camera. From his vantage point, Alex was certain Cletis was getting the incriminating shots. What impressed him even more was the way Cletis maneuvered his crotch so he could feed Camilla while continuing his conversation. In fact, nobody in the bedroom missed a single stroke.

Eventually Camilla's orgasmic screams emptied all thirteen oaks of birds, but the show was far from over. Dooley had no sooner finished than Cletis closed the camera phone and scrambled to take his place. Alex got that on tape too, but when Dooley and Cletis traded places yet again Alex decided he'd seen more than enough and motioned Jolie to follow him to the car.

"May as well get back to town," he said. "That damned music is so loud they'll never hear this engine."

"What about Dooley?" Jolie teased. "He said he wanted to party some more after Camilla left."

"Very funny," Alex said. "Besides, I'm sure Camilla's gonna wear those guys out. I never thought I'd see a nymphomaniac in action, but damn!" He made a face and swallowed the unexpected taste of bile.

"Are you okay?" Jolie asked.

"I guess so. It's just all so . . . so nasty."

"And you know it's gonna get even nastier."

"Yeah, I do." Alex started the car. "I think I better go somewhere to clear my head before sending Daddy his little surprise package."

Jolie was instantly on the scent. "Going back to the Keys?"

"You know me too well."

Jolie patted his knee. "I'm glad you want to patch things up with Cord, but shouldn't you talk to him first instead of just appearing on his doorstep?"

"I don't think so. Even though we parted on such awful terms, I have a real strong feeling about this."

Jolie looked anything but optimistic. "I hate to play the cautionary Greek chorus, but what if he doesn't want to see you?"

"What are you talking about, Jolie? Of course he will."

Jolie tried another tack. "What about your father? Won't he think you're flying the coop again?"

Alex thought a moment, then brightened. "Not if I use the company plane and take Mother along."

Jolie frowned. "How do you plan to pull that off, *bébé?* Karen's a pretty cool cookie, but she's still in the dark about Cord, isn't she?"

"Yes, but I'll think of something to tell her. Now let's see what we've got here."

Jolie knew the subject was closed when Alex stopped the car at the entrance to the driveway and played back his amateur porn video. His first zoom had been successful, yielding a crystal clear shot of Camilla swallowing Dooley's super-sized sausage. There was no mistaking her identity even with her mouth full. Her appetite either.

"Jeez Louise!"

Jolie grunted. "I'm sure I don't want to see."

"No, you don't, and neither will Miss Camilla." Alex chuckled. He peered closer at the tiny screen and shook his head. "Man, oh, man! This is one close-up she's definitely not ready for, Mr. DeMille."

Jolie braced himself as Alex revved the Lamborghini and left a long trail of rubber near the entrance to Thirteen Oaks. "Nor, I suspect, is *le tout La Nouvelle-Orléans.*"

"We'll find out soon enough."

30

All Keyed Up

Alex peered out the plane window. Twelve thousand feet below, a silvery Gulf of Mexico sparkled beneath the early June sunlight. An hour out of New Orleans it already stretched to infinity in all directions, and he found the vista oddly comforting, liberating even, as did his mother's presence in the seat beside him. He felt a sudden rush of affection.

"You're being a really good sport about this, Mom. I mean, not asking a lot of questions about this trip."

"Oh, I enjoy a little adventure now and then," she said, eyes twinkling. "In fact, I can't remember when I've been so excited, especially since I know it's making you happy too. That's enough for me."

"Thanks." Alex leaned over and buzzed her cheek. "One of these days I'll tell you everything."

"Sooner rather than later, I hope."

"I promise." For the first time in his life, Alex actually believed what he was saying. "I also promise I know what I'm doing."

"If I didn't believe that, I wouldn't be here, son."

"I know, Mom. Thanks."

Alex was relieved but not surprised when his mother asked no more questions. She had not only agreed to his suggestion of a couple of days in Key West but claimed it was her idea when she phoned his father at work. Sumner knew it was important because, at his request, she never called his office.

"We've all been under a tremendous amount of pressure, Randolph, and I think a few days in the tropics will do us a world of good."

"Why not visit your mother on St. Bart?"

Karen thought fast. "She'll be coming up for the wedding, and besides, I want some time alone with Alex. He's been so distant after that dreadful incident."

Sumner was suspicious. "Why Key West? The kid was just down there."

"Why not?" Karen countered. "It's close, and we can stay at that fabulous hotel you're always promising to take me to."

Karen had dispensed just the right dose of guilt, and since Sumner was bogged down in a dicey board meeting, he didn't question her further. "All right then. You two run along and have a good time."

"Will you arrange for the plane?"

"Sure."

Wouldn't Daddy have a fit, Alex thought, *if he knew he was facilitating a rendezvous with my male lover?*

The irony gave Alex a special satisfaction as the plane soared south at 300 miles per hour, and his contentment deepened when he imagined, for the thousandth time, how exciting it would be to see Cord again and be wrapped in those powerful arms. He had thought of little else since deciding to make the trip and dismissed Jolie's warning that he should give Cord advance notice. *It's not going to matter,* he thought. *We promised we loved each other, and that will fix everything, especially now that I know Cord wasn't after the ransom.*

Still . . .

Looking due south, Alex found a sprinkling of clouds on the horizon, long stretches of white marring an otherwise perfect, azure sky. Corny as it was, he couldn't help thinking there were also a few clouds hanging over his reunion with Cord. If all went well with his plan to expose Camilla's peccadilloes and force his father to break the engagement, Alex would be freed of all commitments, but how long before the ever-controlling Sumner brokered another marriage for his only son and heir? The solution Jolie relentlessly advocated was for Alex to tell his parents he was gay and face the consequences. Just last night, wearied by Jolie's well-intentioned berating, Alex finally capitulated and promised to come clean when he returned to New Orleans. Jolie was thrilled and did his best to allay Alex's fears that he couldn't eke out a living on his own. Jolie was only partly successful in defusing this crippling self-doubt, and as the biggest cloud of all came back to haunt him, Alex closed his eyes and prayed that once he was back with Cord their unique magic would return and together they could hammer out a solution.

He found some solace in his favorite song from *The Lion King II* and ran the lyrics through his head.

> Now that I've found you
> Love will find a way

Like one of those tunes that permeate the brain and refuse to leave, the lyrics were still threading through Alex's thoughts as the plane touched down at Key West International Airport shortly after noon. Sumner Petroleum had reserved a limo to take them to the Pier House on Duval Street, but his mom knew he had other plans.

"Call my cell if you need me," Alex said as he tucked her in the limo and kissed her good-bye. "I'll be back in time for supper."

As soon as the limo pulled away, Alex raced to retrieve the rental car he'd booked, got directions to Sugarloaf Key, and drove east. By the time he reached Cord's father's house, his palms were damp and his heart thumped in his throat. He calmed down when he saw the little cottage where he had experienced so much joy and freedom, but as he cut the engine and got out he sensed a pall hanging over the place. He steeled himself and walked to the front door. It swung open before he could knock and he was hit in the face with the stink of whiskey and old sweat.

"What the hell do you want?"

Alex swallowed and stepped back. "Mr. Foster?"

"Who the fuck wants to know?"

Alex tried to keep his composure as he absorbed the image of the man who had made Cord's childhood a living nightmare. Except for shortness of stature and piercing eyes, Frank Foster looked nothing like his robust son. Bald and wiry, his face was pocked with gin blossoms, his body wracked by a lifetime of alcoholism. His stale smell and rumpled clothing announced he was in the midst of a colossal bender.

"I'm a friend of Cord's," Alex said.

Foster snorted and swigged from a plastic mug. "Fucking faggot!"

Alex's face blazed at the despised epithet. "Is he here?"

"Hell, no!" the man spat. "I threw his ass out when I found out he was queer!"

Stay focused, Alex told himself. *Don't let this bastard make you lose your cool.*

"Do you know where I can find him?"

When Foster's eyes narrowed like a predator, Alex caught a glimpse of what had terrified Cord and his family. The hideous image made Alex want to beat this pitiful excuse for a human being to a pulp, but he reminded himself this was not what brought him there. He took a deep breath and repeated his question.

"I might," Foster replied after another long swig.

Alex's mind raced as he sought and found a way out of this cat-and-mouse game. "I owe Cord some money," he lied.

"Well, then, young man," Foster said, greed spreading across his maroon face. "You can give it to me. I'll see that he gets it."

When pigs fly, Alex thought. "I'm afraid I can't do that." He reached into his wallet, pulling out a wad of bills brought along for the trip. He dangled it in Foster's face, actually enjoying the look of unbridled avarice. Money is power, his father was fond of saying, and in this case Alex agreed. "But if you tell me his whereabouts I can certainly make it worth your while."

Foster was practically salivating at the sight of so much money. "Uh, sure. He moved down to Key West. I've got his address somewhere." Alex waited while Foster stumbled back inside his cottage and, after a great deal of racket, reappeared with the information.

"Fourteen DeSoto Lane," he said. He propped himself against the doorjamb and held out his hand. "Now how about passing over some of them twenties?"

"Fuck you!" Alex snarled. "Goddamned child beater!"

"Wha . . . what?"

"You heard me, you sorry bastard!"

A look of incredulity flashed across Foster's face as the ancient rage shot to the surface and drove him for revenge. Alex deftly stepped aside as the old man lurched from the porch, lost his balance and landed face down in the yard. Foster's nose exploded with blood as he struggled to his feet, reeled blindly, and fell again. Disgusted by the spectacle, Alex climbed into his rental car and drove away, but not before treating himself to a final satisfying glance in the rear view mirror. He never imagined he could derive pleasure from seeing an elderly man sprawled helpless and bloodied, but he could only think that what goes around comes around. How many times had Cord and his brother been in that same predicament?

"Serves you right, asshole!"

Alex found a map in the door's side pocket and discovered that DeSoto Lane was one of several cul-de-sacs dotting the small island. After driving around the cemetery twice, he stopped a beefy jogger and, to his surprise, got an invitation for sex along with the necessary directions. He politely refused and five minutes later found the street number and pulled up before a Victorian house dripping with gingerbread and flaking paint. Only the upper floors were visible, the ground floor obscured by a jungle of banana trees, hibiscus, and the most enormous fig tree Alex had ever seen. Its grandeur was elusive, making him wonder whether the house was destined for decay or being rescued from the brink of ruin.

He parked across the street, got out, and approached the dense undergrowth. A strange whirring, metallic sound penetrated the hot stillness, and Alex paused when he glimpsed a half-naked figure through the leaves. He caught his breath when he recognized Cord wielding an old-fashioned push lawnmower. Shirtless, body gleaming with sweat, he was, for Alex, more irresistible than ever.

"Dear God!" Alex murmured. "How could I have been such a fool?"

⟿ 31 ⟾

You Really Can't Go Home Again

Alex was stopped cold, mesmerized by Cord's rugged beauty and the raw power it radiated. The reality of the looming confrontation was both exhilarating and terrifying. It made him dizzy, until finally, through sheer willpower, he ordered his feet to move. He inched toward the iron gate and gripped its rusty spikes for support.

Stalled again, he watched and waited.

Although the lawnmower had no motor, it made quite a racket until Cord stopped and pulled a bandana from his hip pocket. Alex watched him wipe his sweaty forehead and scan the yard, as though sensing an intrusive presence. Cord squinted in the tropical glare until the silhouette by the gate came into focus. He took a few steps forward, then stopped as recognition washed over him. His voice cracked with disbelief.

"Alex?"

"Yeah. It's me."

"But how did . . . what are you doing in Key West?"

"Because you're here."

"How did you find me?"

"I went to the cottage and your father told me you'd left."

"He did, huh?" Cord's face went dark and he looked nowhere in particular. "Did he also tell you he tried to kill me?"

"No," Alex said, wrestling with more mental overload. "He . . . he was pretty drunk."

"So what else is new?"

"I guess." Alex rediscovered his strength and pushed the gate back. He winced when it squeaked in protest. "Sounds like this thing could use some grease."

"Uh, yeah," Cord said. He mopped his brow again and shifted his weight from one foot to the other. "Just one of a thousand things that need to be done around here." He looked toward the derelict house. "Need to clean out those gutters too."

Alex frowned. He was dying to rush into this man's arms, aching to be told everything was alright and that all was forgiven and that they could start over again right here and now. Instead, Cord was reciting a laundry list of house repairs. Making matters worse, he backed away when Alex approached, retreating until his heels hit the front steps. Only then did he fully address a visitor's presence by offering lemonade. This mundane gesture of Southern hospitality pierced Alex's heart like an ice pick.

"C'mon, baby," Alex purred. Even in the awkwardness of the moment, he couldn't help noticing Cord's pecs were more tanned and buffed than before. "You don't think I came all this way for lemonade, do you?"

Cord winced, looking more uncomfortable by the minute. "I'm sure you didn't, Alex, but I don't know what else to say."

"Try."

Cord looked at his feet, at the fig tree, the lawnmower, at everything except Alex. "I think we said everything the last time we saw each other."

"We need to forget all that."

"I can't Alex. You called me a liar and—"

"And you said I was nothing but a CNN blurb. Just thinking about those awful words makes me sick to my stomach, which is why I need to forget them. *We* need to forget them."

Sweat dripped from his forehead as Cord hung his head. "We said some pretty terrible things."

"Yes, we did." Alex was encouraged by Cord's markedly gentler tone. "But everything changed when Daddy told me you'd refused the ransom. I realize now that you wanted me and not the money."

"I told you that a dozen times, Alex. You never listened."

"But don't you see, Cord?" Alex was growing frantic, pleas emerging in a single one long run-on sentence as he struggled to make his case. "It was all because I was so damned scared and didn't know who to trust or what to believe, and I was running for my life and I made a dreadful mistake."

"Yes, you did. We both did."

"That's why I'm here, Cord. So we can fix that mistake."

"Oh."

Cord looked up as a pair of wild parrots fluttered between coconut palms, assaulting the quiet with ear-splitting shrieks. Alex thought absently of Sazerac, then nearly swooned beneath the ponderous silence that followed. When it became evident that Cord wasn't going to talk, Alex nodded toward the generous veranda with its jumble of wicker furniture and broken overhead fans.

"Could we at least sit down and talk about it?"

"I . . . I'm not sure there's anything to talk about."

Alex fought this newest thrust to the heart with another desperate overture. "Then how about that lemonade?"

"Sure." Cord said. "Have a seat. I'll get the pitcher and be right back."

The wild vegetation seemed increasingly surreal as Alex settled onto the settee and grimaced when his sweat-soaked shirt stuck to him. Until now he had not noticed the escalating humidity. The air was absolutely motionless, palm fronds hanging limp and still, the rusty paddles of the broken fan seeming to mock him. Even the feral parrots looked wilted as they slumped against one another and dozed.

"This is a bad dream," Alex murmured. "It's that bad dream where I can't wake up and can't find my way home. I'm Scarlett running through the fog again, looking for something that I'll never—"

"Alex? My God! Is that really you?"

Yanked from his stifling reverie, Alex saw a vaguely familiar figure waving from the gate. In a few long strides, it traveled the sidewalk and leapt up the stairs. "Better late than never as they say. Damn, it's good to see you!"

Alex's jaw dropped as he was enveloped in a bone-crushing embrace. Adding to the unreality of the moment was the appearance of someone he had totally forgotten about, someone who brought back a flood of erotic memories and more.

"Chandler!" he gasped. "Chandler Wilde!"

"In person!" Chandler said, beaming. "It's good to see you, but why on earth didn't you tell us you were coming?"

Us, Alex thought weakly. He said *us,* not *me.*

Chandler released him and chattered on. "After that crazy business last month, I figured I'd never see you again. Bitsy must've given you my new address, huh?"

No, Alex thought miserably. *She didn't.*

Oblivious, Chandler swept his arm across the property. "Pretty amazing, isn't it? Of course it needs a ton of work, but Cord and I are doing our best to bring it back to its former glory. He's an absolute wizard when it comes to carpentry and landscaping and . . . well, listen to me running on and on. How are you, buddy? You didn't go through with that damned wedding, did you?"

Alex opened his mouth, but nothing came out. His silence, coupled with a pained expression, made Chandler realize his mistake.

"Didn't . . . didn't Cord tell you he called me when his father threw him out and that we've been together ever—?"

"I didn't have time, Chandler." Cord stood in the doorway with two glasses of lemonade, looking as though he were staring down the barrel of a gun. "Alex appeared out of nowhere about five minutes ago and . . . Alex, wait! Stop! Let us explain!"

Alex heard nothing else as he leapt from the porch and fled to his car. The blue sky and verdant vegetation were an aquamarine blur as he sped down the street, cursing himself when he drove into the cemetery again. In his sorrow and confusion, he stumbled out of the car and into the cemetery. Nearly blinded by tears, oblivious to the stares of a caretaker and handful of sunburned tourists, he wandered aimlessly among the tombstones and mausoleums. Eventually his knees gave out and he collapsed onto the hard, sandy soil where he lay sobbing until he thought his heart would break.

Over and over again, Alex considered the irony of the moment, how he had come all this way to finally admit the truth about himself and embark on a new life with the only man he had ever loved. He finally found the courage to open the closet door only to have it slam in his face.

Is this it? He wondered. *Is this what I've been running through the fog to find? Is this the final fucking payoff?*

Alex didn't know how long he lay there, but when he finally opened his eyes and squinted into the intense Florida sunlight, something shimmered and blurred and slowly came into focus. Staring him right in the face was an epitaph that somehow made everything else irrelevant. He read it aloud.

I TOLD YOU I WAS SICK.

His tears turned to uncontrollable laughter.

PART FOUR

"Curioser and curioser!" cried Alice.

Lewis Carroll,
Alice's Adventures in Wonderland

⚞ 32 ⚟

Alex Doesn't Live There Anymore

Duncan approached the bed naked, a cup of hot coffee in each hand, heavy equipment swinging lazily between his thighs. Alex couldn't resist reaching out and giving Duncan a playful caress.

"Damn, man! This thing never ceases to amaze me." As he continued massaging Duncan's flesh, it slowly stiffened and swelled until the python approached maximum striking length. Alex licked his lips. "I swear if I had that kind of generous endowment I'd fund my own university."

"Invest away." Duncan trembled pleasurably from the wet heat of Alex's mouth. "Mmmm."

He let Alex enjoy himself a little longer before slipping back into bed. Since Alex returned from Florida the night before, they had been in the Ritz half of Duncan's split-personality house on Dauphine Street, lustily indulging themselves to the max. Both forgot the steaming coffee as they devoured each other yet again and rocked the bed until the headboard banged against the wall. Twenty minutes later they were in the shower together, washing away a new coat of sweat.

Duncan couldn't resist some good-natured teasing as they toweled off. "For someone who's getting married next week, you're sure leading the life of a gay blade." He chuckled at his own bad joke. "Pun intended."

"Very funny," Alex said. He scurried back to bed and grabbed his Café du Monde coffee. The familiar aroma of chicory reminded him of home and he grew pensive. "I feel more like a condemned man than a gay blade."

Duncan slipped in beside Alex and draped an arm around his shoulder. "As someone who has definitely 'been there, done that' I understand completely."

"I know," Alex said. He snuggled against Duncan's heavy frame, and, feeling more secure, made overtures of a different sort. "There are a lot of questions I'd like to ask you, Duncan."

"Fire away."

"How do you keep up this constant juggling act? I mean, one life is difficult enough but two must make you crazy sometimes."

"I won't lie to you." Duncan sipped his coffee thoughtfully. "It's never been easy, living with the constant fear of exposure, not to mention blackmail. I'm playing with people's lives here, and that makes for an enormous amount of pressure. Guilt too. The only reason I keep it up is that there's a light at the end of the tunnel."

"What do you mean?"

"In a few more years, Chuck and Leslie will be out of school and on their own. When that happens I'm going to divorce Felicity and move to the Quarter. Start over, so to speak." Duncan sighed heavily. "Or maybe stop lying to myself . . . and everyone else."

"What will Felicity and the kids think?"

"Felicity knows I've had affairs, but she doesn't know they're with men. Either way, she can hardly complain. Before I admitted an attraction to men, I had my share of women, and believe me when I say my wife is one of those gals who absolutely hates sex. I swear she's the closest thing to frigid I've ever seen."

"Are you serious? Wow!" Although Alex no longer slept with women, he liked and admired them, and, like most men, he considered Felicity Stone a knockout. She exuded raw sexuality and had a killer figure for someone in her forties. "That's a surprise."

"No one was more surprised than myself when I discovered she was a virgin on our wedding night. Felicity believed everything her mama said and comes from that old school of 'submitting because a man has animal desires.' Well, I was from the 'Southern Gentlemen School' myself, so I respected her wishes for years. When I finally got tired of the nightly refusal, not to mention constant complaints that she couldn't handle something so big, I started looking elsewhere for fun." Duncan grunted and shifted his bulk. "I had quite a few affairs with women, including my secretary for God's sake, and then one night after a long drinking bout with old fraternity brothers I ended up in the Quarter and got my first taste of man-on-man sex. I never looked back."

Alex remembered his own stumbling out of the closet. "Do you mind if I ask who the guy was?"

"Promise you won't laugh?"

"I promise."

"A cab driver, for God's sake. I was too drunk to drive so my buddies put me in a taxi. That cabbie was a cute Cajun kid about your age, and within minutes we were headed for his apartment in the Bywater. Hottest ass I'd ever had in my life." Duncan smiled and scratched a hairy nipple. "And no complaints that my dick was too big either."

"I'll bet." Alex thought for a moment. "You didn't know you were gay when you got married?"

Duncan's happy memories evaporated as the subject turned serious. "On some level, I've probably always known, but like you I was so damned suffocated by all that family honor and noblesse oblige crap that I suppressed it. What happened to me was the spin of the old genetic clock. I've since learned about a slew of gay cousins over in Lake Charles and I've always had suspicions about my sister. I mean, if she wasn't the world's butchest debutante I don't know who was. Lord!"

Alex silently agreed. Melanie Stone was one of the sweetest ladies he knew, but he wasn't the only one who thought she looked like a football coach in drag.

"In any case," Duncan continued, "I have to be honest and tell you mine is not a lifestyle I would propose for anyone." He hugged Alex close. "Especially you with that watchdog daddy of yours."

Alex enjoyed the warmth of bare flesh against his own. "I appreciate your honesty, Duncan, but I think I'm going to follow in your footsteps."

"Think again, baby. You already know what it's like to live with this deep, dark secret. It seems manageable because you're single, but imagine what it will be like with a wife and kids peering over your shoulder along with Randolph Sumner." Alex visibly tensed against his shoulder. "I don't know Camilla well, but she doesn't strike me as the kind of gal you can leave home alone. In fact, I've always suspected there was a lot of heat smoldering behind that Miss Goody Two Shoes facade."

You don't know the half of it, Alex thought.

He also thought about Cord and how strongly he hoped and believed they would have a life together and wondered how he could bear the loss of such a wonderful dream. He wished now that he had listened to Jolie and contacted Cord before confronting him and facing Chandler and thoroughly humiliating himself. With no possibility of a future with Cord and, more important, the strength that relationship would have given him, Alex reneged on his promise to Jolie that he would come out to his parents and instead slipped back into his father's controlling fold.

What now? he wondered glumly.

Alex forced his mind away from Cord and reevaluated what Duncan had said as it might apply to him and Camilla. Alex knew he could function with a woman, unnatural though it may be, but he knew damned well he'd never keep Camilla satisfied. With her voracious carnal appetite, which he had witnessed firsthand, he had no doubt she would continue her sleazy affairs, and for the first time wondered if they might not strike a compromise. He had never considered telling her about his sexual orientation, but decided she might be amenable if he agreed to her separate affairs. As long as a certain level of discretion was maintained, they could give the illusion of a happy marriage, which would please their fathers and ensure their joint inheritance. Of course, telling Camilla he knew about her nymphomaniac past (and present) would raise a lot of questions he wasn't certain how to handle.

Damn, Alex thought. *Where is Jolie when I need him? Why did he have to go rushing off to Paris for one of his madcap weekends?*

"Are you listening to me?" Duncan asked. "You look like you're a million miles away."

"I'm sorry, Duncan. I just thought of something that might solve my problem, but there are so many variables involved."

"There are no simple solutions because it's not a simple situation," Duncan said. "Like I said, people's lives are involved."

"I know."

Alex's mind raced faster as he plotted the possibilities. Jolie or no Jolie, he realized with the wedding only five days away there was no time to lose. *I'll get Camilla alone tomorrow night after that dinner party at the W,* he decided. *I'll confront her with the truth about her past, but before she freaks out I'll confess the truth about my past as well. Maybe we can find a compromise and some mutual respect for our most private desires. Yeah, that's it. That'll work. And if we play it right it's a win-win situation.*

"I've lost you again," Duncan said. He pretended to knock on Alex's head. "Anybody home?"

"Sorry, Duncan. I think I just saw that light at the end of the tunnel you were talking about."

Duncan frowned. "Alex, please don't tell me you're going back to the status quo with your old man calling the shots. That's a rough place to be."

"No way, my friend."

"You're sure this time?'

"Oh, yeah." He leaned over and kissed Duncan's chest and slowly, steadily worked his hand south onto the happy trail. "Alex doesn't live there anymore."

⤬ 33 ⤬

End of Discussion

Camilla's insecurity level was on high alert. "What's gotten into you, Alex?" she demanded as he hustled her out of the W Hotel and into his car. "You've been acting peculiar all evening. If I didn't know better I'd think you were mad at me."

"I just need to talk to you," he replied, slipping a big bill to the parking valet. The awestruck guy was still basking in the afterglow of driving a Lamborghini. "But I couldn't do it until we were alone."

Camilla frowned. "You sound so serious."

"Nothing to worry about, honey."

Alex patted her knee before revving the engine and gliding up Poydras Street. It was the first time he had seen Camilla since her performance at Thirteen Oaks, and he still hadn't quite processed what he had witnessed. He was disgusted by a hypocrisy he now knew was both genuine and unapologetic, and steeled himself against the coming confrontation.

"It's a 'good' serious," he promised.

Out of the corner of his eye, Alex watched Camilla fidget. As usual, she was unhappy not being the center of attention and was especially displeased if anyone had secrets. Totally understandable, he reasoned, with her checkered past.

"It's about our future," he said as he turned onto Magazine Street and headed uptown. "There are some issues we need to discuss."

Camilla spun toward him, eyes blazing. The softness she had cultivated for the evening's well-wishers was displaced by a hard, biting tone. "Issues? What issues? You'd better not be getting cold feet or thinking about calling off this wedding, Alex Sumner, because if you do I guarantee you'll regret it for the rest of your life."

"Calm down, Camilla. I have no intention of calling off the wedding. In fact, what I want to discuss should make us the happiest married couple in New Orleans."

Feathers smoothed, Camilla retreated. "I'm listening."

Alex had rehearsed a short, carefully planned speech about being true to one oneself and honest with one another and planned to hint, as discreetly as possible, at what he knew about Camilla's raunchy past. He began by praising her personal qualities, laying on the flattery and soft-soaping her until she was almost pliable. By the time he finished eulogizing her beauty, she was purring.

"You always know the right thing to say, darling."

"I guess because they seem to come so easily around you," Alex said. "Anyway, while Mother and I were in Key West, I did a lot of thinking about us, and—"

"So that's what you two were up to!" Camilla snarled. "You and your mother were talking about me behind my back!"

Camilla had blindsided Alex before, and he had certainly watched her go postal over the most trivial things, but this was something else. The air inside the car crackled with tension as he witnessed an emotional overreaction eclipsing anything he had seen. He tried desperately to short-circuit it.

"For heaven's sake, calm down. Mother has nothing to do with it. I was just trying to tell you that—"

"Don't you dare touch that!" Camilla slapped Alex's hand when he retrieved his vibrating cell phone. "The only person you're talking to in this car is me!"

"Sorry." Alex despised his meek retreat but knew he had to control his temper with his whole future at stake.

"I suspected something the moment you two left town!" she continued. "Why, I asked myself, would my fiancé abandon me right before the wedding and go tooting off to Florida with his mother? What could possibly make dear, sweet Alexander embarrass me in front of my friends by disappearing without warning? I racked my brain trying to figure it out and the only thing that makes sense is that you were having second thoughts and wanted your mommy!"

Alex decided she had set a record for skewing far and fast from reality. He had no doubt those long years of living a double life had bequeathed her a streak of paranoia as deep as the Mississippi River.

"You're being ridiculous, Camilla. We were—"

"So now I'm ridiculous, eh?"

Easy, Alex thought. *Take a deep breath and count to ten. If she pisses you off you'll drop the damned ball.*

"I only meant that you're overreacting a little. We were only gone overnight, and I told you I needed a little downtime after the kidnapping. I thought you of all people would understand that."

"I understand only that you've made some kind of big decision without consulting me, and how selfish is that?" Her eyes narrowed. "Just what did you tell your mother? I know she's never liked me!"

"Camilla, if you'd stop being hysterical for one minute—"

"So now I'm hysterical, am I?" Camilla was seething. "What other nasty accusations are you going to make? Is this what you wanted to discuss? My faults? *My faults?*"

Alex took a deep breath, struggling to stay calm and restore sanity to a situation spiraling further and further out of control. If he lost his cool, he'd blow everything he and Jolie had so carefully planned. He diverted himself by spinning one of his biggest lies yet.

"Sweetheart, Mother has loved you since we were children, and I assure you, Key West didn't change her feelings. I honestly can't understand why you're so upset." He paused, testing the waters with his next carefully calculated phrase. "I mean, it's not like you have anything to hide."

"Of course not!" she sniffed. Alex's subtly pointed query had the desired effect, and Camilla's dulcet tones suggested the paranoid outburst had passed. "My life's an open book, especially where your family is concerned. All I want is to make you happy and give your parents a devoted daughter-in-law they can be proud of."

Alex knew her skills in playing this scene were honed to perfection, and she didn't disappoint him. Camilla could never have imagined her silky smooth lies so sickened him that he almost felt nauseous.

"I just want you to know that I'm not the kind of girl who can handle secrets. If you want to go somewhere or do something apart from

me, then I expect you to tell me about it. Mama says sharing is the secret to every happy marriage." Camilla's voice turned even silkier as
she reached across the gleaming console to pat Alex's arm. "You
know I only want the best for us, sweetie pie, and the only way we'll
have that is complete and utter honesty. Don't you agree?"

"Of course I do."

Alex groaned inside as she moved in for the kill. "Now then, you
don't really have any issues to discuss, do you, honey?"

"No, I guess not."

"I didn't think so."

Alex didn't need to see Camilla's face to know she was smiling with
self-righteousness. In fact, her saccharine condescension was so ripe he
could almost smell it. At that precise moment, he knew he could
never tell her the truth about himself or confess what he knew about
her secret life, much less expect any sort of honest compromise.
Camilla's audacious duplicity, flaunted while she accused *him* of being
the bad guy, was more than he could stomach, and whatever feelings
he had left for this woman metamorphosed from indifference to loathing. More clearly than ever, he saw Camilla as the self-consumed,
amoral bitch she really was, someone who would unhesitatingly cuckold her husband and make fools of his family, all in the name of greed.

This, Alex decided, *means war.*

Their good-night kiss was the most difficult he had ever delivered.
As Camilla pressed their lips together, the bile triggered by her lies
stirred again, but somehow he managed to get back to the car without gagging. He'd barely cleared the driveway when his phone vibrated again. This time he answered.

"Darling boy!"

"Jolie! I thought you didn't get back until tomorrow!"

"There were rumors of security threats and cancelled flights at
Charles de Gaulle so I left a day early. I phoned about half an hour
ago, but got no answer."

"Uh, Camilla and I were having words," Alex reported.

Jolie's hope leapt. "Was it about Cord? Did you see him? Did you
patch things up? Is he moving to New Orleans? Is the wedding off?"

Alex's heart sank. "No, yes, no, no, and no."

"Oh, dear," Jolie sighed. "You want to come over for a heart-to-heart?"

"I'm too tired," Alex insisted. "In fact, I feel like I've been hit by the St. Charles streetcar and dragged fifteen blocks."

"I'm whipped too, but mine's only jet lag."

"Was Paris fun?"

"More than I ever expected. I met the most divine couple who . . . well, you'll meet them soon enough. They'll be here in a week or so."

"I'm not sure where I'll be in two weeks," Alex said.

"Uh-oh. Did you send Daddy the photos? Has the shit hit the fan?"

"Not yet. I've got a better idea."

There was a long pause. "You sound pissed."

"I am. Royally."

"Pissed enough to so something rash?"

"You've taught me better than that."

"What then?"

"Something even more spiteful."

"Tell, tell!" Jolie pressed. "I'm dying over here!"

"Let's put it this way," Alex said. "By the time I'm finished with the duplicitous Miss Camilla Spivey, the Garden District will be rocked right to its swampy foundations!"

Jolie cackled so hard Alex moved the phone away. "You go, girl!"

❦ 34 ❦

Audience Participation

It was approaching zero hour the day of the wedding. Alex paced his room, alternately nervous and exhilarated. If everything unfolded as planned, he would be a free man by noon, and Camilla would be deservedly disgraced. More than once he had asked himself if he was doing the right thing, if what he planned was too harsh. He had only to look at the photos of Camilla *in flagrante delicto* and all guilt evaporated.

"Quid pro quo, Clarice," he muttered.

His father was, as Alex expected, on cloud nine. At eleven o'clock at St. Patrick's Church, the unofficial merger of Sumner Petroleum and Gulf South Oil would be cemented and the last piece of his master plan would finally fall into place. Alex's scheme to unravel that plan was the deepest secret of his life, one shared by only two other people. Even Jolie was in the dark. He tried hard to dislodge the facts, but Alex wouldn't budge.

"You act like I'm a security risk," Jolie had pouted on the phone.

"Nothing of the sort," Alex insisted. "It's just that I know you love surprises and this one's gonna be a humdinger."

"And you're sure there's absolutely nothing I can do to help?"

"Actually, it would help if Tatiana came to the wedding. I don't really know why, but she would give me moral support."

"Oh, my! This is just like that time Maria Callas was nervous about her latest comeback and asked her pal Elizabeth Taylor to come to the opera late and distract everyone. It's so exciting!"

Alex struggled to be patient as Jolie babbled on. "Is that a yes?"

"Tatiana will be there with bells on!" Jolie crowed. "I happen to know she just bought something devastating in Paris and this will be the perfect occasion to debut it."

"Thanks, Jolie."

"Any time, kiddo. See you in church!"

Remembering that conversation made Alex smile as he went downstairs to join his mother in Sumner Petroleum's vintage Rolls Royce. As soon as he slid in beside her, Karen sent Jedediah inside to hurry up her husband and seized the opportunity for a private word with her son.

"You're in awfully high spirits this morning," she ventured.

"Why not?" Alex grinned and gave her a hug, careful not to muss her hair or corsage. "It's my wedding day."

"I know. That's why I'm surprised you're smiling."

Alex feigned shock. "Why, Mother dear! What a dreadful thing to say to a bridegroom."

"To any ordinary bridegroom, yes," Karen conceded. "But you hardly fit that category."

Alex's paranoia went into overload. Had his mother overheard something? Did the housekeeper find the photos of Camilla stashed at the bottom of his sock drawer? Or did he just look like he was up to something?

"What does that mean?"

"Well, for one thing you're cool as a cucumber even though your father's still on the phone with that Venezuelan oil deal. We'll barely get to the church on time as it is." Karen toyed with the ribbons on her corsage. "I was also thinking about how determined you were to avoid marriage to Camilla and how you're now hell-bent on going through with it. This sudden about-face has me very intrigued." Before Alex could reply, she said, "This wouldn't have anything to do with our trip to Key West, would it?"

"Sort of," Alex confessed. He took her hand. "Remember when we were on the plane, and I promised I'd tell you everything sooner or later?"

"Of course I do. Is it sooner or later yet?"

"Somewhere in between I think."

"My dear Alexander," she said, squeezing his hand. "Do you have any idea how lucky you are to have a mother who lets you keep so many secrets?"

"You sound like Jolie," he said. "He's always singing your praises, and, yes, I do know how lucky I am. You have the patience of a saint."

"Well, Saint Karen's patience was wearing pretty thin in Key West, but this morning I got a feeling that something's about to happen. Something big. Something life altering."

Alex was more curious than ever, especially about his mother's uncharacteristic choice of words, but he said nothing. "And why is that?"

"Because mothers know things, my darling." She squeezed his hand again and smoothed her long skirts as Sumner and Jedediah appeared at last. "We can only be fooled for so long."

"All right, Jedediah!" Sumner boomed, sliding in beside them. "Let's get this show on the road, eh?"

Despite the supposed joyousness of the day, the Sumner family raced down Prytania Street in complete silence. Alex knew it was because each was consumed by deep personal concerns. While his mother fretted over an enormous unknown and his father dreamed of empires merged, Alex went over his secret scheme for the umpteenth time. He closed his eyes and silently thanked Camilla for insisting the ceremony be videotaped. If all went as planned, he'd have something to cherish for the rest of his life, and it sure as hell wouldn't be a new wife!

"Here we are," Jedediah announced proudly, drawing the Rolls up before St. Patrick's Church. He beamed as he hopped out to open the door. "All delivered safe and sound for Mr. Alex's big day."

Karen wasn't kidding about running late. The wedding consultant, Samara Sarpy, maintained a frantic vigil on the church's front steps. She rushed to the car before they even climbed out and began barking orders.

"Mother of the groom down the aisle!" Miss Sarpy snapped. She glared at Alex and his father as though they were on the FBI Most Wanted list. "Groom and best man, to the altar now! Father Gregory is waiting! Everyone's waiting! Hurry, people!"

As his mother was hustled into the church, Alex glimpsed something lacy and white and realized he had seen Camilla. "Uh-oh," he muttered.

"What's wrong, son?" Sumner asked as they hurried to the church's rear entrance.

"Isn't it bad luck to see the bride before the ceremony?"

"Bullshit," his father grunted. "It's going to be nothing but smooth sailing for you and Camilla." He clapped Alex on the back in a show of affection that was light years too late. "I guarantee it."

"Right, Daddy."

The moment Alex and his father followed the priest to the altar, he scanned the sea of faces and smiled when he spotted Tatiana Yussupov seated right behind Karen. She was a symphony in teal satins and feathers, face largely concealed by a blue veil draped from a picture hat. Jolie winked and gave a discreet gloved wave before Alex looked elsewhere, immeasurably relieved when he found the party he sought toward the rear of the sanctuary.

"Thank God!" he murmured.

Alex tensed, then relaxed as Phaedra Swanson commenced the dreaded "Oh, Promise Me." Phaedra was the size of the Superdome, but he agreed she had the voice of an angel. After that, the ceremony was a blur as Camilla's dozen attendants floated down the long aisle, followed by the bride and her father. Then everyone except Camilla seemed to recede until he and she were alone with Father Gregory. Alex went through the ceremony by rote, occasionally nudged by Camilla and prompted by the priest when his mind wandered. He didn't start paying real attention until the priest approached that moment in the liturgy when he asked approval of the congregation.

"If there is anyone among you with reason why this man and this woman should not be joined in holy matrimony, let them speak now or forever hold their peace."

Because Alex and Camilla faced away from the congregation, they could not see what happened next. Their eyes were riveted on Father Gregory's beaming face as he gave the crowd the requisite cursory glance, never dreaming anyone would respond. Satisfied, he looked back at Camilla, then at Alex, smiled nervously and paused.

The next moment was longest in Alex's life.

Father Gregory looked away from the bridal couple and fixed an unbelieving gaze somewhere between them. A dull rustling broke the stillness, a sound Alex knew could be only one thing. Then the priest spoke in a badly shaken voice.

"Young . . . young man? Have you . . . have you something to say?" There was another interminable pause and more rustling. Someone coughed and cleared his throat. "There are . . . *two of you?!*"

For Alex, time lapsed and everything unfolded in slow motion as Camilla faced the congregation. He turned too and saw, at precisely the same moment as Camilla, two men in ill-fitting suits who were decidedly not on the guest list. They stood a good fifty feet away, but Camilla had no trouble recognizing them. She made an unidentifiable noise and then pierced the vast sanctuary with a screech of raw hysteria. Alex caught her as she fell into a dead faint. Then, prompted by a burst of chivalry, he swept her into his arms and off the altar.

He looked up just in time to see Cletis and Dooley making a mad scramble for the front door.

35

Candid Cameras

The New Orleans Police Department often referred to Mardi Gras as "controlled chaos," and Alex decided the same label applied to the atmosphere in the tension-packed rectory. Camilla, in a sort of suspended animation, languished in one corner while her mother and father hovered like courtiers attending a tragic queen. Slumped in an enormous Gothic chair, face as pale as her wedding gown, she reminded Alex of a photographic negative.

His parents were there too, along with the bewildered Father Gregory who looked anxiously from one set of parents to the other, praying for someone to explain this catastrophe. After Alex volunteered that he knew nothing about the mysterious men fleeing the church, all attention shifted to the bride. Sumner, to no one's surprise, took charge.

"All right, Camilla," he began. "Who the hell is that swamp trash and what were they doing here?"

Camilla shook her head, unable to reply. Her mother leaned close and whispered, "Randolph has asked you a question, dear, and your father and I would like an answer too."

With Camilla's silence, except for the occasional whimper, and Sumner's growing impatience, the tension jacked up a couple more notches. When everyone turned to Alex for help, he dutifully knelt at her feet.

"You must tell us why you're so upset, my darling," he said, praying his voice wouldn't crack with inner glee. "Are those men criminals or something? Are you frightened of them?" He squeezed her icy hands. "Please let us help you."

Camilla's eyes flickered to his face, and in that single fleeting moment Alex felt a lifetime of loathing. He wondered if she suspected he

had a hand in this expose or if she was merely appalled by his unend-
ing ignorance. He shook his head and moved back to his corner to
wait for the approaching train wreck.

Slowly, her lips began to move. "I . . . I can't—"

Sumner's notorious impatience simmered to the surface. "Look
here, Camilla. We've got a church full of people out there wondering
what the hell happened. They deserve to know something and so do
we!"

"Calm down, Sumner," Cleve Spivey said, breaking his paternal
vigil. "Can't you see the poor girl is scared half to death?"

"Of course I can!" Sumner snapped. "I just want to know why.
Maybe we need to call the police. I mean, am I the only one here who
thinks those guys looked like they just broke out of Angola?"

"Yes!" Camilla cried, reclaiming all attention.

What everyone else saw as the beginning of the truth Alex recognized as her convoluted solution to this mess. "What do you mean?"
her father asked.

"Call the police," Camilla muttered. "Those men . . . those men—"

"What about those men, dear?" her mother urged.

Camilla sat up and assumed a commanding posture Alex had seen
innumerable times. Knowing she was a drama queen at heart, he
braced himself for a shocker. He wasn't disappointed.

"Those . . . those men attacked me!"

"You mean they raped you?" Sumner asked.

"Yes!" Camilla cried, voice a calculated amalgam of rage and terror. "They raped me! And I think they're escaped convicts!"

Dear God, Alex marveled. *Is there no end to her audacious lies and deceit?*

"But how . . . what . . . when did—?" Cleve Spivey stammered.

"It was at the fishing camp, Daddy." Camilla took his hand, her
mother's too, and held tight as she spun her fanciful tale. Only Alex
knew she was making it up as she went along. "You see," she told the
Sumners, "I go up there for nature hikes. I was so stressed over the
wedding and Alex's kidnapping that I needed to get away from everything and these guys came out of nowhere. Before I knew what was
happening, they . . . they dragged me into the house and . . . oh, it was
too horrible!"

"Why didn't you tell us, dear?" her mother pleaded.

"Oh, mama!" Camilla buried her face in her hands and trembled terribly. "I'm . . . I'm so ashamed. I can't . . . I just can't talk about it."

Spivey enfolded his daughter in his arms while Camilla gushed crocodile tears. Everyone focused on the poor girl's sorrow and shame, each weighing the horror of what she had confessed. Ivy grew so pale that Father Gregory helped her to a seat, and Cleve Spivey was visibly shaken. Sumner looked equally unsettled while Karen drifted to the window and admired a magnolia tree loaded with white blossoms. Alex, of course, knew Camilla was delivering another of her Oscar-caliber performances. *Well,* he thought, *two can play this game.*

He knelt at her feet again, annoyed that, unlike Camilla, he couldn't conjure tears on demand. "We'll find those animals, my darling," he vowed. "We'll find them and send them back where they belong."

Camilla's response was so hokey he came dangerously close to chuckling, especially when she rested a hand on his shoulder and spoke in a quavering voice. "You mean . . . you mean you still want to marry me after learning that I'm . . . spoiled?"

"I want to marry you more than anything in the world," Alex said, poker-faced. He brushed her damp cheek with a kiss then turned to the priest. "May I use your phone to call the police, Father Gregory?"

"Of course, my son."

"Call nine-one-one," Cleve Spivey said. "Those bastards are still on the loose!"

Alex was reaching for the phone when a loud knock at the door made everyone jump, him too even though he expected it. Father Gregory opened it a discreet crack, and the panic in Samara Sarpy's eyes warned the drama was about to escalate another notch.

"Yes?" asked the priest.

"I have something for Mr. Sumner," she said breathlessly. She brandished a white envelope. "Those dreadful men who ruined the service gave it to me as they rushed out. One said it was urgent."

"Which Mr. Sumner?" asked Father Gregory.

"Give it here!" Randolph Sumner growled.

He pushed the priest aside and snatched the envelope from Miss Sarpy. He tore open the envelope and pulled out a sheaf of photographs. Fearing he'd lose his cool if he watched his father's reaction to Camilla cavorting with the rednecked dynamic duo, Alex drifted to his mother's side and sought escape in the beauty of the magnolias.

Sumner's roar was heard inside the sanctuary. "Jesus H. Christ!"

"Randolph!" Ivy Spivey gasped. "Remember where you are!"

Sumner was speechless when he saw the first photos. His face flooded red with embarrassment as he shoved them back in the envelope and motioned Cleve Spivey to join him in the hall. Alex wasn't surprised at being excluded. *After all,* he thought, *this marriage has nothing to do with the bride or groom.*

"What on earth was in that package?" Ivy asked in a small voice.

No one ventured a guess. In fact, no one spoke until the men returned and Sumner announced their findings. "Camilla was telling the truth. These photos are of her and those two hooligans."

Camilla sprang to life, leaping to her feet and snatching the envelope from Sumner's hands. "They didn't!"

Oh, yes, they did, Alex thought. Or rather, *we* did! But with Camilla's unexpected accusation of rape, he wondered if it had all been for nothing.

"No!"

Once again, Camilla fainted away, but this time Alex didn't help as she crumpled in a heap of white silks and satins. While everyone swarmed around her, he picked up the photos and pretended to thumb through them for the first time. He felt sick to his stomach Instead of his passport to freedom, he now saw them as evidence to convict two men of rape. Although she was clearly enjoying herself, Alex knew Camilla would claim she was threatened, bullied, and forced into feigning pleasure while being brutalized. With her father's money and his father's connections, they'd doubtless engage the most high-powered attorneys in the country, and Alex would be right back to square one.

"Damn!" he muttered.

His father looked up. "I know it's a terrible shock, son, but I promise you justice will be done." The bizarre circumstances dawned on him before anyone else. "Wait just a minute. Why would those men send us these incriminating photos?"

Alex shrugged, defeated, and started to shove the pictures back in the envelope. He stopped when he glimpsed one he'd forgotten about. He gave it a second look and as he examined those underneath it the balance of power shifted yet again.

Holy shit!

"Daddy?"

"What?"

Alex jerked his head toward the hall and, once they were alone, handed four sequential photos to his father. "Did you see these?" As Sumner perused the photos in shock, Alex said, "I hate to question Camilla, Daddy, but . . . well, this doesn't much look like a woman about to be raped." He paused. "Does it?"

Sumner's jaw dropped at the picture of Camilla getting out of the Porsche in a whorish get-up making Anna Nicole look like aristocracy. He grimaced at the next shot of her smiling and flashing her tits, but the final, most damning photo of all caught Camilla kissing Dooley while groping his crotch.

Sumner was disgusted and outraged when he realized the truth. "Shit, son!" he growled. "We've been had!"

Alex nodded with exquisitely feigned gravity. "My thoughts exactly, sir."

"I'll handle this!"

As Sumner stormed back into the office, Alex turned toward the bewildered wedding consultant lurking in the shadows. He smiled. "Daddy always takes good care of me, Miss Sarpy."

For another fifteen minutes, the mystified congregation was treated to more loud voices from Father Gregory's office, predominantly masculine shouts punctuated by the occasional feminine wail. Rumor and speculation spread like wildfire until a shaken Samara Sarpy appeared on the altar. She raised her hands to quiet the buzz, and, after much throat clearing, made the shocking announcement.

"I have been asked by the families of the bride and groom to—" A loud hiss turned her head to stage left where Sumner gestured frenetically. "Uh, I've been asked to announce that the father of the groom has called off the ceremony."

Bitsy Covington and Puddin' Dupree let out dual shrieks that deafened those in adjacent pews and set every dog on Camp Street howling. Tatiana Yusuppov bowed her head, discreetly lifted her veil and dabbed her eyes. To the casual observer, her shoulders shook from weeping, but in truth Jolie quivered with laughter.

"The families thank everyone for coming," Miss Sarpy continued, "and now bid you a good morning."

Miss Sarpy's frantic nod to Phaedra prodded her to her chubby feet and, after a quick confab with the organist, the soloist seized the opportunity to vocalize for the wedding to follow the ruined Spivey-Sumner nuptials. While everyone filed out, Jolie remained seated and hummed along with a gloriously intoned version of Beethoven's "Ode to Joy." By the time Phaedra finished, the sanctuary had emptied, and, as Jolie expected, Alex came looking for him.

"Well?" Jolie asked.

"It's a done deal," Alex said, giving his friend the short version for the time being. "Daddy saw the photos and hit the ceiling."

"I heard," Jolie said. "We all heard. In fact, I'll be surprised if they didn't hear across the river in Algiers."

Alex shook his head. "If there's anything Daddy hates, it's losing a business deal or being double-crossed. In this case it was a bit of both. I swear, Jolie, I've never seen him so mad. I think he would've killed Cleve Spivey if I hadn't convinced him the poor guy was as shocked as himself."

"Not altogether true, but a moot point at this juncture," Jolie opined. "What about our delicate little Camilla?"

"In the midst of all the commotion, she gathered up her skirts and hit the road. Last I heard, she and the Porsche were peeling rubber out of the parking lot."

"Good riddance to bad rubbish as the Brits say."

"Amen to that."

"Where are your folks?"

"Jedediah drove them home. I told them I needed some time to think, and Daddy was so consumed with rage that he didn't question me. He's also consumed with humiliation. You're not going to believe this, but he gave me a look that was almost apologetic."

"As well he should," Jolie said. "If anybody's going to meddle in your affairs, it's going to be me!"

"What do you mean?"

"Well, the important thing is that you make another positive step as soon as possible. Maintain your momentum so to speak. Dear boy, I have just what the doctor ordered."

"I'm scared of that!"

"Nonsense, *mon ami*. Think about it. What better to replace a wedding than another wedding?"

Alex chuckled. "I think your girdle's too tight."

"I'll have you know I'm not wearing a girdle," Jolie sniffed. "I'll also have you know thanks to my trip to France I have for you and you alone the absolute proposition of a lifetime. The deal of the century as it were."

"Thanks, Monty Hall, but whoever or whatever it is, I can't think about it right now." Alex looked toward the altar as Phaedra delivered a haunting "Ubi Caritas." "In fact, all I can think about is what Martin Luther King Jr. said: 'Free at last, free at last, thank God Almighty, I'm free at last!'"

"In that case, I suggest we celebrate that newfound freedom with a trip to the country club. It's two-for-one day and they have a new bartender who mixes the most divine cosmos."

"Fine," Alex agreed. He was too tired to make any more decisions.

Jolie took his arm as they rose and headed for the door. "I suppose there's an irony in our walking down this aisle together, dear boy, but I'll need a drink to ferret it out."

Alex paused in the vestibule and looked back toward the altar banked with Camilla's favorite, calla lilies. Although he had no regrets, Alex felt a twinge of something discomfiting. "I guess it's really over, huh?"

Jolie squeezed his arm as Phaedra's voice soared toward heaven. "No doubt about it, my pet. The fat lady's singing her ass off!"

~ 36 ~

Let's Make a Deal

"Forget everything you've ever heard about French arrogance," Jolie insisted, basking in the grandeur of the Windsor Court. "I swear submission is a secret passion for those guys, at least in *le boudoir*."

Alex had another theory. "Maybe it just took someone like you to coax it out. Or in or up or wherever."

"Maybe. God knows I was never one of those Iraq War hawks screaming 'Fuck the French,' but in retrospect I suppose I did my share for their cause."

"Sounds like you were just giving people what they want." Alex smiled, enjoying his first good mood since walking out of St. Patrick's church two weeks ago.

"More likely it just proves tops are a rare commodity in France," Jolie theorized. "In any case, I have tons of phone numbers for our trip to Paris."

"Since when am I going to Paris?"

"You'll find out soon enough, dear boy." He flagged a passing waiter. *"S'il vous plaît, garçon. Encore de champagne."*

While the waiter refilled their flutes, Alex pondered the ongoing scenario. At Jolie's insistence, he had dressed to the nines and agreed to rendezvous at the Windsor Court for afternoon high tea. Such a time and place signaled special occasions, but Jolie revealed only that it was a surprise.

He looked up as Jolie chuckled. "What's so funny?"

"I was just taking inventory," Jolie replied, sweeping a hand over the handsomely appointed room, "and I see patronage is largely limited to little girls in ruffles, their doting *grandmeres*, and pretentious fairies."

"Present company excepted."

"Not really. I only have a few snooty oats left, but for some reason the Windsor Court always makes me want to sow them. It's rather nice though. There are so few places left where quality folk can still gather and—"

"Better recheck your program," Alex interrupted. "There's about to be a serious change in the line-up."

Alex nodded toward a couple of chic beauties threading their way through a maze of tables brimming with china, crystal, and silver. The women looked to be in their late twenties and might well have stepped from the pages of *Elle*. The taller of the two, a svelte brunette, glittered with good gold jewelry while her petite flame-haired companion sparkled with vintage diamonds that screamed old money. Both wore smart white frocks perfect for the steamy New Orleans summers, but Alex doubted they were locals. Jolie's reaction confirmed his suspicions.

"That's your surprise!"

Alex frowned. "My surprise is a couple of babes?"

"They're hardly babes," Jolie hissed. "The redhead is Mademoiselle Jacqueline Bertier, *le Comtesse de Baudouin,* and the other is Denise Riviere. Denise is one of those Provence beauties that come along once in a lifetime."

"She looks like Juliette Binoche."

"A little." He rose to take Jacqueline's hand, bowing as he brushed her knuckles with a kiss. *"Madame le Comtesse! Enchante!"*

"For heaven's sake, Jolie," she said, pale cheeks coloring. "You know I detest unnecessary protocol."

"Je regret, ma chérie, but you must remember we Americans don't have nobility, and sometimes we get carried away." He indicated Alex. "This is the young man I told you about. Madame le Comtesse, this is Alexander Sumner."

She waved away the formal introduction. "Please call me Jackie."

"Thank you." Alex was surprised by the firm handshake. "You must call me Alex."

"I will," she said, giving him a conspiratorial nod. She stepped aside to present her companion. "Alex, this is Denise Riviere."

"Her other half," Jolie said a bit smugly. Bomb dropped, he waited for a reaction.

Alex was stunned. His exposure to lesbians was limited to a few coarse diesel dykes he'd seen at the bars. He'd heard there were all kinds of gay women, but this was the first time he had met what Jolie termed "lipstick lezzies." They were that rare, ultrafeminine breed who mystified straight men because they preferred their own sex. Their penchant was undetectable to all but the best-trained eye, a category Alex didn't belong to. It took him a moment to recover.

"A great honor I'm sure," he managed finally.

"The honor is ours," Jackie said. She and Denise discreetly positioned themselves so the seating was boy-girl-boy-girl. "We've been most anxious to meet you."

"Indeed we have," Denise confirmed.

When Denise's deep husky tones drew looks from adjacent tables, Jolie beamed. "Oh, Alex! Don't you just love that voice? I know a couple of leather daddies who would absolutely kill for it!"

Denise was taken aback. "Is that a compliment?"

"To be sure, *ma chérie!*" Jolie smiled. "Just consider it lost in translation."

Jackie turned to Alex. "Jolie told us all about your ill-fated liaison with Camilla. You know, I've never met a Camilla I could trust. They have a way of skulking about, don't they?"

"Uh, I suppose," Alex said, suddenly uncomfortable. "What else did he tell you?"

"Only good things," Jolie said. "After a delightful weekend at Jackie's country house, I discovered the two of you have a great deal in common. That's the reason I've brought everyone together today."

So the truth finally comes out, Alex thought. "I see."

"Forgive my frankness," Jackie said, "but owing to our shared predicament, I believe it advantageous to get right to the point."

"Please do." Alex glared at Jolie. "I'm more fascinated by the moment."

"Like yourself," Jackie continued, "I was being forced into a marriage not of my choosing. Fortunately I managed to avert it, but I'm afraid it won't be long before my Tante Monette will push me to marry someone else. Ordinarily, dear auntie is crazy as a bedbug, but she always manages to gather her wits about her when it comes to my inheritance."

Denise picked up the conversation thread as though it was rehearsed. "Jackie's an orphan who will inherit a great deal of money when she marries. Her aunt has power of attorney and is determined that her late brother's final wishes be carried out. Obviously, Jacqueline can't marry just anyone."

"Obviously," Alex said. Something flickered in his mind but remained elusive. "I empathize completely."

"When we met in Paris and Jolie learned of our situation," Jackie continued, "he said you might be our salvation if you managed to extricate yourself from this Camilla creature. When he phoned the day of the wedding and explained that you are now a free man, we were wondering if—"

The mental flicker congealed. "You want us to get married?"

"In name only, of course," Jackie said. "It would solve both our problems, allowing us to claim our respective inheritances while pursuing our special lifestyles."

"You could spend as much time as you like abroad," Jolie interjected. "Think about it. All those blond Swedes and swarthy Spaniards and red-haired Irishmen to play with. Plus, you'd be thousands of miles away from Daddy Dearest."

Alex felt three pairs of eyes on him as he weighed the outrageous proposition. He had every right to be annoyed with Jolie for airing his dirty laundry to perfect strangers, but he knew his friend's motives were selfless. Deeper analysis, however, made him doubtful that they could succeed in pulling off such a daring scam.

Daddy as usual.

"I'm flattered and honored and totally tempted, but my father would never agree."

"Why not?" Jolie demanded. "Jackie is French nobility with a father who was the tenth *Comte du Baudouin*. Their roots go back to Charlemagne, for God's sake, so why on earth would your father object to—" Alex's steely gaze stopped him cold. "Sorry. I forgot who we were dealing with."

Jackie looked bewildered. "Pardon?"

"My father's the most obnoxious American chauvinist imaginable." Alex explained. "He hates all foreigners, unless he can make money off them of course. He has never liked the French, and their refusal to support the U.S. in the Iraq war made him despise them more than ever."

Distressed, Jackie turned to Jolie. "You didn't tell us that."

"Mea culpa, darlings. I only knew he hated gays, blacks, and Jews. I didn't realize his bigotry was across the board."

Denise was crestfallen. "Oh, dear."

"I'm afraid this changes everything," Alex said.

Jolie jumped in. "You're being too hasty, dear boy. You're forgetting your mother's in our camp. She told me she loves everything French, and I know she'll absolutely adore Jackie and put in a good word with your father."

While Alex pondered the likelihood of Sumner being swayed, Jackie drew herself up and, intentionally or not, revealed a glimpse of her noble French heritage. "I assure you I have no intention of dealing with someone who disapproves of me or my country."

Alex was mortified. "I certainly don't blame you. My father's a horrible man."

"Indeed." After a ponderous moment, Jackie's arch demeanor vanished, and she weighed in with a proposal that caught even Jolie off-guard. "*Mais,* that's not to say we can't find a compromise."

"What do you mean?"

"You don't need your father's approval or his money." Jackie took his hand and gave him a dazzling smile. "Not with a wife worth around fourteen million."

"That's Euros," Denise added. "Not dollars."

Jolie was astonished. "You'd do that?"

"Why not?" Jackie said. "Denise and I are not greedy. All we want is to spend the rest of our lives together and we're willing to do whatever it takes to make that happen."

"But why not someone French?" Alex asked. "Or another European? Someone with a title perhaps."

"Because there are no secrets among the nobility," Jackie explained. "With an American, it's easier to hide the truth. As Jolie said in Paris, which really started me thinking, New Orleans was a French city, and that offers all sorts of possible embellishments. Perhaps we'll start a rumor that our families have been associated since colonial times."

"But you hardly know me."

"Jolie's told us a great deal, and I like what I've just seen. Especially your honesty and frankness. Denise will tell you I have excellent intuition about people and that I make quick decisions. She'll also tell you I'm not a fool. Sexual orientation aside, I'll naturally require a prenuptial agreement."

Alex liked Jackie more by the minute, especially drawn to her frankness and no-nonsense demeanor. Still, he couldn't help being overwhelmed by this latest outrageous plot to alter his destiny. Armed with this amazing proposition, he could tell his father he was gay and to shove his fortune where the sun doesn't shine. He could also take Karen to France and give her a new lease on life too. It seemed the perfect plan to finally give Randolph B. Sumner his just deserts.

"Well," he said at length, "I guess Jolie didn't exaggerate. This is indeed the deal of the century."

Jolie was ebullient. "And it comes with a title too, eh, Count Alexander?"

"Shall we drink to our partnership?" Jackie asked.

Alex lifted his glass. "To our partnership!"

Denise squeezed Alex's hand. "You'll never know how much this means to Jackie and me. It's a dream come true."

Jackie took his other hand. "Perhaps we can help make your dream come true too. When Jolie first explained about you, he told us about this young man named Cord. Since the Baudouin chateau is quite large, he could join us in France."

"I'm afraid Cord is no longer in my life," Alex said.

Jolie's face blazed. "I'm so sorry, Alex. I forgot to tell them about your trip to Key West."

"Don't apologize. It's no one's fault."

"But that was so careless of me to—"

Eager for the awkward moment to pass, Alex lifted his glass again and smiled. *"Vive la France!"*

The women were so engrossed in the moment that they didn't notice the flash of melancholy in Alex's blue eyes. He seemed as exuberant as Fat Tuesday, but behind the facade Jolie saw a soul as somber as Ash Wednesday.

37

Mothers Always Know

Alex raced upstairs to his mother's bedroom and found her poring over paint chips. To maintain sanity in her sumptuous prison, Karen Sumner repainted, remodeled, or redecorated the house on a near continual basis. She held up an array of colors for her son's perusal.

"What do you think of mauve, darling? I read somewhere that it was the Czarina Alexandra's favorite color."

"I think I'd think again," Alex said, recalling Jolie's faux Russian provenance the night they met. "She was murdered by Communist revolutionaries, remember?"

"Oh, that." Karen waved a hand dismissively. "I'm certainly not going to let some nasty historical facts interfere with my decorating. In fact, I want a mauve boudoir just like hers. With newer furnishings of course." She put the chips aside. "You have such a strange look, Alex. Is something wrong?"

"No. In fact everything's right." He closed the door. "Where's Daddy?"

"At his club," she replied.

"And Jedediah?"

"Visiting his sick sister. Why?"

"Because I want to talk to you alone." Alex sat beside her and looked into eyes like his own. "I've met her, Mom. I've met the woman I want to marry."

Those eyes widened. "Oh?"

"Jolie introduced us," he explained, carefully laying the groundwork for the long-overdue confession about his sexuality. "Her name is Jackie Bertier and she's a bona fide French countess visiting from Paris."

"I see." Karen went to the window and peered into the garden. "I must say this is quite a shock, son. After Camilla, I didn't expect you to be interested in another woman for . . . well, for quite a while."

"Why do you say that?"

"Oh, I don't know, darling. I suppose because the whole thing was such a fiasco, and Camilla's the type who could put a man off women for good. After all she did, I wouldn't be surprised if you decided to never marry."

"That's an odd thing to say."

"Is it?" Karen fidgeted with the draperies.

"Yes. Very." Alex knew his mother well, and the edge in her tone put him on high alert. "Are you trying to tell me something?"

"On the contrary." Karen faced him, expression enigmatic and not a little pained. "I'm trying to get *you* to tell *me* something."

At that moment, Alex recognized the unthinkable. He saw in his mother's face the acknowledgment of what he had struggled so many years to hide. He also saw acceptance and caring and the quality of love that made him feel ashamed and foolish for being anything less than honest with her. His response arose from somewhere deep in his soul and bubbled to the surface, bursting in the freest, most exhilarating manner imaginable.

"You know I'm gay, don't you, Mom?"

"Of course I do, darling." Karen came to him, arms outstretched. "Mothers always know."

As he embraced his mother, the gamut of emotions roiled through Alex, so many that none gelled before being replaced by something else. He was alternately teary and joyous, empowered and yet a little frightened. Mostly he was relieved, and he remembered Jolie's prediction that when he came to terms with who and what he was, he would feel the weight of the world lifting from his shoulders. It was true.

Mother and son held one another for a long time, each lost in thought, both rejoicing in a moment too long in coming. Alex recovered first and apologized.

"I'm sorry, Mom. I should have told you a long time ago."

"Not really," Karen said. "You had to wait until you were ready."

"But when . . . what . . . how did you know?"

"There was no one great epiphany if that's what you mean," Karen replied. "A thousand different things I suppose, although I will say the signs intensified these past few months."

"Really?"

"Oh, honey. There was much more to your running away than panic over Camilla. It was a cry for help that had little to do with marrying a woman you didn't love. When you sought refuge with Jolie, well, there's something in him that reminds me so much of one of those boys on *Queer Eye for the Straight Guy*."

"You watch that?!"

She chuckled. "I watch a lot of things when your father's not around, which is most of the time. I also fool around on the Internet and a while back I started doing some research. It's absolutely amazing how much information is available on being the parent of a gay child. It was very comforting to know I wasn't alone."

"Just like it's comforting for gay men and women to know we're not alone too," Alex offered.

"Yes, I learned that too. Thank God for Elton John and Chastity Bono and Ellen Degeneres, not to mention Alexander the Great and Michelangelo and Tchaikovsky and—"

"Wow! You've really been doing your homework!"

"I guess I have." She frowned with mock gravity. "By the way, dear, do you really think there's a gay mafia?"

Alex burst out laughing and hugged her all over again. They reveled in their special moment until he remembered what had brought him to her room in the first place.

"Did you also read about lipstick lesbians?"

"I did indeed. And leather daddies and twinks and drag queens and rice queens and trannies and—"

"Whoa!" Alex said. "You know more than I do!"

"Well, I must say it's a whole other world," Karen confessed. "Is this Jackie a lipstick lesbian?"

"Yes. With an equally beautiful lover named Denise."

Karen was suddenly serious. "And the reason for this marriage?"

"Jackie's in the same boat as myself," he explained. "She's an orphan who can't claim her inheritance unless she marries, and her old maid Aunt Monette has a firm grip on the purse strings."

"And a wedding will loosen them up, eh?" Alex nodded. "Well, that's fine except for one thing, honey."

"Daddy?"

"Exactly. You know he hates foreigners, especially the French. He wants you to get married, but he'll never allow his fortune out of America."

"I don't care if he cuts me off," Alex announced. "Jackie's so rich we don't need his damned money."

"And she's willing to share with a perfect stranger?"

"She's an amazing woman, Mom. You're going to adore her. Denise too."

His mother's good mood darkened. "Will you move to France?"

"In the beginning, we'll have to. You know, for appearance's sake. You can visit as often and as long as you like. Jackie has an apartment in Paris and a chateau in the Loire Valley. It's a dream come true."

Karen's spirits lifted only slightly. "Well, you know I fell in love with France when I was in school there, and you're very sweet to want your old mother tagging along but—"

"No 'buts,'" Alex insisted. "We want you with us and that's that. We'll also need your support since Daddy's going to oppose us."

Karen held out her hands, palms up. "No, you don't. You're legal age, dear, and if you want to get married, there's nothing your father can do about it. Especially if you're giving up your inheritance."

"That's not what I mean. We have to be very discreet until after the wedding, and I need you to come to Paris to help me charm Aunt Monette. Use your best French and lay it on that you went to school at the Sorbonne. Once Jackie has the money, she can tell auntie to take a hike and I can tell Daddy I'm gay." The look on his mother's face told Alex she was having trouble processing so much so fast. "Are you with me, Mom?"

Karen nodded. "Have you set the date?"

"As soon as possible. The longer we wait, the more chance for trouble. The girls are staying with Jolie. We'll go over tomorrow so you can meet them, okay?"

"Of course I'll do anything I can, dear, but . . . well, there is something I'd like to ask."

"Sure."

"About our trip to Key West. You behaved so strangely when we flew home after your mysterious mission. I knew you were hurting and I hurt too because there was nothing I could do. Was it . . . was it a man?"

Alex nodded. "You're on target again, Mom. His name is Cord Foster and I met him on the bus ride to Florida. The guy bailed me out of a bunch of scrapes, and somewhere along the way we fell in love."

Alex watched more truth dawn on his mother. "Did you say Cord? Wasn't he the young man who turned you in?"

"Exactly. After that, I thought the guy was a fortune hunter, but when Daddy told me he refused the reward money I realized I was wrong. I mean, this guy doesn't have two nickels to rub together, and if anyone needed the money, he did. I couldn't believe he refused it."

"So you went back to Key West to fix things?"

"I tried, but I was too late. He's involved with someone else."

"And that's why you were so crestfallen."

"Yes. I'm still kicking myself for being such a first-class jerk. Jolie kept telling me to grow up and stop lying to myself, but I wouldn't listen. I acted like a spoiled brat around Cord, and he called the cops. I can't say I blame him."

"You're still not over him, are you, darling?"

Alex shook his head, suddenly exhausted. "He was my first real love, Mom. I don't think you ever get over those."

"No," Karen said wistfully. "You don't."

Alex wanted to pursue her curious response, but noise downstairs ended the discussion. "Mmmm. Daddy's home."

"Are you going to tell him about Jackie now?" Karen asked.

"No reason to put it off," Alex offered. "Besides I'm sort of on a roll, don't you think?"

Whatever Karen started to say was lost when her husband burst into the bedroom. "What's going on in here? You all know I hate closed doors."

"Hi, Daddy," Alex muttered. Karen said nothing. "How was your day?"

Alex had intended his question as small talk, not something to unleash a diatribe. "Just got back from the River Club," his father said, "and did I get an earful from some of the other members. You won't believe what certain idiots and perverts are up to. As if we don't have enough problems with terrorists, those illegal spics are getting amnesty and the queers are legalizing marriage and the niggers are—"

"Please, Randolph," Karen said. "You know I hate that kind of talk."

Sumner sneered. "Missy, you'd be singing a different tune if you knew some of the things these twisted pinko left-wingers were planning."

"For God's sake, Daddy. You sound like Joe McCarthy."

"McCarthy was a good man," Sumner thundered. "The good old U.S. of A would be a lot better place if we had more like him!"

"And we'd be living in a society crippled by censorship, bigotry, and Nazi tactics," Alex ventured.

His father gaped. "What?!"

Alex retreated. "Listen, Daddy. I need to talk to you about something—"

He was wasting his breath. Further provoked, his father delivered a vitriolic rant making Rush Limbaugh and Jerry Falwell sound like liberals. It was hardly the first time Sumner exploded without warning, unleashing his bigotry in a bone-wearying frenzy. Alex, as usual, tuned much of it out, telling himself to keep quiet until after the wedding when he could, once and for all, tell his father what he really thought, but he was stirred to action by Sumner's final horrifying announcement.

"So I just sent a half a million dollars each to the Organization for Fair Family Values and the Rights for White Americans Association. That ought to help to stem this sickening tide, eh?"

Alex was appalled. "Daddy, you can't be serious! Those are nothing but hate groups, and they're both under investigation for—"

Sumner's eyes narrowed. "More left-wing propaganda!" he snorted. "I won't listen to it, not in my house." He grunted something about a drink and stormed out, leaving Alex and his mother in silent commiseration.

"I guess now's not the best time to tell him about Jackie," Karen said.

"Not when he goes crazy like that."

"I know. Sometimes I don't think I know him anymore. He wasn't like that when we got married."

"So you've said." Alex shook his head. "Man, he really knows how to push my buttons."

"Don't let him get to you, sweetheart. Not this time. Not when a miracle is about to occur for both of us."

"You're right, Mom. It's time to accentuate the positive."

Karen beamed. "I'm so anxious to meet Jackie and Denise. Jolie too. I was beginning to wonder if I'd ever meet him."

"Actually," Alex said slowly, "you already have."

"What do you mean, dear? We've only talked on the telephone."

"Brace yourself, Mom."

"I'm braced," Karen said. "I think."

"Remember at the wedding there was an older lady in a teal dress with a big picture hat and veil?"

"Why, yes. Everyone was trying to figure out who that exotic creature was. I just assumed she was on Camilla's guest list."

Alex rolled his eyes. "Well, Mom, it's like this . . ."

38

Camilla the Hun

The two months since Alex came out to his mother passed without incident. Karen had been thoroughly charmed by Jackie and Denise and returned the favor by courting and winning over Tante Monette when they visited France. Karen's Southern flattery delivered in flawless Parisian French proved irresistible to the dotty old lady, as did her handsome, attentive son who lavished almost as much attention on her as he did on Jackie. Carefully coached by Jolie, Alex's devoted, smitten suitor was so convincing Denise privately joked that she was getting jealous. The Sumners not only secured Aunt Monette's blessing but an unexpected announcement that the wedding should be held in New Orleans.

"A city I've always wanted to visit," the old lady revealed. "Along with Saigon and Algiers of course."

"Poor Tante Monette forgets we French no longer have an empire," Jackie explained later.

"*Vive le France,*" Alex said.

"You mean *vive la lunatique!*" Denise added with a wink.

"I suppose," Alex conceded. "But you know something? I can't help liking the old lady. She only wants what's best for her niece."

Jolie smiled and lofted his glass of Lillet. "And thanks to a little fairy dust, dear tante's fondest dreams will come true."

In August, the engagement was announced in the *Times-Picayune* alongside a stunning photograph of Jackie. Wanting to give the Garden District and Camilla a noble bone to gnaw on, Jolie overrode Jackie's decision not to include her title so everyone knew Alex Sumner was to wed a French countess on October 11. To please her future mother-in-law and be appropriately feted, Jackie planned to arrive

223

two weeks early but insisted on a small chapel service restricted to family and close friends. Along with Denise and Tante Monette, she took suites at the Maison de Ville, a chic French Quarter hostelry known for insulating celebrity guests like Tennessee Williams and Elizabeth Taylor. As Jolie hoped, the French-obsessed Old Guard buzzed with the news, and parties honoring Mademoiselle Jacqueline Bertier, la Comtesse de Baudouin, became the hottest tickets in town. Even the French Ambassador got in on the act with a reception in the couple's honor. Alex was thrilled but hardly surprised when Jackie's beauty, grace, and old-world charm won over everyone.

Except Camilla Spivey and Randolph Sumner of course.

Since the public was still in the dark about why Alex's father had called off the marriage, Camilla initially garnered all the sympathy as a bride jilted at the altar. Speculation ran wild about Sumner's shocking decision, but the truth remained a well-guarded secret until the damning photos surfaced on the Internet. According to Jolie, Camilla & Company were rivaling Paris Hilton in the porno popularity polls, and Camilla was persona non grata above Jackson Avenue. After that, she dropped off the social radar.

"How did this happen?" Alex asked. "God knows Cletis and Dooley don't know how to operate a computer!"

"The Cyber Age is as enigmatic as deep space," Jolie replied. Whether or not he was responsible remained a mystery, because he clammed up whenever Alex pressed the issue. Alex had never seen him so secretive.

Sumner was as low-key as Camilla, a major surprise to everyone considering his well-known Francophobia. Of course, he exploded when Alex told him about Jackie, but his condemnation was defused when Alex calmly renounced his inheritance. Insult was heaped on injury when Alex added, "Jackie's even richer than you!" It was a lie, but it stunned Sumner into an ongoing silence. He wasn't boorish enough to refuse to meet Jackie, but his icy reserve paled in comparison to her imperious indifference. Alex and Karen shared the pleasure when Sumner more than met his match, but his quiet retreat made Alex uneasy.

"I don't trust him when he's like this," Alex told his mother. "I've watched him in board meetings, and when he shuts up it means he's looking for a weak spot and waiting to pounce. You know how he can be."

"Don't worry about it," Karen said, basking in her newfound confidence. "This is one time when your father's not going to get his way."

"How can you be so sure, Mom?"

"Trust me, sweetie pie," she said, patting him on the cheek.

With both Jolie and his mother acting so mysterious, Alex felt like his wedding was the setting for a whodunit party. He tried to ignore his misgivings and concentrated on cinching the deal of the century. Once Jackie, Denise, and Tante Monette arrived, he devoted every ounce of energy toward that end, and all went smoothly until he and Karen made the mistake of taking them to lunch at Galatoire's. They had barely been seated when Alex saw his mother go pale.

"Mom, what is it?" He grabbed her hand. "Are you feeling faint?"

"In the corner. Heading this way—"

"What?"

Karen took a deep breath, working hard to maintain her composure. Luckily, the three Frenchwomen were immersed in their menus and didn't see the panic in her eyes. "Camilla!" she hissed.

Jackie was not so engrossed that she didn't hear a name she knew was cause for alarm. As their friendships deepened, Jolie and Alex had shared the details of Camilla's sexual peccadilloes and the fishing-camp caper, a story Jackie and Denise found hilarious and thoroughly justified. Given Camilla's background, Jackie also knew this was someone to be reckoned with, but she remained focused on the menu.

Forks paused in midair and conversations ceased as Camilla approached Alex's table. Although not everyone had the dirty Internet details, Galatoire's patrons all knew about the disastrous Sumner-Spivey wedding. Camilla's face was an unreadable mask until she caught Alex's eye and dazzled him with a smile he knew meant utter insincerity. He also knew she was out for blood.

"Darling Alex!" she said, offering her cheek for a kiss.

He rose and picked up the gauntlet. "Hello, Camilla."

"Long time, no see," she said. "What's new?"

As if you didn't know, Alex thought. "I'm getting married next week."

"Oh, that's right. I remember hearing something about that." She scanned the table, dismissing Karen with a curt nod, ignoring Jackie and Denise, and looking right at Monette. "This must be the lucky girl!" She thrust a hand in the old woman's face. "I'm Camilla Spivey, Alex's ex-fiancée."

"Eh?" Aunt Monette ignored her hand and muttered something in French.

Alex was seething. "Save it, Camilla. She doesn't speak a word of English."

"How silly of me!" Camilla said with a fake giggle.

"Indeed it was," Jackie said smoothly. She set aside her menu and extended her hand. "I'm Jacqueline Bertier, Alex's new fiancée."

"Oh, of course. Why, your pictures don't do you justice, but newspaper photos never do, do they? Now let's see. You're a duchess or something, right?"

"Or something," Jackie replied.

"Forgive me," Camilla said, smile stretched much too thin. "We don't have titles in America."

"Or manners apparently," Jackie observed with almost tangible condescension. Before Camilla could continue, she said, "Have you come here to insult me, mademoiselle?"

So it's out in the open, Alex thought. He took a step back and crossed arms over his chest. *Well, then. Let the games begin.*

"Actually I just came over to warn you, honey. He left me at the altar, or did he not tell you?"

"He told me." Jackie paused before delivering the next word with deadly aplomb. "Everything."

Camilla tried to ignore the implication with a coquettish giggle that fell flat. "Why, Alex, darling! I never knew you were one to kiss and tell."

"He isn't," Jackie. "But the Internet is. We have it in France too, you know."

Camilla blanched. Alex cleared his throat. Karen covered her smile with a napkin. Denise stared. Tante Monette said, "Eh?"

"I'm . . . I'm sure I don't know what you mean," Camilla stammered.

"Oh, I think you do," Jackie said, closing in for the kill. "I agree that newspaper photos are poor, but Internet pictures can be remarkably clear. I had no idea you were such a gymnast, my dear."

Camilla dropped her voice to a whisper. "Fuck you!"

"Trés charmant," Jackie purred.

Alex winced as Camilla grabbed his forearm and dragged him toward the front door, leaving a wake of gapes and gasps. She didn't let go until they reached the sidewalk. There, in broad daylight, on Bourbon Street of all public places, she unleashed her full fury. For the first time, Alex saw the real Camilla, and he was unnerved as her face contorted and her words spewed like venom.

"All right, you low-life sonovabitch! It's time you told the truth. You're behind those photographs, aren't you?"

"You're crazy, Camilla."

"Lying bastard!"

Alex almost laughed at such hypocrisy. "You're a fine one to talk about telling lies. How do you think I felt when I saw those photos? Christ, Camilla! You made me the cuckold of all time!"

As he expected, she shrugged off the accusation. "I looked at those pictures carefully and some were shot through the window. Those two bastards had an accomplice, and I think it was you!"

Alex told himself to stay cool, that she was grasping at straws. He started to claim that he didn't even know where her father's fishing camp was, and that he didn't own a camcorder much less know how to use it. He plumbed for a whole string of alibis before realizing they would only drag him down. Instead he put the ball back in her court by demanding a motive.

"Why would I do such a thing to my fiancée?"

"So you could marry Miss French Dressing in there!" she snarled.

"Get serious, Camilla. I didn't meet her until after Daddy called off the marriage. None of what you're saying makes sense!"

Camilla retreated only slightly before launching a counter attack. "Well, maybe you didn't have anything to do with those fucking pictures, but I'm sure as shit going to find out who did. Dooley and Cletis are a couple of lowlifes, and all I have to do is dangle some money in their greedy little faces and they'll talk."

Alex had heard enough. "I'm going back inside."

Camilla grabbed him again. "It's not over, Alex. Not by a long shot! Think about that when your priest asks the fatal question to the congregation and keep thinking about it when you hear my voice."

"You're crazy, Camilla. There's nothing you could possibly say to—"

"Don't be so sure!" Her grip tightened. "I warned you, Alex. I told you if you ever called off our wedding you'd regret it for the rest of your life. I meant every word I said, asshole!"

Alex felt sick to his stomach. The combination of Camilla's wild accusations and the noxious heat of Bourbon Street were taking their toll. "Good-bye, Camilla."

He wrenched free and left her on the steaming sidewalk, praying she wouldn't follow him back inside Galatoire's with more invective. He paused in the cool foyer to regain his composure and wait for his racing heart to slow. His light silk suit felt clammy, and his forehead gleamed with sweat as he rehashed the hideous exchange and tried to make sense of it.

What had Camilla meant? Did she really know something or was she bluffing? Could she possibly have found out he was gay or was he just being paranoid? What made her suspect he was the accomplice outside the window? All this and more tumbled in his fevered brain, until two names floated free and terrified him all over again. Cletis and Dooley. There was no doubt Camilla could bribe those two-bit hustlers to reveal his presence at Thirteen Oaks, and once she had the facts. . .

"Damn!" Alex dabbed a handkerchief against his damp forehead before retrieving his cell phone. "You got me into this mess, Jolie, and you're sure as hell gonna have to get me out!"

~ 39 ~

Goin' to the Chapel

The morning of the wedding dawned sunny and cool with the sort of azure Louisiana skies poets and painters rhapsodize over. Such crystalline majesty, however, was lost on Alex as he paced the parking lot behind St. Michael's Chapel, alternately glaring at his watch and silent cell phone. It was almost four o'clock, and since Jolie had promised to call over an hour ago, Alex grew more anxious by the second. Camilla's vicious threats still dogged him, and although Jolie had promised to handle the situation he remained maddeningly vague about when, where, and how. On top of this, he was a no-show with the service scheduled to start in ten minutes.

"God!" Alex almost jumped out of his skin when the phone beeped and J. MENARD popped up on caller ID. He yelled into the phone. "Where the hell are you?"

"Agent Double-O-Seven-Up-Yours checking in," Jolie answered in a voice light as air. "And I've got a big newsflash from Mexico."

"Cut the comedy, Jolie! I'm a nervous wreck!"

"This is no comedy, dear boy. It's the real deal and will definitely cheer you up."

"Talk fast!"

"Well, it took me forever to find those slippery little swamp rats, Cletis and Dooley. It seems they've temporarily taken up with some lonely trailer trash housewife across the river in Gretna, shudder, and—"

Alex felt like his brain was unraveling. "Jolie, get to the point!"

"All right, already. The shorthand version is that Cletis and Dooley are, even as we speak, lazing on a beach in Cancun."

"Cancun?"

"Si, senor. I figured that was a cheap and cheerful place to stash them until after today's big event. You know. Keep them out of Camilla's diabolical clutches and all that. Just think of it as an early wedding present from little old *moi*."

"Thanks, but where the hell's Camilla?"

"Calm down. I'll get to that."

"Jolie!"

"Well, Camilla's a much stickier wicket I'm afraid, and it's better that you don't know any details until after it's over."

With prewedding jitters pushing his nerves to the max. Alex's temper flared. "I'm not a child, Jolie!"

"I'm well aware of that, *mon ami,* but in case things fall apart, you can talk to the police with a clear conscience."

"The police?!"

"Isn't kidnapping is a federal offense or something?"

"Kidnapping?!"

Jolie was as cool as ever. "Take a chill pill. It's not exactly kidnapping. It's sort of . . . mmmm, borrowing someone's time."

"Dear God!"

"Now, I know you think that's extreme but so was what we did at the fishing camp. It's also like when you ran away from home. You remember. Desperate situations call for desperate measures and all that."

"I'm sweating bullets," Alex moaned.

"You are? How about me? If you only knew what I've been doing this past . . . hey! What the hell are you doing?"

Alex was further frustrated by muffled voices and the sounds of a scuffle. "What's going on? Where are you?" He heard a loud crash. "Jolie!"

"Hate to miss the wedding, darling, but I really must dash! I'll try to make the reception. Promise!"

"But—"

"A bientôt!"

Beep. Silence. "Damn!"

The cell phone was Alex's last hope for salvation, and when it went dead he was sustained only by a very rickety blind faith. *Please God,* he prayed. *Help Jolie pull off another miracle.* It would hardly be the first time. Since their fateful Twelfth Night meeting, there seemed to be no end to the actions and reactions Jolie could conjure. Thanks to him, Alex had finally addressed being gay, run away from home, experienced first love, and left a bride at the altar. As if that weren't enough, there were CNN bulletins, kidnapping allegations, blackmail, duplicity, deceit, subterfuge, and some plain old-fashioned lunacy, and in just a few minutes he, a gay man, would be marrying a French lesbian he barely knew. The scenario was easily enough for a half dozen soap operas, and if Alex hadn't been petrified Camilla was going to sabotage this latest chapter of *Alex in Wonderland,* he would've laughed at the absurdity of it all. He felt trapped, like he was tumbling down the rabbit hole again, and was hungrily eyeing the Lamborghini when his father came out of the chapel.

"It's time."

"Okay, Daddy."

Sumner gave him a long look. "Son, you look like you're about to face a firing squad." His hollow chuckle was sickening because Alex guessed what was coming next. "It's not too late to call it off. I'll even make the announcement if you—"

"For God's sake!" Alex said, fighting the temptation to tell his father to go fuck himself. "Once was enough."

"You sure?"

"It's just wedding-day jitters," Alex lied. "I'll be fine once I get to the altar and see Jackie."

"Suit yourself."

Sumner grunted and headed back inside, mood as sour as the day he learned about Jackie. Alex ignored him and sought comfort in his mother's promise this was one time his father wouldn't get his way. As he followed Sumner into the chapel and took his place on the altar, Alex's lips moved in a silent prayer that this was true. The last thing he needed was another barrier to the wedding.

To his delight and relief, Alex's offhand remark to his father proved true. The moment he saw Jackie floating down the aisle like Glinda in *The Wizard of Oz,* his spirits soared and he beamed like the proud groom he was supposed to be. Behind her veil of illusion, Jackie glowed too and turned as she passed Denise to send the most discreet kiss imaginable. Karen was just as thrilled, but tears kept washing away her efforts to smile as Jackie took Alex's arm and the two faced the altar. Sumner remained the picture of utter gloom.

"Dearly beloved," Father Dennis began. "We are gathered here to-day to—"

Alex heard nothing else until the priest asked if anyone had reason to oppose the union. In the silence that followed, a dull roar hurt his head as he waited for his father or Camilla to protest. When nothing happened, he again lost himself in the moment and blissfully drifted until he and Jackie were pronounced man and wife. The kiss was brief but genuinely affectionate, and Alex chuckled when his bride of five seconds gave him a big wink before kissing him a second time.

"You go, girl!" she whispered.

For Alex, that said it all.

An hour later, he and Jackie were in a receiving line at the Pavilion of the Two Sisters in City Park. Alex's elation was real, but he was plagued by lingering fear that Camilla might still make an unwelcome appearance. His eyes continually darted along the long line of well-wishers as he searched in vain for Jolie. After that bizarre phone call, he couldn't help worrying something had happened. It just wasn't like Jolie to pull a disappearing act, especially with so much at stake. Maybe Jolie's scheme had gone awry and Camilla had him arrested on kidnapping charges. Or maybe Camilla was heading for City Park at this very moment to open her Pandora's box of bad news. Maybe Jolie was even hurt. Maybe, maybe, maybe.

Alex's imagination was racing into overdrive when the line thinned at last and a familiar voice rose above a Handel largo, a reminder that a chamber music orchestra lurked behind the potted palms. In spite of his anxieties, Alex grinned as a welcome figure raced across the marble floor, arms outstretched.

"Ma chers!"

Angelique Poché was a stunner in vintage black Chanel complete with antique pearls and matching turban. She kissed Jackie and Alex on both cheeks, all the while gesturing dramatically and babbling in an unbroken stream of French. Jackie hung on her every word, smiling, and squeezing Alex's arm as Angelique continued to unfold her incredible tale. Alex's French was minimal at best, but he managed to catch "Jolie," "Camilla," *les gendarmes,* and *le Bastille.*

"In English!" he hissed.

Angelique clutched her breast. "I'm so sorry, Alex. I just got caught up in the excitement of the moment, and so will you when I tell you what's happened."

"Where's Jolie? Is he all right?"

"He's fine and he's on his way." She rolled her eyes. "Unfortunately I can't say the same for my gal pal Camilla."

"Where is she?"

Angelique leaned close to whisper, then reconsidered. "What the hell? The whole town's going to know before sundown. I may as well get the credit for the social scoop of the season." She leaned back, fired up a cigarette, exhaled a stream of smoke and announced to everyone within hearing range. "Camilla's down at central lockup."

"What?" Alex gasped.

"Yes, indeedy," Angelique cackled, obviously relishing this part most of all. "She's in the drunk tank, honey, and believe me she ain't a happy camper!"

✒ 40 ✒

Sunrise, Sunset

"That's so bizarre," Alex said. "I've never even seen Camilla take a drink."

Angelique shrugged. "I guess it's just one more thing we didn't know about her. I must say that girl is full of surprises."

Alex was dying for details. His father had long since disappeared with a couple of cronies, but with his mother's help he signaled an official end to the receiving line. Poor Samara Sarpy, in a reluctant return engagement, tried to announce the cutting of the cake, but Alex told her he and Jackie needed a private moment first. He asked Karen to join them but she insisted on tending to Aunt Monette who was inexplicably plying her with questions about the Louisiana Purchase. With Jackie and Denise in tow, he and Angelique trooped outside where Alex finally noticed the beautiful day. He was so excited he hugged the women all over again.

"Okay," he told Angelique. "What's the scoop?"

"First, I have to give credit where credit's due. This was all Jolie's idea, even though nothing turned out as we expected. Camilla may be cagey in some departments but she's a big fool in others, meaning she still considers me a trusted confidante. She never dreamed I had a hand in the fishing camp incident, and when she said she was out for revenge, of course I reported right to Jolie. He told me to ask her to lunch the day of the wedding and offer to drive her to the chapel to make her big scene. She was so desperate for an accomplice it was pathetic. She has, it seems, lost all her friends." Angelique blew a stream of smoke toward the blue sky. "Pity."

Despite the day's warmth, Alex had a sudden chill. "What exactly did she plan on doing?"

"She was never very clear about that," Angelique reported. "In fact, she wasn't clear about anything except a desire to get revenge and believe me when I say she was out to scorch the earth!" She sipped her champagne. "Since she wanted to be incognito, we went to lunch at Coop's on Decatur Street. It's pitch dark in that dive, and we'd no sooner sat down than she ordered a tequila sunrise. I knew I had to keep my wits about me so I nursed a glass of the worst Merlot imaginable while she slammed down one sunrise after another. After about an hour, I realized this had turned into a liquid lunch and that little Miss Camilla was heading for a very early sunset!"

Jackie and Denise exchanged puzzled looks. *"Comme?"*

"She was drunk," Alex explained.

"Ahhh!"

"So I excused myself and went to the loo to call Jolie. When I told him Camilla was whacked, he said to keep her there until he arrived. And this is the funny part. We're all so used to him being Jolie that we forget he's also Jacques Menard. When he wants to butch it up, he's quite irresistible to the ladies."

"Oh, no!" muttered Alex.

"Oh, yes!" Angelique insisted. "He introduced himself as Jean-Luc Something-or-other, poured on the Gallic charm, and next thing you know—"

Alex grinned. "Camilla came on to him!"

"Like gangbusters!" Angelique laughed. "It was downright embarrassing the way she crawled all over him in the dark, unbuttoning his shirt and doing God knows what with her hand underneath the table. I must say Jean-Luc was a terrific sport and played his role to the hilt. When he told her he had a sweet little *pied-à-terre* right around the corner, she practically drooled into her sunrise."

Alex was horrified. "Is he crazy?! If he took her home and she figured out who he is—!"

"Relax, sweetie pie. Jolie wasn't about to implicate himself. Besides, Camilla was so bloody shitfaced she couldn't tell the difference between Jean-Luc and John Paul II. She was absolutely reeling when we steered her up the street to his house. We both assumed she would pass out and sleep through the wedding and reception, but no such luck. We got her into bed all right, but we'd no sooner gone into the living room and called you when she reappeared stark naked with lovin' on her mind. That's why Jolie had to get off the phone so fast."

"It sounded like a brawl."

"When he tried to get Camilla to lie down, *sans* sex, she got pissed and started throwing things. She's so used to taking her clothes *off*, I guess she's not used to someone telling her to put them *on*." Another sip of champagne and a drag off her cigarette. "Well, you know how Jolie feels about his antiques being tossed about, and that's when we realized we were in over our heads. He finally wrestled her back to bed and held on until she finally passed out. By then the wedding was over but we didn't want her sobering up at Jolie's place. While I helped him get her dressed, we decided to take her down the street to Cabrini Park. She was about half-conscious while we walked her down the street and—"

"No one stopped you?" Denise asked.

"Of course not," Alex said. "Drunks prowl the Quarter night and day so it's hardly unusual to see someone helping a friend who's had too much to drink."

"Our thoughts exactly," said a deep voice.

"Jolie!" Alex cried. He had appeared out of nowhere, resplendent in black tie as he hugged Alex and dispensed kisses all around. Alex smelled bourbon on his breath but figured the guy deserved a drink after what he'd been through. "Thank God you're all right!"

"And you got here just in time to finish the story," Angelique said. "I was just to the part where we got Camilla into the park."

Jolie nodded. "Ah. Well, things got more interesting when I spotted some derelict sleeping it off in the corner and decided to incorporate him into the plan. We eased Camilla down beside him, tiptoed off to watch things from a safe distance, and called nine-one-one. Drunks are never an emergency unless they're violent, so I reported a mugging in progress. Camilla had passed out again when the police got there, and things got really dicey when the cops tried to hustle her and her new friend out of the park. As Tenn used to say, she was 'cross as ten flies.'"

"To put it mildly," Angelique said with a chuckle.

"She fought like a wildcat, and when one rather handsome young officer got kneed in the groin, Camilla got cuffed. That was our cue to *exeunt*." Jolie bowed with exaggerated politeness. "I apologize for being so late."

He and Angelique glowed with pride as everyone applauded, Alex loudest of all. Alex had never been so proud to call someone a friend and told Jolie as much before going back inside. "I'll owe you for this forever," he said. "Thanks to you, it looks like my life is finally going to come together."

"I sure as hell hope so." Jolie draped an arm around Alex's shoulder as they headed toward the wedding cake. "I know how hard this past year has been for you, kiddo, and I'm happy I could help get you through it." His eyes brimmed with tears as he gave Alex a gentle push. "Now get over to that cake and play groom."

When Alex and Jackie finished cutting the cake and posing for the obligatory photos with icing on their chins, they took their first dance. Alex's father was still nowhere to be seen, but the mother of the groom scarcely missed him in the arms of the dashing Jacques Menard. Alex watched them whirl around the dance floor, heart filled with happiness as his mother's laughter floated above the crowd. He knew Jolie had told her about Camilla when she caught his eye and gave him a thumbs up. It was a gesture he never expected to see from his mother, and as Duncan Stone gallantly took Jackie off his hands, he cut in on Jolie.

"Happy, son?" Karen asked.

"Happier than I've been in a long time," he said.

"Me too." She blew a kiss to Jolie who was now dancing with Denise. "I absolutely adore my new daughters-in-law. Aunt Monette too. Which reminds me—she's not as nuts as we think. Oh, she has ditsy moments all right, but I think she's more savvy than anyone realizes. In fact, when the truth comes out about you and Jackie, I'll bet she's not bothered at all."

"Oh?"

Karen nodded against his lapel. "It's not much to go on, but after the ceremony she told me she knew her niece was happy which was all she and her brother ever wanted."

"And you don't think she'll care whether Jackie finds happiness with a man or a woman?"

"Not really. I know it's cliché, but life really is full of secrets. Lord knows we Sumners have more than our share."

"What do you mean?"

Karen smiled and whispered in Alex's ear. "Timing is everything, my dear."

PART FIVE

"I could tell you my adventures—beginning from this morning," said Alice a little timidly, "but it's no use going back to yesterday, because I was a different person then."

Lewis Carroll,
Alice's Adventures in Wonderland

~ 41 ~

The Tennessee Waltz

"I must say we I absolutely adore this hotel," Jackie said. Far more sober than Jolie and Alex, she and Denise deftly dodged furniture as they waltzed around the intimate suite. "You couldn't have picked a more charming spot."

"I've always loved the Maison de Ville," Jolie enthused. "Tenn and I thought it was the most romantic old hotel in the Quarter. He used to stay in Number Nine."

"Who is this Ten?" Denise asked. "You mentioned him before. Something about being 'cross as ten flies.'"

"Tenn was Tennessee Williams's nickname."

"You knew him? How wonderful!"

"Not always, Denise." Jolie closed his eyes a moment. "Tenn was the quintessential tortured genius. He could be pretty difficult, especially toward the end."

"I'm sure you have good memories too," Jackie offered.

"*C'est vrai.* Tenn could be charming and very, very funny. He once remarked that gay men in the French Quarter didn't 'come out of the closet' but 'stepped out of the armoire.' And of course we had some really wild times in his place on Dumaine Street. If his old brass bed could talk we'd have to shoot it!" He lifted his glass by the window and caught the last rays of sunlight. "Cheers, old friend. Wish you were here."

Alex chuckled. "Know who else I wish was here? Jerry Falwell!"

Jolie snorted. "Why would you want to see that hateful old bigot?"

"Because the sight of that beautiful bride dancing with her beautiful maid of honor would give the bastard a stroke. Just look at them, Jolie!"

The women were utterly lost in each other's eyes, at that moment unaware of anything hateful or homophobic in the world. Alex saw something else too, a mutual love and contentment that was almost tangible, and although he was happy for them he couldn't help being envious. He inevitably thought of Cord, and before he grew dangerously introspective announced it was time to go.

"Jolie and I better hit the road."

No one questioned his decision. The four had been in Jackie's suite for almost two hours, dancing, toasting each other with Möet, and reminiscing about the day's monumental events. For appearance's sake, Alex had booked another suite in the nearby Audubon Cottages under Mr. and Mrs. Alex Sumner, and the look on the women's faces told him it was time he used it.

"It's been an amazing day, ladies. Thanks for making it possible."

"Denise and I are the ones who should be grateful," Jackie said, rising to give him a kiss and hug. "We've been looking for someone like you a long time. You've no idea."

"She's right," Denise said, blinking away tears as Alex embraced her. "Who would've imagined we'd have to venture all the way to New Orleans to find our liberator?"

"Let's not forget Jolie's part in all this," Alex said.

"Enough hugs and tears," Jolie said. He opened the door and stepped into the lush courtyard with its sun-splashed fountain. "Keep that up and the hotel will call the schmaltz police."

Alex paused in the doorway. "Breakfast tomorrow, ladies?"

Jackie blushed. "Better make it brunch. Denise and I have some serious celebrating to do."

"Alex and I do too," Jolie said, lifting his champagne flute high. "Better make it lunch."

The women laughed and blew kisses. "*Á bientot!*" they chorused.

"What a couple of dolls," Alex said as they walked down Toulouse to Dauphine Street. "You know what? I think I've fallen in love with both of them."

"So did I. The first time I met them."

"It's amazing what they have together, Jolie."

"Agreed. It's what most people want I suppose."

"You don't?"

"Not anymore."

"What a strange thing to say."

"Not really."

The comment dogged Alex as he unlocked the gate to the Audubon Cottages and led Jolie to a suite at the rear of the courtyard. In all their months of confidences and shared experiences, Alex still knew precious little about his best friend's past relationships. The more he thought about it, the more he realized Jolie steered the conversation elsewhere whenever matters turned personal, and this time he challenged it.

"What did you mean back there? About not wanting what the girls have?"

"Just what I said. I've already had my one great love, and I know I'll never have another one." He swallowed the last of the champagne as they crossed the courtyard. "Why kid myself, kiddo?"

Alex had never seen Jolie look so serious. "Do you want to tell me about it?"

"You won't laugh?"

"Of course not."

"I might need a *soupçon* more champagne."

"That's no problem." Alex unlocked the suite and selected a bottle of Laffite Rothschild from the honeymoon gift bottles. He knew he was drinking too much but asked himself if this wasn't a special day, what was? "Well?"

Jolie held the flute beneath his nose and enjoyed the bubbles before taking a hearty swig. "It was Tenn."

Alex was surprised, but not altogether. Jolie referred to Tennessee Williams often, usually when relating tales about famous and infamous men who'd crossed his path over the years. Some of the facts didn't always ring true, but Alex knew Jolie and Williams had been more than ships passing in the night. Proof was in a photo on Jolie's nightstand. A shirtless Jolie dangled his legs in a swimming pool with Tennessee Williams kneeling behind, chin resting on Jolie's right shoulder. Both men squinted against harsh sunlight, but the photograph still froze a happy moment in time.

"I was twenty-six when we met back in 1978. Tenn was speaking at the Theater for the Performing Arts and I was in the audience. There were terrible rains that night with flooding everywhere, but I was such a fan I was right there in the front row. I was so starstruck it was love at first sight, at least on my part. I mean, the man was a legend in his own time and, corny as it sounds, when I saw him the next night in Lafitte's I swooned all over again. Of course lots of guys were hitting on him because of who he was. I wanted him too, but I was also concerned because he was so drunk. I bullied my way through the crowd and got Mr. Williams out of there. It was still pouring, but he didn't mind getting wet and handed me his keys when we got to Dumaine Street. I'll never forget what Tenn said as I unlocked the door. He actually quoted himself!"

Considering the seriousness of story and moment, Alex was surprised when Jolie laughed.

"Tenn chuckled and said, 'Whoever you are, I've always depended on the kindness of strangers.' He later confessed he wrote that famous last line to get a laugh, and was disappointed when it never did. He delivered it as it had been intended, and for one fragile, fleeting, rainy New Orleans moment he became Blanche DuBois. To this day that's my favorite memory of the man, and to think it happened the night we met."

This was one story that Alex didn't doubt because he knew it came straight from the heart.

"I stayed with him exactly one week," Jolie continued. "The most glorious seven days of my life. Then he went back to New York and I saw him intermittently when he came to town. Usually he had some new guy with him but when he didn't I happily shared his bed. To be honest, he was usually so whacked that sex wasn't possible, but I didn't care. I didn't even care when he was abusive because I knew that was the booze and pills talking. When Tenn was sober, he was extraordinary, flaws and all, but so, so lost. He reminded me of that old spiritual. You know the one. 'Sometimes I Feel Like a Motherless Child.' And you know what else? It never once bothered me that he was forty years older."

"When was the last time you saw him?"

"In 1983. Tenn came down to sell the house on Dumaine and he had one of his boy toys in tow. He was in terrible shape, totally irascible, almost blind." Jolie's voice cracked and he swallowed hard, warning Alex the story was growing painful. "He sort of dismissed me, but like all people in love I made excuses and blamed the addiction, not the addict. I loved him as much as ever, but I knew he was a drowning man. No one could save him. Not me. Not anyone. A month later, he was dead."

Although two decades had passed, Jolie's story was told with such poignancy that the playwright's death seemed recent. Alex was deeply moved. "I'm so sorry."

"I'm not. At least Tenn's demons were finally stilled."

"I wish I'd known him," Alex said.

"Me too. Oh, how Tenn would've loved those blue eyes and all that blond hair." Jolie coughed and cleared his throat. "Sometimes I wish . . . no, never mind. The champagne is making me melancholy and I detest anyone feeling sorry for themselves, especially drunks."

Alex could never tell when Jolie had drunk too much, but he wasn't taking any chances. "Know what? Suddenly I'm famished. Let's get something sent over from the Bistro and have a pigfest."

Jolie looked at his watch. "No, thanks. I want to go home and get in my own bed and not wake up until it's time for lunch with the girls."

"I'll walk you home," Alex insisted.

"I'm fine, Alex. I promise I'm much more tired than drunk and it's still light outside."

"But—"

"No 'buts.' Besides, you need to stay here. Whoever heard of a newlywed groom prowling the French Quarter on his honeymoon night?"

Alex was unnerved. The events of the day, coupled with Jolie's moving confession about Tennessee Williams, suddenly overwhelmed him and the idea of being alone was unbearable. "Please don't leave, Jolie. I'm too keyed up to stay by myself." He threw himself in Jolie's arms. "I'm so upset I'm shaking. Can't you feel it?"

"You have no idea how much you sound like Tenn. He was like a child afraid of being alone at bedtime." Jolie folded him in his arms and hugged him until the trembling slowed and stopped. "That's my boy. You've had one helluva day, and you're feeling the unavoidable letdown. So am I, and I'll admit it's a dilly!"

"Jolie, please don't leave."

Jolie was adamant. "I have to go, *bébé*. I'm dead on my feet, but I'll call you when I get home. If you don't feel better, I'll come back over."

"Promise?"

"Promise."

Alex stood in the open door until Jolie disappeared into the deepening shadows of dusk. He didn't step back inside until he heard the gate clank shut on Dauphine Street and knew he was really alone. He closed the door and paced the room until his feet hurt. He poured another glass of champagne and flopped back down on the couch. He sipped and made a face.

"Warm."

Alex stuck another bottle in the fridge but as he lay there waiting for it to chill he decided he didn't want more alcohol. What he wanted was what Jackie and Denise had. He wanted someone to hold him and say I love you and all those hokey things that Jolie dismissed and he craved. Sure, Jolie could be cavalier it because he'd had his one great love, and the possibility that Alex had lost his chance with Cord was unbearable. Fear and loneliness rushed back, this time coupled with a powerful anxiety.

Alex tossed off his tie and stretched out on the couch, hoping the ugly moment would pass. *If not,* he thought, *I'll call Jolie and tell him to get his ass back over here. I can't fucking stand this!*

The feeling didn't intensify, but neither did it pass. As though he could physically fend it off, Alex grabbed a pillow and covered his face. He tried to focus on positive things, on the liberation he would find with Jackie's inheritance, the satisfaction that would come from telling his homophobic father he had sired a gay child and the freedom of finally being true to himself. It helped, but Alex's mind was so cluttered that his brain shut down and he dozed off. Unfortunately it was a restless sleep giving him no peace, riddled with the kind of hideously vivid nightmares that awoke him over and over only to reclaim him again. More than once he was awakened by his own terrified moans. Then came the loud, insistent beeping.

"Someone make it stop!"

By the time Alex realized it was his cell phone, the signal had stopped. The room was dark and his tuxedo shirt was soaked with sweat. He sat up, trying to remember where he was when the phone sounded again. The deep voice at the other end plunged him back into the nightmares.

42

Love Will Find a Way . . . Maybe

"My God!" Alex moaned. "Why won't they stop?!"

"Alex?"

Alex shook his head, trying to vanquish the terrible dreams. He heard his name crackle and fade over the phone again.

"Make them stop!"

"Alex? Can you hear me? You're cutting in and out."

"Cord?" Alex was still struggling to register the voice. Cord was the last person he expected to hear from, today of all days.

"Yeah. It's me. What's wrong with you? Why won't *what* stop?"

As reality slowly settled in, Alex heard rain in the courtyard and distant, breaking thunder. "I . . . I was having nightmares."

"You're sleeping at eight thirty?"

"I must've nodded off." Alex rubbed his eyes, trying with limited success to sort his thoughts, but Cord's next words muddied his mental waters even more.

"I'm passing through New Orleans and thought I'd call and say hello."

"You're what?"

"I'm on I-ten. There's an exit for Elysian Fields coming up."

"My God! You're so close. Almost to the French Quarter."

"Is that where you are?"

"Yeah. I'm . . . I'm in a hotel."

"Really? Did you finally move out of your folk's house?"

"Uh, not exactly."

"Want to get together for a drink?" When Alex didn't respond, Cord said, "I really need to see you, Alex."

"I don't understand, Cord. I mean, what are you doing here? And where's Chandler?"

"Back in Key West. I'm heading back to Texas, Alex. For good."

Alex frowned, trying to stay focused and decide if his nightmares were ongoing. "What the hell does that mean?"

"It means Chandler and I have split. On good terms, but a split's a split."

Alex's heart leapt, but he forced himself to stay grounded. The last thing he needed was another disappointment from Cord. "What happened?"

"Oh, it's way too complicated to go into over the phone." His voice faded, crackled and returned. "I just passed that exit, Alex. Want me to get off at the next one?"

There was a long pause as Alex desperately sorted his thoughts. "I . . . I can't figure out if this is real or not, Cord. It's been . . . it's been one helluva day."

"I'm real all right," Cord said. "I promise."

This time there was no hesitation as Alex was nourished by the optimism in Cord's voice. "All right then. Listen carefully. Your next exit is St. Bernard. Get off there."

"I already see it."

Alex finished giving directions, tore off his tuxedo, and hopped into the shower. It would take Cord about fifteen minutes to get there, just long enough to chill a bottle of Möet if he stuck it in the freezer. He realized too late he hadn't brought a change of clothes, and since his tuxedo shirt was soaked with sweat his only choice was a white terry bathrobe emblazoned with Maison de Ville. *Not my first choice for greeting an ex-boyfriend, but what can I do?*

Alex went back into the bathroom and combed his damp hair again, deciding to go commando beneath the robe and forego the underwear he'd worn all day. Then he returned to the living room and paced. He felt like he'd been pacing all day, starting that morning in the parking lot at St. Michael's, and he forced himself to stop by sitting on the couch. He considered calling Jolie about this unbelievable turn of events but changed his mind when he remembered his last encounter with Cord. *There may be nothing to tell,* he told himself. *You're*

jumping to all sorts of wild conclusions. The guy didn't say anything about get-
ting together again and even if he did, are you sure that's what you want? Are
you kidding? You know you'd take him back in a heartbeat. But so much has
happened since Key West and you've got a whole new life planned in Europe.
Oh, shit! What's Cord going to say when I tell him about the wedding? Do I
wait for him to ask what's new and then casually mention that I got married a
few hours ago?

"Shit!"

Alex started pacing again. He patted his damp hair for the umpteenth time, telling himself he was going to brush himself bald if he
didn't stop. He gargled with mouthwash again and was about to apply more deodorant when he heard the buzzer. He rushed to the
intercom.

"Cord?"

"More like a drowned rat."

Alex buzzed him in, took a deep breath and opened the door. The
rain was coming down in sheets as the shadow hurrying through the
courtyard turned into Cord. When he reached the light, Alex gasped.

"Man, you weren't kidding." He stepped aside so Cord could come
out of the rain. "About the drowned rat I mean."

They stood silent for a moment, just looking at each other. Even
with Cord's wild hair clinging to his face and his nose dripping water,
Alex found him sexier than ever. The feeling deepened when Cord
peeled off his windbreaker to reveal a wet T-shirt. He was soaked to
the skin, pecs abs and nipples prominent through the thin cotton. The
rest of the package, encased in wet jeans and boots, was equally, un-
deniably appetizing.

Alex smiled and nodded. "You look great, Cord."

"So do you."

A second, more awkward silence fell. Alex was about to suggest
Cord dry off and change into a robe when reason was vanquished by
the feel of the other man's arms around him. He thought of nothing
except the hardness of Cord's wet body and a familiar insistence that
flooded him with erotic memories. Cord leaned down as Alex looked
up. Their lips were barely an inch apart.

"Cord, what are we—"

"Don't talk, baby."

When that critical inch disappeared, Alex knew he was a goner, and he returned Cord's kiss with fervor. They clung tight, like children lost in the storm, separating just long enough to strip and scramble under the covers. As they rediscovered each other's naked flesh, Alex was thrilled to find Cord even more aggressive than he remembered. He gave himself eagerly as Cord took control, and the moment grew a little frantic before it peaked and passed like the storm howling outside. They were drained and exhausted, still clinging with labored breathing. Alex recovered first.

"Well," he murmured in a dreamy voice, "the perfect end to a perfect day."

Cord propped himself on one elbow and ran a hand through the tangle of blond curls. "I spent all day on the road. What did you do?"

Alex caught himself before blurting the truth and weighed the ways to tell Cord about Jackie. Past history warned him how Cord felt about arranged marriages, and Alex didn't want to unravel what had just happened.

"Just promise you'll hear me out before saying anything or jumping to any conclusions."

"I promise." Cord was massaging the base of Alex's skull. "Feel good?"

"It feels wonderful, Cord, but please listen. This is important. There's a reason I'm in this hotel."

"Does it have something to do with the tuxedo hanging over there?"

Alex cursed himself for not closing the armoire. "Yes. Yes, it does. I . . . uh, went to a wedding today."

"Obviously a fancy one."

"I did more than go to it, Cord." Alex took a deep breath. "I was . . . I was in it."

Cord's fingers tightened on Alex's neck. "Please tell me you were a best man or an usher or something. Please don't tell me you were the groom."

Alex was getting panicky. "Remember, you promised to hear me out. Cord?" When Cord turned, Alex kissed him and lost himself in eyes much darker and more intense than he remembered. "I did get married but it's definitely a good thing."

"A good thing?" Cord pulled away and folded his big arms across his chest. "Suppose you cut the Martha Stewart crap and tell me what the hell you're talking about." Alex tried to snuggle closer, but Cord pushed him away. "On second thought, I don't want to hear it. I'm not ready for another of your crazy roller-coaster rides. Not after Chandler told me you'd left that girl at the altar and—"

"I married someone else," Alex interrupted. "But she's a lesbian, and it's all part of a plan to—"

"I should've known better," Cord grunted. "I should've known I'd just be walking into another chapter of Alex in Fucking Wonderland. Man, you've got to be the craziest dude I ever met." He rolled out of bed, shaking his head as he stomped naked into the living room and grabbed his wet T-shirt off the floor. He wrung a puddle onto his bare feet. "Shit!"

Alex tugged on his robe and found another for Cord. "Put this on and we'll worry about those wet clothes later. I've got a bottle of Möet chilling, so why don't I pop the cork and explain what happened?"

Cord was flabbergasted. "Are you serious? Didn't you hear what I just said?"

"I heard every word, but remember you promised to hear me out." Alex's heart was racing at the thought of losing this man again and he struggled to sound calm. "Please, Cord. What have you got to lose?"

"Only my sanity," Cord muttered. He put on the robe and flopped on the couch while Alex popped the champagne. "I ought to have my head examined."

For the next half hour, Cord listened with a mixture of bemusement, disbelief, and outright shock at Alex's audacious tale. When Alex finished with Camilla being thrown in the drunk tank, Cord realized he'd been entertained in spite of himself. He had also drunk half the bottle of champagne and was floating on a very pleasant buzz. He gave Alex one of his crooked half-smiles.

"Not just one goofy stunt this time but a whole bunch of them. Man, your friend Jolie has got some damned big balls."

"I know it sounds preposterous, Cord, but things just got curioser and curioser and Jolie kept finding ways to get me out of the next fix. I wouldn't believe it myself if I hadn't lived through it."

"Oh, I believe it after some of the things we did on that damned bus ride, but I do have one question."

"Fire away."

"Where was Ethel Mertz during all these shenanigans?"

The joke came as an enormous relief. Alex even believed his story had salvaged the situation, but Cord's next question torpedoed those hopes.

"Why haven't you told your father you're gay?"

"I will!" Alex said quickly. "As soon as Jackie has her money, that frees me to tell the bastard off once and for all."

"So it's all about the money and not about honesty."

Alex was uneased by Cord's edginess, dangerously reminiscent of what precipitated the fight that drove them apart in Florida. "C'mon, honey. Don't you see it's only a means to an end? The honesty will come, I promise. Until then you can come to France with me, and we can start all over again." He reached for Cord's hand, heart sinking when it was pulled away. "Cord, please don't—"

"We're right back where we started from, Alex. Same song, second verse, and frankly I'm tired of the tune."

"Well, you know what? I'm tired of it too," Alex retorted, temper slipping. "Why is it so damned important for me to come out to my father? There's no law that says everyone has to do it and lots of people don't. God knows, you never did!"

Cord sloughed off the accusation. "As usual, you're taking the easy way out." Alex watched in horror as he dropped his robe and pulled on the wet tee shirt. "You always have and you always will."

"And you're not?" Alex shot back.

"What the hell's that supposed to mean?"

"What happened between you and Chandler? That's got to be one of the shortest romances on record. Did you get going when the going got rough? Huh? Is that it, Cord?"

Cord snorted. "You don't know what you're talking about."

"I know one minute you two lovebirds were restoring a house together and the next minute you're heading back to Texas. How'd you get here anyway? Did Chandler give you a car as a going-away present?"

"I pay my own way, pal, remember?" Cord unleashed a string of expletives and glared at Alex as he struggled into wet jeans. "I'm driving my old man's truck. Some fancy fucking legacy, huh?

"Your father's . . . dead?"

"As a doornail. And for your information he'd stashed a few thousand bucks around the place, so Darcy and I had two reasons to celebrate."

"What . . . what happened to him?"

"The bastard fell off the front porch and hit his head. One of his neighbors saw him later and figured he'd passed out. The guy took his sweet time calling the paramedics but it didn't matter because Pop was already gone." Cord zipped the soaked jeans with difficulty. "In fact, it happened that day you came by the house. The way I figure, you were one of the last people to see him alive."

Alex's stomach turned over. "Jesus, Cord! I . . . I was there when he fell!"

"Huh?"

Alex sat down hard as realization washed over him. "We had a sort of argument. He wouldn't tell me where you were unless I paid him and after . . . after I got the address I refused to give him the money and told him to go fuck himself. He lunged at me and . . . and fell down the steps." Alex's face streamed tears. "I left him lying there, Cord. I swear I didn't know how badly he was hurt. I figured he was just an old drunk who fell down all the time."

Cord sat too and put his arms around Alex. "That's exactly what he was, and you sure as hell shouldn't blame yourself. It would've happened sooner or later, and frankly, I'm glad you had a hand in it."

Alex dabbed his eyes with the cuffs of his robe. "That's an awful thing to say."

"No, it's not. It's retribution, plain and simple. An eye for an eye, and it makes me feel a lot closer to you."

"Really?" Alex frowned. "It gives me the creeps."

Cord's smile was fleeting. "Let me tell you something else. The last time I saw you I said my old man tried to kill me, remember?" Alex nodded. "I was too big for him to beat anymore, but that didn't keep him from heaping on the verbal abuse: what a failure I was, how I would never amount to anything—shit like that. He told me I ought to get the hell out of his house and move to Key West with the rest of the fags. He was just trying to hurt me because he didn't know I was gay, and when I told him the truth he went nuts. He grabbed a butcher knife and said he wanted to kill every queer in the world, starting with me."

"Sweet Jesus!"

"He was so damned drunk I didn't have any trouble getting away, and that was the last time I saw the sonovabitch."

Alex said, "It just gets crazier by the minute."

"Now you know how I feel when I'm around you." Cord thought for a very long moment. "Maybe I'm certifiable, Alex, but do you think maybe we're meant to be crazy together?"

Alex was reeling. "Please tell me you're serious."

"Serious as a heart attack."

"But what you just said, about me always taking the easy way out—"

Cord shook his head. "A minute ago I ignored what you said about coming out to my father, but I was wrong. Talking about him made me realize I was a hypocrite. There was no fortune at stake and I still couldn't face him. I had to be pushed to the max to tell him the truth, and I now realize how you handle it is your business."

"*Our* business," Alex said. He almost fainted with relief as Cord hugged him. "Whoa! You're freezing me. Get out of those damned wet clothes and let's get back in bed. I want us to make some plans."

Cord stripped again and hurried after Alex. Back in bed, they nestled spoon-fashion with Alex's back against Cord's chest. Cord toyed with the blond curls. "If you're thinking about going to France, I don't have a passport."

Alex grinned. "Certain people might not agree, but you don't need a passport to go to the Garden District."

"Isn't that your folks' neighborhood?"

"Yeah."

"Why would I want to go there?"

"Because it's time Mother met you, and time I told Daddy Dearest I was gay. Let's see. Tomorrow's Sunday so he should be home."

Cord was dumbfounded. "After all we just talked about, you want to come out to your old man right now? Won't that screw up everything with Jackie? I mean, what about the money?"

"Don't worry. I'll keep Jackie's secret. Once Daddy knows I'm gay I'm betting he won't want to have anything to do with either of us, but if he does, I'm ready for him. I'll probably get thrown out of the house, but that's fine too because I can leave with a clean conscience. You and I can sail off into the French sunset and live happily ever after."

"I just hope you know what you're doing."

"I was never so sure of anything in my life, Cord. This whole day has been filled with miracles. I feel rejuvenated and reenergized and I see no reason why the magic can't continue." He snuggled closer and hummed a few bars of "Love Will Find a Way." "I still can't believe we're back together. The Man Upstairs sure saved the best surprise for last."

Cord shifted his weight. "The Man Upstairs had nothing to do with it, Alex."

"How do you know?"

"Instead of thanking God, you should thank your friend Jolie."

Alex sat up. "Huh?"

"He called me in Key West last week and told me I owed it to myself to see you one final time. He didn't mention Jackie or the wedding or anything else for that matter, and when I told him Chandler and I were going our separate ways I felt like it was some kind of sign. The only real coincidence is that I arrived on your wedding day. I was supposed to get here yesterday but I had trouble with that damned old truck."

"God, help me," Alex moaned. He slid down in bed and pulled the covers over his head. "I feel like I'm falling down that damned rabbit hole again!"

Cord slipped under the covers too. "Don't worry, baby. I'll pull you back out."

"Promise?"

Cord gathered him into his arms. "Always."

❧ 43 ❧

Fasten Your Seat Belts!

"Wow!"

As the Lamborghini turned into the driveway and glided to a halt, Cord leaned out the window and gawked. Restoration work with Chandler had given him a crash course in nineteenth century Southern architecture, and he recognized a masterpiece. The Sumner house was two stories of 1850s Italianate splendor set behind a fence of wrought iron morning glories. More iron grillwork wrapped gracious galleries, and fountains and sculpture dotted Karen's antique rose gardens.

"Damn!" he said. "I guess this is the fanciest house I'll ever get into without having to buy a ticket."

"Well, don't get too excited." Alex parked the Lamborghini and climbed out. "It won't be long before we're thrown out of it."

Cord followed him up the steps and caressed the floral ironwork. "This is really a work of art, baby doll."

"Yeah, I guess." Considering the confrontation staring him in the face, Alex couldn't focus on historic architecture. He unlocked the front door. "C'mon, honey. It's show time."

Cord whistled at the opulence of the foyer's black and white marble floors, a French chandelier twelve feet tall and a mahogany spiral staircase. "You know what, Alex? Now that I see all this up close, maybe we should rethink things. I mean first that incredible car out there, and now this house—"

Alex's next words put everything in perspective. "Careful, Cord. You're sounding like the old me!"

Cord looked sheepish. "You're right. Now I really understand how all this glamour could turn a guy's head." He whistled again. "Wow!"

"Who's whistling down there?"

They looked up as Karen Sumner waved from above. Since they'd never met, Cord had no frame of reference, but Alex noticed the change right away. Not only did his mother radiate a strange new confidence, but she looked different too. The trademark couturier clothes were gone, displaced by a look that could only be called Jazz Baby. Swathed in silks, beads, and turban, shoulders draped in a fringed piano shawl, Karen channeled Auntie Mame as she descended the grand curved staircase. All she needed to burst into song, Alex mused, was a bugle.

"My God, Mom!" Alex beamed as she reached the bottom step. "You look fabulous!"

"Thank you, darling. A new look for the new me." She offered her cheek for a kiss while giving Cord the once-over. "My word! Who have we here?"

"This is Cord Foster, Mom. Cord, meet my mother."

Cord blushingly obliged when Karen offered her cheek for a kiss. "Nice to meet you, Mrs. Sumner."

"You too, my dear. And please call me Karen." She looked back at Alex. "The young man from Key West, yes?"

"Yes."

Thin, penciled eyebrows rose like question marks. "I'm afraid I don't understand. I thought you two—"

"We patched things up," Cord said.

"Really?" Karen clapped her hands together and beamed. "How wonderful!"

Alex happily memorized the next moment as his mother embraced him, then Cord, then him again. *It's one thing to tell a mother you're gay,* he thought, *and quite another to introduce her to your lover.* Karen handled it as smoothly as he'd hoped, and when she stepped back everyone's eyes were gleaming. Karen stemmed her tears with a joke.

"Will I be needing another mother-of-the-groom gown?"

"No!" the men chorused. Everyone laughed.

"No more weddings," Alex said, "although I'd marry this guy in a heartbeat if he asked."

Karen studied Cord for a moment. "So you're the gentleman who refused the reward money? Well done! I must applaud your honesty."

"Thank you." Cord's humility and shyness made Alex fall in love with him all over again.

"You're welcome." Karen turned back to Alex, suddenly serious. "Since you brought Cord along I assume you have something very important to tell your father."

"You better believe it."

"He's in the library with the Sunday paper, and I should warn you he's in a foul mood. He's been snarling at Jedediah and me all morning. I finally fled to my room for some peace and quiet. Jedediah's holed up too."

"What's Daddy so mad about? Not that he ever needed a reason."

Karen shrugged. "He's probably still steaming over the wedding. He went to his club after the reception and didn't come home until all hours."

"Well, Mom, I'm about to get him steamed up all over again, so if you'd rather not watch the fireworks—"

"Are you kidding?" Karen squeezed his arm. "I've waited for this moment so long I wouldn't miss it for the world!"

The library's double doors were closed, a long-standing signal that the man inside was not to be disturbed. Alex walked right over and pounded with his fists. The response was immediate and thunderous.

"Who the hell is it?"

"Your son!" Alex shouted back.

Through with waiting for permission, Alex opened the door and faced his nemesis. Randolph Sumner was ensconced behind his desk, poring over the newspaper. He looked up and glared as Alex came into the library, Cord and Karen a few paces behind.

Sumner was immediately suspicious. "What are you doing here? Why aren't you on your honeymoon?"

"The honeymoon's over, Daddy. In more ways than one."

Sumner's eyes darted over his shoulder, lighting briefly on Cord before moving on to Karen. He snorted at his wife's colorful ensemble. "What the hell are you dressed up for? Mardi Gras?"

Karen smiled but did not answer. She was, Alex thought, as confident and enigmatic as Alice's Cheshire cat.

Sumner glared at Cord. "Who are you?"

"Cord Foster, sir." It was lost on no one that Cord did not move closer or offer his hand. "We've never met, but we've talked on the phone."

"Is that so?"

Alex knew much of his father's success was due to an uncanny ability to memorize every face and name he encountered. He enjoyed Sumner's momentary confusion before solving the puzzle.

"Cord turned me in and refused the ransom, Daddy."

Sumner rose but remained behind the desk. "So that's it, eh? You've changed your mind and want the reward after all?" He looked at Alex. "Since you're losing your inheritance you've decided to cash in this guy and split the profits. Well, if you think you're going to waltz in here and—"

"I don't want your damned money," Cord interrupted, booming through Sumner's loud accusations. When Sumner hushed, Cord put an arm around Alex's shoulders. "All I want is your son, and I'm going to have him whether you like it or not."

Sumner's gaze narrowed. "What the hell are you talking about?"

With Cord protectively beside him and his mother radiating encouragement, Alex took a deep breath and expelled the truth.

"I'm gay, Daddy!"

The three little words exorcised years of misery, deceit, and self-loathing, and Alex felt more emotional burdens lift away. It was like the day he had told his mother the truth, and he reveled in an exhilaration that was almost cosmic. Its sweetness was made more so by the shock contorting his father's face.

"You're what?!"

"You heard me," Alex said. "I'm a homosexual, or, as you prefer to call us, faggots and queers. Well, this is the fag with whom I plan to spend the rest of my life. We just wanted you to know."

Sumner's fist crashed onto the desk. "Wait just a goddamned minute!"

"For what?" Alex asked with maddening calm. "We really have nothing more to say."

"Except good-bye," Cord added.

They turned to leave, but Sumner leapt like a panther from behind the desk and slammed the double doors. "Who the hell do you think you're talking to?"

Neither Alex nor his mother had ever seen him so enraged, but neither was frightened. As for Cord, Alex knew he had witnessed far worse outbursts but he duly noted the clenched fists.

Sumner's face blazed like someone having a heart attack. "Why the hell would a queer get married? It's Frenchie's money, isn't it? You figured if you were financially independent you could humiliate and embarrass me. Well, you better think again! I'll tell your poor deluded wife the truth, and she'll throw your sorry faggot ass out on the street!"

Alex was coolness personified. "It won't work, Daddy. Jackie knows everything and she doesn't care."

"What?!" Sumner clearly hadn't expected that one. "In God's name, why would a woman like that marry a fag?"

"The Europeans have far less sexual hang-ups than we Americans," Alex replied smoothly. "Especially the French."

"Bullshit!" Sumner boomed. "I may not know much about French morals but I sure as hell know when someone's trying to pull a fast one. I've battled corporate barracudas for thirty years and I can smell a scam a mile away!"

As his father's son, Alex fully expected this argument. "You'd better not stick your nose where it doesn't belong, Daddy. Cord and I were planning on moving to France, but if you keep messing around with my life I'll stay right here and become the most vocal, most radical gay activist in the state of Louisiana!"

"So will I," Cord said.

"Want to know something else, Daddy? Having a gay son won't look so hot to those family values hate groups you've been underwriting. The newspapers will have a field day doing stories about the homophobic tycoon with a gay activist son."

"You're bluffing!" Sumner snarled.

"You wish!" Alex returned fire with both barrels blazing. "I've watched you a lot of years, Daddy. Watched and learned to get as down and nasty as the competition. Remember my schoolmate Stacy Knight? She's a reporter with the *Times-Picayune* now, and I'm sure she'd appreciate an exclusive from an old friend."

"I still say you're bluffing!"

Alex pulled out his cell phone. "Want to watch me make the call?" When Sumner didn't move, Alex put the phone away. "It's finished, Daddy. All of it. And I'm leaving this damned prison for good."

"Atta boy!" Karen said. When Sumner shot her a nasty look, she shot it right back. "Give it up, Randolph. You've finally met your match."

Sumner turned on her like a snake. "Shut up!"

Alex was infuriated but said nothing. At that moment he was concerned with the raw hatred on Cord's face and those clenched fists. Karen never flinched.

"I'll shut up all right," she said. "But not until I've finished speaking my piece."

Sumner glowered. "What the hell are you talking about? Have you gone crazy too?"

"Never felt better, husband dear." Karen turned to Alex and Cord. "You boys stay right where you are. It's my turn to set off some fireworks."

"Mom, what are you—?"

"I know what I'm doing, son. I promise."

For the first time in his life, Alex heard his mother raise her voice. Even more amazing was the fact that she did it right in her husband's face.

"Okay, you hypocritical bigot. Fasten your seat belt!"

~ 44 ~

Mothers Always Know, Part Deux

Karen Sumner closed the doors and looked around the library. She reminded Alex of a college professor about to announce a pop quiz as she paced back and forth, carefully weighing her words.

"I've got something to say, Randolph, and you're going to listen and listen good."

Alex took Cord's hand when his heart began to race. Sumner's response to the gesture was a glare of disgust.

"Our son was right when he said it's finished: your cruelty and lies, your selfishness and intimidation—all of it is finished. Do you want to know why?" When her husband didn't respond, she got in his face again. "Answer me, Randolph!"

"What the hell do you want from me?" he grunted.

"It's very simple," Karen declared. "I want the truth."

"About what?"

"About Pearl Brewster, that's what."

Sumner's stony facade slipped long enough for Alex to glimpse a man snared in his own duplicitous net. The mask was swiftly jerked back into place, but it was too late.

"Who?"

"Oh, I think you heard me," Karen purred.

"Never heard of her!" Sumner snapped.

"Really?" Karen rolled her eyes in feigned shock. "You've never heard of the woman who's been your mistress for over thirty years?"

Sumner's eyes narrowed to slits, then darted around the room as though looking for an escape hatch. "Says who?"

Alex had never seen his father so unnerved and, like his mother, he relished the moment. Karen's pleasure was almost tangible as she took her time unveiling a litany of damning truths to make her husband squirm.

"Unlike you, I don't need a vast network of spies or even a single private investigator to track down the facts. Truth is, the facts came to me." Sumner visibly fidgeted. "You know, you really have no one to blame but yourself, Randolph. You made a big mistake with those big donations to white supremacy groups. Did you possibly imagine that such a thing would go unnoticed by Jedediah?"

Sumner's face flooded redder. "What's he got to do with it?"

"In a word? Everything!" Karen's tone and tactics changed, now reminding Alex of a defense attorney on the scent of a perjuring witness. "Especially since Jedediah is Pearl's father."

Alex gasped. Given his father's flagrant racism, he could scarcely believe the man had an African-American mistress. He was further surprised when his mother articulated his own thoughts.

"You make Strom Thurmond look like a rank amateur, and I can only imagine what your bigoted buddies will say when they learn the truth. First gays and now this. Talk about having a field day!"

"You're all insane!" Sumner said. "This is some kind of crazy conspiracy to discredit me and win back Alex's inheritance. It won't work, people! All it takes is one call to my attorneys, and they'll—"

Karen laughed in his face. "Dear Lord, I wish you could hear yourself. You're the one who sounds insane. This is not another corporate takeover where you hold all the cards. At the risk of making a very bad joke, you've been caught with your pants down, and there's nothing you can do about it." She paused. "Except strike a bargain."

Sumner grunted and muttered a few seconds. "What kind of bargain?"

Karen smiled and resumed pacing. *Now,* thought Alex, *she's moving in for the kill.* The truth gave his mother an awesome amount of leverage, and he watched with pride as she wielded every ounce. Now he understood what she meant on the dance floor about the Sumner family having more than their share of secrets.

"It's quite simple, Randolph. You give our son his inheritance and I'll keep your naughty little racist secret."

Sumner was livid. "That's blackmail!"

"Call it whatever you wish, husband dear. It's all in the family."

Sumner glared at Alex and Cord. "There's no way in hell I'm giving money to those faggots!"

"I thought you'd say that. Well, then, you leave me no choice."

"What the devil are you talking about?"

"I'll simply give them money after the divorce. I'm sure my share of your empire will be considerable considering my grounds will be adultery. There isn't a judge in Louisiana who won't throw the book at you."

"You can't prove a thing!"

"To the contrary. Jedediah is in my camp now, and before you try to buy the silence of your faithful old family retainer, you should know he gave me a notarized deposition about the relationship between you and his daughter. The choice is yours."

For the first time in his life, Randolph Sumner was speechless. So was Alex, who kept reminding himself this tiny, determined dynamo was his mother, and, along with Cord, was riveted as she delivered a devastating coup de grace.

"You've always boasted that there was no one who could outsmart you, Randolph, but at the end of the day you've beaten yourself. Like our son, I studied you closely over the years. Watched and waited for the right moment to use what I learned. The day of reckoning has finally arrived and it's going to involve me writing very hefty checks to the International Gay and Lesbian Human Rights Commission, the NAACP, and PFLAG. In case you don't know, husband dear, those last initials are an acronym for Parents, Friends and Family of Lesbians and Gays."

"This isn't over," Sumner grunted, voice dripping vitriol. He looked at each of them with loathing before storming down the hall. His parting shout rocked the rafters. "Not by a long shot!"

Alex started to say something, but Karen shushed him until she heard the front door open and close. At the sound of Sumner's car speeding down the driveway, she let out a whoop and the three fell into each other's arms.

"Ding, dong, the witch is dead!" Alex sang.

"Not dead," his mother warned. "Only down for the count. We both know your father will come up with some cockamamie scheme before it's all over."

"Yeah, but this time we've really got the old boy!" Alex grinned. "This calls for a huge celebration, y'all. We're all going to Arnaud's for lunch—me, Cord, Jolie, Jackie, and Denise. You have to be there when we tell them the good news."

"Let's do dinner instead." Karen smoothed her turban and gave Cord an admiring look after his enthusiastic hug. "Goodness, young man! You don't know your own strength!"

Alex was insistent. "You have to come right now, Mom! What could be more important?"

"Getting Jedediah's signature on a deposition, that's what."

Alex gasped. "But you just said—!"

"Bluffing, honey. Something else I've watched your father do over the years. While I was delivering the Sermon on the Mount I realized I hadn't covered my tracks. That's why I was so anxious to make sure your father drove off and didn't go looking for Jedediah."

"How do you know he'll sign?"

"Because he's as angry and fed up as we are," Karen explained. "You know he's always been your father's shadow, and when he over-heard talk about those awful racist groups, he came to me. I was surprised since we'd never been close, but we bonded when I assured him I was as horrified as he was. The poor old soul broke down and cried as one confidence led to another, and when he got angry he blurted the truth about Pearl. I almost fainted, Alex. Oh, I knew your father was unfaithful and didn't much care, but I couldn't forgive the hypocrisy. Neither could Jedediah. When he said he wanted to confront your fa-ther, I had the foresight to assure him if he kept quiet he'd never have to worry about financial security. Now I have to go make good on that promise."

"Wow!" Cord said. "What a gamble!"

"All right," Alex said. "We'll take care of Jedediah and then go to Arnaud's."

"Sorry, honey. I'm gospel brunching with Angelique Poché at the Smoking for Jesus church down in Arabi. She assures me it's *trés amusant*."

"That's who those clothes remind me of!" Alex gave her a suspicious grin. "Since when did you two become friends?"

"Since last night after the reception. She invited Monette and me to her home, and we played dress up until dear old auntie nodded off. I felt just like a girl again. Lord, I can't remember when I've had a hangover." She reconsidered. "Oh, yes, I do. It was the night Jolie took me to drag bingo at Oz."

Alex was floored. "What?!"

"My darling, I told you this family was full of secrets! Just because you keep a low profile in the gay community doesn't mean I have to."

"You're a handful, Mom!"

"High time everyone knew it! Anyway, if you're going to have a new life, I want one too. Preferably one that'll give your father apoplexy."

"Hey, Karen." Cord grinned. "Will visiting us in Paris be a start?"

"What mother doesn't dream of being asked to France by her son-in-law?" She took Cord's hands and looked deep into his eyes. "I'll be there with bells on. Thank you for inviting me, and thank you for giving my son what he's been looking for, for much longer than he realizes."

Alex draped one arm over Cord's shoulders and the other around his mother as he left the hated library for the last time. "Sounds like you knew I was gay before I did."

Karen smiled. "Haven't you been listening, my darling? Mothers *always* know."

ABOUT THE AUTHOR

Michel LaCroix wrote *The Edge Guide to New Orleans* and the New Orleans section of *Access Gay USA*. He is also the author of nine published pseudonymous historical, adventure, and romance novels. He divides his time between New Orleans and Pasadena, California. He is currently at work on a sequel to *Alex in Wonderland,* entitled *Through with the Looking Glass.*

Order a copy of this book with this form or online at:
http://www.haworthpress.com/store/product.asp?sku=5257

ALEX IN WONDERLAND

_____in softbound at $19.95 (ISBN-13: 978-1-56023-532-3; ISBN-10: 1-56023-532-2)

Or order online and use special offer code HEC25 in the shopping cart.

COST OF BOOKS_____

☐ **BILL ME LATER:** (Bill-me option is good on US/Canada/Mexico orders only; not good to jobbers, wholesalers, or subscription agencies.)

POSTAGE & HANDLING_____
(US: $4.00 for first book & $1.50 for each additional book)
(Outside US: $5.00 for first book & $2.00 for each additional book)

☐ Check here if billing address is different from shipping address and attach purchase order and billing address information.

Signature_____

SUBTOTAL_____

☐ **PAYMENT ENCLOSED: $_____**

IN CANADA: ADD 7% GST_____

☐ **PLEASE CHARGE TO MY CREDIT CARD.**

STATE TAX_____
(NJ, NY, OH, MN, CA, IL, IN, PA, & SD residents, add appropriate local sales tax)

☐ Visa ☐ MasterCard ☐ AmEx ☐ Discover
☐ Diner's Club ☐ Eurocard ☐ JCB

Account # _____

FINAL TOTAL_____
(If paying in Canadian funds, convert using the current exchange rate, UNESCO coupons welcome)

Exp. Date_____

Signature_____

Prices in US dollars and subject to change without notice.

NAME_____
INSTITUTION_____
ADDRESS_____
CITY_____
STATE/ZIP_____
COUNTRY_____ COUNTY (NY residents only)_____
TEL_____ FAX_____
E-MAIL_____

May we use your e-mail address for confirmations and other types of information? ☐ Yes ☐ No
We appreciate receiving your e-mail address and fax number. Haworth would like to e-mail or fax special discount offers to you, as a preferred customer. **We will never share, rent, or exchange your e-mail address or fax number.** We regard such actions as an invasion of your privacy.

Order From Your Local Bookstore or Directly From
The Haworth Press, Inc.
10 Alice Street, Binghamton, New York 13904-1580 • USA
TELEPHONE: 1-800-HAWORTH (1-800-429-6784) / Outside US/Canada: (607) 722-5857
FAX: 1-800-895-0582 / Outside US/Canada: (607) 771-0012
E-mail to: orders@haworthpress.com

For orders outside US and Canada, you may wish to order through your local
sales representative, distributor, or bookseller.
For information, see http://haworthpress.com/distributors

(Discounts are available for individual orders in US and Canada only, not booksellers/distributors.)

PLEASE PHOTOCOPY THIS FORM FOR YOUR PERSONAL USE.
http://www.HaworthPress.com   BOF04